At What Cost?

LIFE AND LOVE:
A Lesbian Medical
Romance Series

M.T. CASSEN

Copyright © 2023 by MT Cassen

All rights reserved.

No part of this book may be reproduced in any form or by any electronic or mechanical means, including information storage and retrieval systems, without written permission from the author, except for the use of brief quotations in a book review.

CHAPTER ONE

FOR THE CHILDREN

Anne

The world was lost in a soft silence when Anne Silva stepped outside the hospital hallway. She had spent all night restless and hopeful that today would bring smiles to the children's faces. Those fears could only linger as the rain pattered along her bedroom window. *What if the day got rained out?* She could already see the frowns forming on the children's faces when she broke the news. *We'll do it another day, I promise.* The cries would echo through the halls. They needed this. They needed a day away from the sterile antiseptic air of the hospital; they needed fresh air. Anne took in a whiff of the fresh air that she had long promised them and smiled. There was still a scent of rain but not a cloud in sight. All her fears washed away with the last puddle; today would be the day she only saw smiles. The workers from the local zoo were busy organizing the hospital courtyard as they had done for the past three years. Anne made it her duty to ensure that the kids stuck in the Pediatric ward could enjoy themselves but still access their medical care. It seemingly worked.

Anne glanced at her watch and grinned. She tossed her dark hair into a ponytail to get her bangs out of her green eyes. The courtyard would be flooded with children of all ages in just a few more minutes. Many of those children were stuck inside CAPMED for weeks due to their health issues—some with cancer and others with less severe cases of asthma. Anne carefully screened all participants to ensure they were medically fit to participate in the day's activities. Regardless of their health issues, everyone needed a break. It was the beginning of summer, and these kids deserved a chance to spend the day outside, like their peers who would be readying for summer vacation. Anne might not be able to give them a whole summer camp experience, but she could provide them with a day where they could just be ... kids. Anne turned and hurried to the elevator. And now, the best part was grabbing the children from their beds and pointing out the zookeepers and animals already filling the courtyard. There was a miniature pony, a face-painting station, and a small pen full of bunnies. Two baby goats munched on the overgrown grass. Today was just as exciting for Anne as for the young ones. She laughed as she stepped off the elevator.

Anne stepped into Willow Bixby's room. Willow, an inquisitive seven-year-old cancer patient, was already sitting in her bed. She had a round face framed by a blonde bob and large brown eyes. She looked like a cherub. "Is it time?" she exclaimed. Her enthusiasm was hard to contain.

Anne laughed. "You know it!" She wheeled the chair over to her and helped her to get seated. "Are you ready?"

"You betcha!" She clapped her hands together. "Mommy and Daddy are coming during lunch. I'm so excited!"

Anne laughed and leaned in, brushing her lips against the young girl's top of her head. "Same here."

The little girl giggled, and they exited the room. Already, the Pediatric staff had worked to gather the kids from their rooms, and Anne looked around at the organized chaos. "Cecilia," she called, waving her hand. Cecilia, a supervising nurse and one of Anne's old mentors, came over. She was tall and slender; she carried herself throughout the hospital with an undisputed air of grace that spoke to her experience. "Did you grab Maria?"

"No, she's the next on the list. I'll grab her and take Willow down to the courtyard for you. You're needed downstairs."

Anne frowned. "Downstairs?"

"HR." Cecilia shrugged. "But I'll take care of the rest."

"Alrighty then," Anne mumbled. She watched as the elevator was loaded with more patients and turned to head toward the stairs. What would they need her down in HR for? She shrugged it off and hurried down the stairs, as no one liked to keep that department waiting. As she drew closer, it hit her. They probably needed to verify the count of children so they got the payment correct. Clarissa looked up from the front desk the moment Anne entered. "Hey, Clarissa. I've been summoned." Anne laughed lightheartedly, but Clarissa didn't budge.

"They're expecting you. Go on in." She motioned to the boardroom, and Anne frowned. It seemed silly to make such a big entrance for a simple question they could have asked over the phone. But as she drew nearer, she thought even harder. And it was odd that they would need to have a count, as she was sure she had included that in her budget request. She shrugged and entered the room.

Robert Tucker sat at the head of the table. He was a burly man with ruddy cheeks, the CEO who kept everyone on the edge of their seats. He only made his presence known if there was a huge issue. Around the table sat Bill Bristow, the union rep, along with Henry Martin, her other mentor, who had a sort of Mister Rogers air about him. There were a few other faces that Anne could place, but she wasn't quite sure of their relation to the hospital. Callie North was also seated at the table, the nurses' representative. She was at least a friendly face. "Have a seat," Robert stated, motioning to an empty chair.

"Um, well, I don't know what this is about, but I have a courtyard of children waiting outside, and I'm supposed to make a speech welcoming the families. So, can we make this quick?"

"Please have a seat, Anne," Callie started. "That's what this meeting is about. It won't take long. Just have to get some things out of the way." Anne glanced at Callie, and she gave an encouraging smile and motioned to the seat beside her.

Anne slid into the seat and glanced over at Robert. "Alright, what's this about?"

"It's come to our attention that this event costs triple your proposed budget," Robert started.

Anne narrowed her eyes. In the last ten years she had been employed at CAPMED, she had never been in such an awkward situation. In the previous five years in the Pediatric department, her career at CAPMED had soared, and things had never been better. Now, everyone stared at her as if they were ready for her to break right before them. She shifted in her seat, the awkwardness gripping her muscles.

"The staff was going through your portfolio, and while the depth of your organizational skills never ceases to amaze us, it seems that this year you had several unaccounted expenses." Anne frowned. She had gone through everything three times before submitting it. "Well, things come up," she hedged.

"The budget for snacks was double what it was last year." He pushed two papers out in front of Anne, and Anne picked up each one. She surveyed the one list, then the second, "The catering company raised their prices! Plus, this year, more than half the kids are gluten-free; that's going to be more expensive, but I didn't want anyone to feel left out." Anne looked over the list and nodded. "That's fair, but on page three, you'll see that the cost of the tents was double what it was last year as well."

"I had to find a new company! The other one went out of business because of COVID," Anne didn't want to sound like she was making excuses, but she couldn't shake the feeling that Robert was blaming her for circumstances beyond her control.

"I fixed it, though! Instead of renting folding chairs, I used the spare folding chairs in the storage room behind the cafeteria."

"And now there are no chairs for art therapy this morning," Robert finished.

"You see, Anne…." Robert pulled the lists back in front of him. "CAPMED, like all hospitals, is going through some tough times. Usually, mistakes like these would be permissible. However, the hospital board met last week to discuss the budget for the upcoming year, and we have to make some cuts. We need to cut some of the non-essential services, starting with family fun days." Anne sighed. "But Robert..." she began.

He arched an eyebrow. "There's no need for discussion. We went over the budget every way we could." A weight was heavy in Anne's gut, and she looked down at her hands. She could feel the children's disappointment when she announced today was the last Family Fun Day. "This will be the last one. Please inform the children and their families that our Halloween Haunt is canceled this Fall as well."

"You can't be serious." Anne glanced up and stared at him. "The children rely on these moments. You're letting the budget of all things snatch it away from them?" Robert didn't budge. Anne turned to Henry. He was always reasonable, but his gaze dropped to the table. She mentally groaned and turned back to Robert.

Robert shrugged. "The decision has been made. The hospital can't have any more events if we want to keep our doors open, especially the PEDS wing."

Anne cringed. "And there's no way that these cuts could be made in, say, the donor luncheons?" She crossed her arms in front of her.

"We are being reasonable here, Anne. I don't want your arguments, as they will only waste your breath." He grabbed his papers together and stood up from the table. "Now, if you'll excuse us, we have another meeting."

Anne stood up from her table, her head down as she exited the room. Clarissa's eyes were on her as she hurried from the HR office. This was ridiculous.

Willow grinned and waved at Anne when she arrived in the courtyard. "Nurse Anne! Come see the bunnies!" She called.

She was holding hands with a taller blonde woman who was most likely Willow's mother.

Anne walked over to the wooden hutch containing a giant gray bunny.

"They're the cutest ever," Willow gasped.

"They are pretty cute," Anne agreed.

"Thank you so much for organizing this. I'm Ella, Willow's mom," She extended her hand, and Anne shook it.

"It's lovely to meet you."

"Seriously, I can't thank you enough. You have no idea how much it means to my husband and me to have a chance to be a normal family for a day." Ella gushed.

Anne's stomach sank. How was she supposed to explain to all these people that budgetary concerns were crushing their one chance at normalcy?

CHAPTER TWO

ROUGH MORNING

Anne

The radio played as Anne entered the kitchen; her cat, Whiskers, a gray-striped tabby, was not far behind. He meowed and nuzzled up against her, and she laughed and leaned down to ruffle the back of his neck. "Are you hungry, Whiskers? Is that what you're trying to tell me?" She ruffled the fur on his neck more, then walked over and grabbed a can of cat food from the cupboard. Whiskers proudly stood by his bowl when she walked over with the can and scraped it in. "Make it last. Mama's gotta work today." She smirked, then moved to the counter to pour herself a cup of coffee.

The clock on the wall read 7:05. She still had plenty of time to enjoy her morning before taking the ten-minute drive to the hospital. She leaned back against the counter and sipped on her coffee, glancing around where she had called home for fifteen years. What started as a dilapidated two-bedroom on the outskirts of Chicago quickly turned into her oasis. The first year was a lot of work. First, she ripped up the carpet to uncover the original hardwood floors. She replaced the grimy linoleum in the kitchen with chic laminate tiles she found online. She swapped out the Landlord special off-white paint for a soothing Robin's egg blue. On weekends, she scoured every corner of the Internet and every garage sale in the Chicagoland area for upcycled furniture. She found her round kitchen table in Bridgeport. The yellow velvet sofa was a cast-off of her sister, who couldn't risk a velvet couch with two young children. Her white iron bed frame was from an estate sale where she found her quilt. And while Whiskers didn't care about the decor, Anne adored the iron bird feeder shaped like a tiny cottage she stuck on the tree outside the kitchen window. It didn't take long for it to feel like that, a home. She took another sip and sighed. One more mortgage payment and the place would officially be hers, paid in full. Scrimping and saving down to the last dime hadn't been easy. She doubled her monthly payment so she could pay it off in half the time. But it had finally been worth it. She could imagine walking into the credit union and handing over the last installment. She planned on having two parties, at least. After all, her friends, co-workers, and sister would be happy to celebrate the joyous occasion with her. She finished the last of her coffee and placed the mug into the sink. Her life didn't have everything she desired, but had all the necessities. Now that Anne could pay off her house, perhaps she could find a woman to share it with.

Meow. Anne looked down and laughed at Whiskers as if he had read her mind. "Of course, she'll have to be a cat person."

She knelt and scratched behind his errors. "Mama's off to work."

Anne never imagined she would be one of those parents who treated her pet as if they were human. But Whiskers was different. She met him a year ago on a date at a cat cafe with her ex-girlfriend. The girlfriend broke up with her a month later, but Whiskers was her friend for life.

Anne longed for a family one day. She knew that most therapists would tell her it stemmed from Anne's tumultuous childhood. Her father left them when she was still in elementary school. He said he fell out of love with her mother. Anne and her sister, Melanie, thought that was a lousy excuse. What about them? Did he not care what happened to his children? He was cheating with his secretary, a fact that only came out two weeks before the divorce was final. Anne and Melanie never did forgive him for deserting them. Where he wound up was simply a mystery.

Their mother, however, didn't let the divorce get her down. She worked as a government official in the Postal Service. Her friends at the post office rallied around her mother and family, ensuring they never had to do without. Unfortunately, as Anne was getting out of college, her mother was involved in an accident, killed by a drunk driver. The driver ended up in prison, but Anne vowed to preserve her mother's legacy of kindness, generosity, and being a great friend.

As for Melanie, Anne liked to believe she had gone down the same road. However, Melanie married a man named Josh, who was similar to their father. Yet, she didn't want to be the one who forced Melanie out of the marriage. Melanie would ultimately resent her, and her sister's relationship was the most important one she had, other than her relationship with her nieces. The four of them regularly got together for game nights and movies. She enjoyed getting to see her nieces grow up right before her eyes. That relationship was way too important to let it falter. Hopefully, one day, Melanie would realize the jerk Josh was, and Anne would be there to help Melanie and the girls get back on their feet.

Anne turned up the radio and began singing along to a Lady Gaga song. Traffic was light, which enabled her to go at her speed, and she started singing along. She was so close to paying off her house, which made her feel unusually buoyant. She was slowing down to ease onto the exit when she heard a loud crash, and her car jolted forward.

"Shit!" she groaned. Her car halted, the motor shutting off. She looked in the rearview mirror. She couldn't make out any features of the driver but saw a burgundy ribbon hanging down from the rearview mirror. The car stayed there, with no movement coming from the driver—a few cars whizzed by, but no one offered to stop. Anne reached for her phone and sighed. Not exactly how she wanted to start her morning, she grabbed the door handle, but before she could get out of the car, the driver backed up and sped around her, tearing off onto the exit and disappearing. "You've got to be kidding me!" Anne slammed her fists against the wheel and stared back at the now-empty spot.

Anne looked in her rearview mirror. There weren't any cars coming, and she opened the door and braced herself, walking around the car and looking at her bumper. The bumper was askew. There was a huge dent right where the two cars collided. Now, all responsibility was on her shoulders since the perpetrator had fled. She tilted her head from one side to the other.

Maybe it wasn't that bad, and she could get by. If she planned on fixing it, she was looking at derailing paying off her house. She covered her face and shook her head as a truck whizzed by her, blowing on the horn.

She walked around and slipped back into the front seat. So much for the great big party she had planned. First, she didn't want to waste time getting it into the shop to be repaired. If only her car still drove. When it started, the radio resumed, and the engine roared to life. At least there was one plus. She drove off onto the exit, where the car disappeared, and looked around as the road drew to a T. She looked both ways, surveying each direction for a car that matched the red vehicle, but she rolled her eyes. She knew nothing about cars and couldn't differentiate one from the other. It was pointless.

She would call the shop later and see when she could get her car in and then worry about calling the insurance company. What was done was done. She had to get to work; she had never missed a shift. It'd been two months since hospital management shredded her budget, and the last thing she needed was another disciplinary meeting. Besides, there were times to shirk responsibility, and this wasn't one of them. She had to keep the pay coming, even more so now with an insurance estimate and repairs looming.

CHAPTER THREE

HIT AND RUN

Taylor

Taylor's grip tightened on her steering wheel, and she stared straight ahead. Her mind was fuzzy as she headed to the parking lot. She was too afraid to leave her car and see the damage she had done. A hit-and-run was far from her finest moment. But the car came out of nowhere. Then again, she was distracted, and her music was playing louder than a rock concert. It was the only way she could stay awake. She would have a long day ahead of her, and the neighbors had been in a screaming match all night.

Taylor slowly released a grip and opened her door. She stared at her front bumper and covered her face. The one good thing was that her car was still running. She groaned and got back in the car, slamming her door shut. A text dinged on her phone, and she grabbed it, spotting her brother's message.

> **GAVIN:**
>
> Hey, Sis. I just wanted to wish you a great first day on the job. You're going to rock it.

Gavin was just sixteen, a junior in high school, and her rock. Taylor believed that she should be the grown-up in the scenario. Their father was out of the picture when Gavin was only a baby, and their mother struggled with drugs and alcohol.

> **TAYLOR:**
>
> Hopefully, the day goes better than it started. Ugh.

> **GAVIN:**
>
> Who do I need to beat up?

> **TAYLOR:**
>
> You don't need to worry about anything. I got in a bit of a fender bender this morning.

> **GAVIN:**
>
> Oh no. Who's fault?

> **TAYLOR:**
>
> You're talking to her.

> **GAVIN:**
>
> Tay...please don't say...you can't afford that. You don't have insurance. How much damage?

> **TAYLOR:**
>
> I wouldn't know. I left the scene of the accident. I feel awful.

> TAYLOR:
> If I knew how to find them, I would gladly reach out and help them out. I'm a coward.

Taylor and Gavin had been in an accident before. One that left them in a homeless shelter as their mother tried to detox. The detox didn't work, and the accident left Taylor afraid of driving. Eventually, she overcame her fear enough to get her license, but panic lingered every time she merged onto the highway.

> GAVIN:
> Don't!! I'm guessing you bumped into an old dude with billions lying around.
>
> GAVIN:
> Let it go, Sis. You're better off.

Taylor laughed. It was easy to suggest letting it go, but was that even possible? She let go of a breath and tried to shake out her jitters. She couldn't lose this job before it even started. She was trying to save up for a nicer apartment for her and Gavin. It was nice that their aunt let them stay with her when Taylor was working her way through college, but her aunt's house was tiny. Taylor longed to move her family to a better neighborhood and life. Taylor got out of the car and looked over at the banged-up bumper. She did a number on it. She glanced down at her watch and heaved a sigh—only ten minutes to get the lay of the land of her new job. No pressure. Taylor started running toward the front of the building, leaving the accident behind her. She was about to reach the curb when she tripped. Taylor flew face-first toward the pavement. In the nick of time, she grabbed onto a pole to steady herself. She groaned, hopping from one foot to the other, a throbbing pain shooting up the heel of her foot and to her shin. If only no one saw her, she could shake it off and get inside.

"Are you alright?"

No such luck. Taylor grimaced and turned on her heel. Taylor's jaw dropped when she saw who was asking the question, a woman who looked to be in her mid to late thirties. Her complexion was flawless, her olive skin glowed, and her hazel eyes shone. Flecks of gold stared back at her from those captivating eyes. Her curly brunette hair was up in a messy ponytail, but she looked like she had just stepped out of a magazine.

The woman tilted her head. "Are you sure? I know curbs tend to jump out in the middle of nowhere."

Taylor was stunned. This woman was so gorgeous she couldn't think straight. Taylor cleared her throat and shifted her feet. "All better. It's just been a day, and that was the icing on the cake."

"Tell me about it. I'm having one of those days myself. I hope yours gets better. I hate to jet off, though. I'm running behind schedule. But, if you're sure you're alright..." Her words trailed off, and Taylor nodded, dazed. "Take care!" She waved and then rushed off, disappearing into the building.

Taylor snickered. Out of all the people she had to make a complete fool in front of, it was that dazzling woman. But it was nice to know there were still friendly people in the world. The woman didn't need to stop to make sure she was okay. She rolled her shoulders back and adjusted the burgundy ribbon she wore wrapped around her blonde hair. Who could blame her for trying to look nice on her first day?

Taylor slipped her purse back on her shoulder and picked up the pace to get into the hospital. She hadn't a clue where she was going and was already a few minutes behind. If only the day would improve.

CHAPTER FOUR

WE MEET AGAIN

Anne

"You're scowling," Cecilia said, breaking into Anne's thoughts as she stared at the computer. She had tried to put the accident out of her mind when she entered the hospital. Yet suddenly, in the stillness of the Pediatric floor, the accident came rushing back to her. Who would just up and leave an accident like that? Someone with no conscience. As Cecilia raised an eyebrow, Anne released a groan and shook her head.

"Long morning."

Cecilia checked her watch. "It's just a minute past eight. I'd say the morning hasn't even begun."

Anne laughed. "You would think, but let me tell you about the start of my day. I'm on the highway, about to get off the exit, when *Bam*." Cecilia jumped, and Anne leaned back in her chair.

"I was rear-ended. As if that wasn't bad enough, the person left the scene so that I couldn't get their registration, license, nothing." She threw up her hands. "They left. Sped so fast that I couldn't even get the license plate number, as if my brain was even thinking that far ahead."

"Ugh," Cecilia grunted. "Could you make out the person? Male, female, make of the car, anything?"

"Red two-door. Does that help anything? If my head had been in the right place, maybe something would have stuck, but nope." Anne sighed. It didn't even help to talk about it. What would help is if she could go back to the highway and start over. She would have been more prepared. She would have snapped a picture.

"Sorry, Anne. That has to suck. People are downright rude." A light lit up at the nurses' station, and Cecilia backed up from her. "I have to grab the call. But chin up, stay positive. You always do."

"Thanks, Cecilia." Anne watched as she disappeared into a room and returned to her work. She was right. Things would improve as the day went on. It couldn't get much worse.

"Anne?" Anne looked up and saw Hailey, a fellow nurse, approach the nurses' station. She was younger than Anne and shorter. She had large brown eyes and blonde hair that she wore in a loose ponytail. Hailey clasped her hands together. She fidgeted from one foot to the other. She tossed a look over to the elevator and then back to Anne. "Do you have a few minutes?"

"Sure. What's up?" Anne leaned back in her chair, tearing her eyes away from the computer. Hailey appeared like she needed Anne's attention more than the computer did. Her eyes darted down to the floor, then back up. Anne nodded. "Are you nervous about training the new hire?"

Hailey sighed and even broke through a smile. "How'd you guess?"

"We all are there at some point in our careers. It's a tough job having to train someone. You want to ensure you don't forget anything, yet you also don't want to overwhelm them, especially on their first day. Just remember, everyone had to start new at some point. And it's a great pleasure that they think you're prepared enough to take on this challenge."

"Do you?" Hailey leaned against the counter. "Think I'm prepared, I mean."

"Absolutely! They asked me for a suggestion, and I instantly gave them your name. Hailey, you've got this."

"Do you have pointers?" she asked. "Advice on what to point out, what I can't forget, etcetera?"

"My advice would be to think about what you wish you would have known when you first started. Then make sure you do that. You'll want to give her a tour on her first day. That way, she does not feel like she's thrown to the wolves in a completely new place. Sometimes, it's the little things that make the biggest difference."

Hailey nodded, mentally taking notes of Anne's advice. "I don't know why I'm so nervous. I've been doing it long enough."

Anne smirked. "It's just one of those things. You have been doing it so long, but that's when you tend to forget. It's like a routine. When you do the same thing repeatedly, you can do it in your sleep. However, when you start talking about it, you can miss things." By the end of the talk, Hailey was back to her smiling and cheerful self. "But you're going to be fine. We all have faith in you."

Hailey smiled, her dimples returning. "Thank you, Anne. I needed to hear that."

"Anytime." Anne watched as the younger woman walked away.

She stared back at her computer and eased into the flow of the day. She had an initial consultation meeting with a new patient coming in for evaluation. That should take twenty minutes, then the rest of the morning, she would be free to work the patients through their usual routine. It shouldn't be too hectic, at least not until after lunch.

The elevator opened, and Anne glanced at the woman exiting onto their floor. Her jaw dropped as she stood up, trying to mask the obvious questions she wanted to delve into.

CHAPTER FIVE

GETTING THE TOUR

Taylor

H ailey was personable and left Taylor feeling comforted. The minute they left the desk, Hailey had Taylor on a full-fledged tour of the Pediatric floor. Taylor was in awe of how the floor catered to the pediatric patients. The walls were attractively decorated, from the bright and vibrant colors. Each hallway contained a new theme, along with the age groups that housed those rooms: oceans, jungles, cityscapes, and farm animals decorated each corresponding hallway. It was as if the hospital wanted to guarantee that the children wouldn't be bored if they were stuck inside all day. Taylor couldn't help but enjoy the view.

"Our motto is that if kids have to spend their nights here, we want to ensure they don't have to stare at drab surroundings."

"And I would say you do a fine job." Taylor traced the

outline of a horse decal on the wall and glanced at Hailey. Hailey beamed, clutching her growing baby bump.

"I look like I'm about to pop, don't I?"

"What?" Taylor exclaimed. "Not at all. Quite the opposite. How far along are you?"

"Six months."

"Wow! You don't look old enough to have a child."

Hailey beamed, standing next to a room at the end of the hall. "That's a nice compliment. It's my first child. My husband and I were high school sweethearts and knew right after high school we'd get married. I worried that going to nursing school would be our demise. I heard horror stories about how being married and going to college full-time, only amounts to debt and arguments. Yet, it never happened to us." She giggled. "Mike is truly my best friend."

Taylor smiled. She would have given anything to have a relationship like that. But Taylor spent high school parenting her brother. She loved her brother dearly, but it was still a bummer that she spent high school playing Mom because her own mom couldn't step up to the plate.

"Do you have kids?"

Taylor shook her head. "My mother was a single mom who wasn't home often, so I helped raise my brother. It's not the same thing."

"Don't sell yourself short," Hailey argued. "I'd have to say that it's just as hard raising a sibling as raising your kid." Hailey touched her stomach. "I'm blessed to have this little bean right here. But it helps to have Mike in my corner. But I love kids. If you want to make it as a Pediatric nurse, you have to."

"You have a valid point there. I'm excited to start. I love kids, too. I think peds is a great fit for me."

"I imagine you're going to fit in great." Hailey grabbed Taylor's arm and gave it a slight squeeze. Taylor smiled, grateful to be part of a team of kind, dedicated people. Hailey walked over to the elevator and pushed the down button. They rode to the second floor. "This is medical records. We use electronic records most of the time, but we still have some paper records in case EMR goes down." Hailey explained when the doors opened. "It's all alphabetical, so quite easy to find what you're looking for. And if you need any help, you can be sure to ask any of us. We'll be glad to help you out. That's one thing about this department, everyone loves helping everyone else."

Taylor grinned -- another great sign. To her, it was as if they were looking at a family and not a workplace. She hoped she didn't relax too much; she had to remain on her A-game today. After Hailey finished her tour, they rode back up to the peds floor.

"We'll see if we can introduce you to some of the department staff. Dr. Newsome should be getting out of the room at any moment. They left the room and were headed down the hall, just as a door opened and an older woman exited the room. She glanced toward Hailey and nodded. "Speaking of…" They stopped next to the woman and Hailey made the introductions. "This is Dr. Newsome. She's been in the department for twenty years. The most senior physician the hospital has on staff.

Dr. Newsome was tall, with a neat silver bun secured on the top of her head. She rolled her eyes. "Hailey likes to make it sound like I'm ancient. I remember when the dinosaurs were roaming the halls."

That made the three of them laugh, and Taylor felt another wave of relief. In college, she heard stories about how you sometimes couldn't joke with the physicians because they always had to keep things serious. But with Dr. Newsome and Hailey, it felt like two friends hanging out.

The two of them continued their easy banter back and forth as Taylor watched them. "It was nice to meet you, Taylor."

"Likewise, I'm sure we'll be working more together in the coming days," Taylor remarked.

"I'll leave you two to finish up the tour." She waved and then turned a corner.

Taylor glanced at Hailey. "Are all the staff so easygoing?" she asked.

Hailey shrugged. "Mostly. Dr. Pohler can be a bit temperamental, but he is a great physician. You can get him to smile a few times, but mostly, good luck trying."

Taylor snickered. That might be a personal quest. She would have to consider it along the way. Anything was possible. Hailey and Taylor rounded the corner and Anne stood behind the nurse's station again. She was mortified when she realized that the one person who saw her outside, making a fool of herself, was the same person she would be working with. It almost felt like she was on a hidden TV show. What was more confusing was that the woman had this glow that left Taylor a tad speechless. She would have to figure out how to get over that quickly.

Taylor and Hailey made their way to the nurse's station, and Anne looked up. "So, how'd the tour go? Do you have the layout memorized?"

Taylor gave a soft laugh. "Hopefully. Guess I'll find out."

Anne nodded. "Good luck to you. Holler if you need

anything." She hurried off. Taylor watched after her and didn't look away until Hailey cleared her throat. When she looked at Hailey, Hailey arched an eyebrow.

"What?" Taylor asked, sitting in the chair that Hailey had rolled over for her.

Hailey snickered. "You're not the first person to be enamored by Anne. She is one of the nicest and sweetest people to work in this department. And let's talk loyal. No one could even compare. The patients love her. The parents love her." She shrugged. "There's no one that doesn't."

"Enamored is such a strong word," Taylor mumbled.

Hailey laughed loudly, tossing her head back and her whole face lighting up. "I don't mean anything by it. She's wonderful. I can't find anyone with anything bad to say against her."

"Well, I know I'm new to the group, but you seem rather nice yourself."

Hailey blushed. "Flattery. It will get you everywhere. Now, this is the computer. You be nice to it, and it will be nice to you." She shrugged. "Sometimes."

Taylor laughed. Hailey was quirky. She liked that. She leaned in to study the computer as Hailey worked to guide her through the system. By the end of the computer tutorial, her head was spinning. She hoped to retain enough info to look like she wasn't a complete dunce. With notes going over everything, she was one step further in the learning and ready to make a difference like the rest of the staff.

CHAPTER SIX

GENUINE CHAT

Anne

A nne stepped into the cafeteria. She took in a whiff of the fish and scrunched up her nose. Today, she needed something less filling. She walked over to the sandwich bin, grabbed a chicken club, grabbed bottled water, and went to the cashier.

"Hey Kelly, how's it going?"

Kelly nodded. "It's been a busy morning. I'm looking forward to the lunch crowd dwindling. How are you?"

Anne wanted to lament about her car and how her day had started rough, but with any hope, it could only improve. However, there was a line behind her, and talking about her crummy day would only make her want to cry.

"The day is half over. So gotta love that."

Kelly smiled. "Yep. Enjoy the rest of it." She grabbed her

sandwich and water and stepped away from the cashier. She was two seconds away from telling all about her morning. But she was relieved that she somehow let it go. There was no use complaining to anyone else. She glanced around the busy cafeteria until she spotted Taylor in the corner. She had her eyes pointed down at her cell phone and ate alone.

Anne glanced around again to see if anyone would go over and sit with her. When she was satisfied that Taylor was alone, she walked to the booth. "Hey."

Taylor looked up, her eyes wide. "Oh, hi, Anne." She shifted in her seat, quickly pocketing her cell phone.

"I don't want to interrupt. If you're busy, I can sit somewhere else. But truthfully, I tend to feel awkward eating by myself. So, if you wouldn't mind having company, you'll be helping me out."

Taylor quickly shook her head. "Not at all." Her cheeks grew a slight shade of red. "That's why I was staring at my phone. Somehow, I didn't feel so awkward being here alone." She smirked. "There you have it, my truth."

Anne sat down across from her. "Now we both don't have to feel so awkward." She looked at Taylor's sandwich and held up her own. "Welcome to the turkey club, club, I guess." She joked dryly.

Taylor sat up straighter, and her smile widened. Anne got to see her rosy complexion and bright eyes when she smiled. Her eyelashes were long and full. Her blue eyes shone as she stared back at Anne. She was a pretty woman. She was most likely in her early twenties, just straight out of college, but she held her head up in confidence, which is why it was odd to see her hiding behind her phone.

"How's your first day going?" Anne asked, opening up the plastic container that held her sandwich.

"Great! Everyone has been super nice to me, and I'm finding it easier than I could have hoped to acclimate myself to the area. I know it's only been five hours, but I feel like I will get a handle on my responsibilities."

"That's a positive note. Just remember that everyone has good and bad days. How you handle the bad days really makes a person."

They sat and talked for a bit, an easy chit-chat back and forth that surprised even Anne. When they first came into the department, most people were quieter and reserved, testing things out and ensuring they knew how the other co-worker would respond. But Taylor was laughing and joking around with her, almost easier than Anne could. They had good chemistry.

"What made you choose Pediatrics'?" Anne asked.

"I guess you could say Pediatrics chose me." Taylor popped the last bit of her sandwich into her mouth, and Anne stared at her, confused by how that one phrase sounded. She had said that multiple times, but no other person seemed to understand the same motivation. "I love kids. If ever I'm lucky enough to be a mother, I would want their nurse to be someone who cared for them as much as I cared for them. When contemplating what departments to do my residency, it was the only one that made sense."

"Inspiring," Anne mumbled. Taylor looked down, still blushing. "It takes a special person to see it through that way. It's rough to see kids suffering, and you will one day experience a loss you never thought you'd ever feel. And trust me, you never truly get over that loss."

Taylor stared at her, but Anne couldn't move her gaze away. Their eyes were locked, and Anne dared herself not to blink first. However, Anne failed and dropped her gaze to her water. She could feel the tension in the air between them. She was pretty sure if she touched Taylor, sparks would fly. And oh, how she longed to reach out and touch her. Taylor let out a breath and then started to laugh. That chortle brought Anne's eyes back up to Taylor's. Her jaw dropped slightly.

"I don't mean to laugh." Taylor covered her mouth. "I'm just reminding myself of how we first met this morning, with me practically diving face-first into the concrete."

Anne snickered. "You caught yourself. It was quite an impressive catch, indeed."

Taylor shook her head. "It was a rough morning. That was just the icing on the cake. I wouldn't have been surprised if I face-planted and broke my nose." She sighed. "But I am grateful I caught myself."

"Believe me, I know rough mornings," Anne groaned, suddenly thrust back into the accident that nearly left her late to work. Taylor stared at her, compelling Anne to share the story. She sipped on her water. "I was—." Her phone dinged a text message, breaking into her conversation. She glanced down at it and saw her sister's name, with a crying emoji as the text.

Anne groaned, then slipped her phone into her pocket. "I have to go." Without so much as an explanation or apology, Anne got up from the table.

She felt Taylor's eyes on her as she rushed away, dropping the trash into the nearest can and rounding the corner out of sight. She fished her phone out of her pocket and stared at the text again. If Melanie was upset, then she had reason to be. She called her and anxiously waited for her sister to answer.

"H...he...hello?" She sniffled, cutting deep into Anne's core.

"Mel, what's wrong? I got your text."

Immediately, the sniffling got louder, and Anne heard sobs. "I didn't mean to call you at work."

"Where are you? Are you in a safe place? Where's Lily and Rose?"

"Anne, will you stop?!" Melanie whined. "The kids are at the park with their friends, and I'm home alone. I didn't text you to get the third degree. I need someone to talk to and hoped you would listen."

Anne sighed. She would have to do her best. Josh wasn't the epitome of a great guy or even mediocre. In her eyes, he was the scum of the Earth, but Melanie loved him. She always defended him, and Anne sometimes needed to remind herself that she shouldn't be the motherly figure at that moment. She needed to be the friend.

"I'm sorry. I'm here to listen. What's going on?"

"Josh was out late last night. He said he had car trouble and needed to find a way home. It just doesn't add up. I smelled perfume on him. His car was fine this morning."

Anne sighed. If only Melanie would wise up and leave the loser. She released a breath, aching to spew all the hatred she could about her brother-in-law.

"Anne?" she inquired. "I know you want to tell me how much you despise him."

"I won't say those words," Anne replied. "But, Mel, you deserve better. That's not criticizing him. That's merely stating the truth. And I hope that you know you deserve better. He doesn't appreciate you."

"I love him." Then the whining resumed, and Anne could only stand there and listen, leaning against the wall, waiting for Melanie to stop crying over him.

"There's only so much love you can give someone that continues to treat you like that." She sobbed on the other end, but Anne left it at that. As much as she hated to hear that her sister and her husband were experiencing difficulties in their marriage, it reminded Anne that she wasn't the only one with problems. Melanie would cry for hours, possibly all day. Josh would apologize, and Mel would forgive him. It was the sad truth when it came to her sister's marriage. Anne could only hold onto hope that Melanie would eventually know that her happiness and the children's happiness were the most crucial things, and Josh wasn't the one to provide that happiness.

She returned to the floor and saw Taylor at the nurse's station. The conversation was still heavy on Anne's mind. If her sister didn't get out of the house quickly, who knew the damage Josh would cause? Not only to Melanie but to her nieces.

"Everything alright?" Taylor inquired.

"Yeah. Why?" Anne tried to play it off in the most lighthearted of ways.

"Well, you rushed off, and I thought we were bonding. Just wanted to make sure you were doing okay."

Anne sighed. "It's been a long day. I need to get back to work. And so do you."

CHAPTER SEVEN

FOR SHE'S A JOLLY GOOD LADY

Taylor

As the rest of the day went on, Taylor attempted to catch Anne's eye. See if there was some recognition of the moment they had spent together at lunch. It felt like they were talking, experiencing good chemistry with one another, even opening up in ways Taylor had never been able to do. Sure, she hadn't told Anne everything. There had to be more than just a few minutes between them before she was comfortable to dive in. Yet, things shifted the minute Anne ran away from the table. Was she paranoid?

With the day winding down, she saw Anne and prepared to catch up to her. She could be wrong, but she felt this pull toward Anne, and it seemed like Anne was even going to confess her darkest secret until something on her phone had her scurrying away. Although she wanted to catch up to her, Anne disappeared from the elevator.

Taylor frowned. Was Anne always this elusive? What happened to the friendly woman she met at lunch?

"Hey, Taylor. Heading out?" Hailey asked.

Taylor forced a smile and nodded. "Getting there." She hesitated. "So, Anne…" Her mind raced. Maybe it wasn't wise to bring up someone else's business. Hailey arched an eyebrow, waiting in angst as Taylor contemplated letting Hailey in. She shook her head. "Never mind."

"Are you sure?" Hailey tossed her bag over her shoulder. "If you are concerned, we can talk about it."

Taylor shook her head. "No, I'm good."

"Alrighty." Hailey reached into her bag. "I made a copy of your schedule for you. I nearly forgot it, so I'm glad we bumped into each other. First off, you did great today. I know the first day on any job can be a bit stressful, so good job."

"Thanks, Hailey." Taylor looked over her schedule, and her eyes widened. "Is this schedule for real? I have a ton of hours. If I weren't overwhelmed before, this would do me in."

Hailey laughed. "Trust me; there will come a time when you wish you had these hours." She shrugged. "I guess they just want to get your feet wet in all aspects. That way, you have the training. Just appreciate them for now because it won't last forever."

"If you say so," Taylor mumbled. She wasn't used to working full-time, and this gig had several double shifts. She had to remind herself that it was only getting her warmed up to learn all responsibilities. Hailey would know best.

"I have to run. I'll see you tomorrow." She tossed a wave over her shoulder and hurried to the elevator. Taylor looked back down at the schedule and groaned. This would leave virtually no time for activities outside of work. Sure, she had a couple of days off, but it was harder to maneuver around a work schedule so packed.

Taylor waited for the elevator to pick her up, then got on and took the slow ride down to the break room. She had gotten a locker and was able to house her personal belongings. It was bare when she got to the break room, or so she thought. She rounded the corner to the lockers and heard a muffled voice.

"Come to my place: you and the kids. You shouldn't be home with him. Who knows what he'll do?"

Taylor backed up, jamming her elbow against the metal door with a loud CLANG. She cringed, holding her breath. Anne peeked her head around the corner and stared at Taylor. "I'm sorry," Taylor whispered.

"It's fine," Anne mumbled. She pocketed her phone and then turned to a locker. Taylor stopped at her locker, the silence deafening at that moment. Taylor swallowed and glanced at Anne, who was fiddling with the combination. She groaned, moving the combination around several times. Taylor opened her mouth, ready to offer her assistance, when the locker fell open. "Finally," Anne grumbled. Taylor turned back to her locker and quickly grabbed her things from it. When she had her locker closed, she turned to Anne.

"Work tomorrow?" Taylor asked.

"Yep, bright and early. 6:00 A.M."

"I'll see you tomorrow, then." Anne turned and nodded, and then a smile slowly brushed her lips. "Have a good night!" Taylor quipped, then turned and hurried toward the door. If Anne wanted to be cold with her, that was her prerogative. After all, she did nothing wrong. At least nothing that she could recall. The phone call clearly soured Anne's mood. There was torment in Anne's voice.

Taylor entered her car and turned the key. Her car made a noise, then stopped. She groaned. Her car was pretty reliable in most situations. It was an older Toyota Camry, though. One that sometimes liked to be a tad picky. She tried the key again, pumping the accelerator and closing her eyes. All she needed was a little more gas. It started, and she released a sigh. She just needed to know how to work the vehicle.

When Taylor exited onto the highway, even though her radio was playing, she was more mindful of the traffic. It was when everyone got off work, and the highway was busier than in the morning. She tapped on her steering wheel and sang along to the song but focused on the traffic around her. She had to be careful because there wasn't any way she could handle getting into another accident. She was already letting the guilt settle in for the accident that morning. Someone out there was being forced to take care of damage they didn't cause. Why wouldn't she feel guilty?

Thirty minutes later, Taylor pulled into the driveway of her aunt's house. During the daytime, it wasn't anything to write home about. It needed a fresh coat of paint. The roof looked like it could cave in at any given moment. The street leading to the house was filled with potholes. The neighbors liked to get drunk, party, and have loud fights in the middle of the night. But since her aunt didn't force her to pay rent, it was the best she could find. However, she always dreamed of getting out of her house and into a better neighborhood, of course, taking Gavin with her. Maybe even find a place nearby that her aunt could afford if Taylor helped her out. They were all dreams but something to strive for.

Taylor approached the door and fumbled with her purse to find her keys. Before she could get her key out, the door swung open, and Gavin appeared in the foyer, wide-eyed, with a big smile. At seventeen, the baby fat had melted away from his face, revealing an angular jaw. He was starting to bulk up, too. He had biceps and a buzzcut. He played on the football team at his high school, a far cry from the kid who used to hide behind her whenever there were thunderstorms.

"Hey, Sis! It's about time you got home." He pulled her into the foyer, and Taylor smiled. Her aunt stood there with a homemade cake. She was still wearing her sea foam polyester work uniform from the restaurant. She was slim and in her late fifties, with smile lines bracketing her mouth and kind green eyes. She wore her hair in a loose ponytail. Her hands were red and raw from cleaning tables.

Gavin and Kristi both started singing For She's a Jolly Good Lady.

Taylor laughed when the song came to an end. "What's this for?" she asked. The lettering was sloppy, but the cake had writing sprawled across it, which read We're So Proud of You. She flicked a tear away, which had attempted to crawl down her cheek.

"Can't you read?" her aunt asked, laughing. "We're proud of you, and it's celebrating your first day on the job.

"And I'm starving," Gavin moaned. "So, let's have cake."

Taylor rolled her eyes. "After dinner." When he scowled, Taylor snickered. "I know. I'm so mean. Wash up. Aunt Kristi and I are going to make something delicious."

"I'm on it." He hurried out of the foyer, and Taylor reached for the cake.

"I hate that you feel the need to help," Kristi began. "You should be relaxing. After all, today was your big day. Besides, Gavin told me."

Taylor followed her aunt into the kitchen. "He told you what exactly?"

Taylor put the cake down on the counter and leaned back against it. She would have hoped they could have had a few minutes of quiet, where Kristi didn't know that Taylor had fled from an accident.

"You know I don't approve of people that shirk their responsibilities." She held up a finger and wagged it in front of Taylor. Taylor felt like a little kid, ready for her scolding. She looked down at the floor as Kristi continued. "The truth is, I understand you felt it was your only option. But, honey, you have to remember that I'm here."

"I know, but you work two jobs to keep this house. The last thing you need is to help me out of a bind. Are you disappointed in me?"

Kristi opened the refrigerator and pulled out a casserole she had made special for the occasion. It was Taylor's favorite—sausage and hash browns, fit for dinner and breakfast. "I wouldn't say disappointed, exactly. You're a grown woman, worthy of making up her mind. Just think before you leap next time. I'm always on your side." She winked. "Set the table, and I'll warm this up."

In a way, it was a relief to have the truth out in the open. It could have been worse if she had waited to tell Kristi the truth or if Kristi had found out another way. So, ultimately, Gavin had done the right thing. Now, if only she could ease her guilty conscience.

Taylor stared at the fire as the glow towered over the living room ceiling. Gavin was in bed, and at any minute, she'd have to be going, too. It was hard staying up, especially with a 7 A.M. call time. And seven o'clock was going to come soon. Besides, she had fourteen hours scheduled for the next day. She already felt the exhaustion.

"Want me to top off your water?" Aunt Kristi asked, startling Taylor from contemplating the fire.

"Just a bit." Taylor yawned. "I need to go to bed in a few minutes." She smirked when Kristi laughed. "What? You don't think so?"

"You're the one who lived off of coffee and energy drinks for the entirety of college." She winked, and Taylor snickered, sipping on her water.

"I'm different now that I have a job and real responsibilities. It's great to dream, but you sometimes have to be practical."

"Oh. So, this is practical, Taylor?" Aunt Kristi winked and sipped on her coffee. Taylor turned back to the fire. A lot had changed since she dreamt as a child. Back then, the world was hers to conquer.

"We haven't even talked about your day," Aunt Kristi began. "How was it? Outside of the accident, I mean."

Taylor snickered. "Yes, outside of that. But the day was good. You should have seen some of those kids that I worked with. And to see what they're going through; it just breaks your heart."

"And that's why you're meant for pediatrics, my dear."

"There isn't anywhere I'd rather be." Taylor sipped on her water.

"And your co-workers. I trust you're working with a great group?" Aunt Kristi arched an eyebrow, always the motherly figure. It gave Taylor great comfort to know that Aunt Kristi would always be there for support as she navigated her new job.

"Hailey is the one that trained me. She's six months pregnant and oh so tiny. She has a great heart. I lucked out when it came to working closely with her. I couldn't have asked for a better trainer to get me through my first day." Taylor dropped her gaze to the fire and thought back to the hours before when she started, not knowing where anything was, and left the day confident she could make this job work. "The physicians seem friendly enough. I heard there's a doctor that can be a bit temperamental, but I've seen plenty of guys like that."

"The neighbor in the back to mention one," Kristi teased.

Taylor laughed. "Mr. Landrin. Yep. He just might be one I was thinking of." Always yelling about the rickety fence that crossed their paths in the back. Even though it was on his property, he was insistent it was their nuisance. He and Aunt Kristi had yet to come to a resolution.

"There's always one grouch in the bunch," Aunt Kristi added. "Anyone interesting?"

Taylor's cheeks flushed, and she looked down at her glass of water. It was as if her Aunt had already read her mind. It was true; their bond was like no other, but she hadn't even breathed a word of Anne, and her Aunt was there to drag it out of her.

"Come on, Taylor. I see that sparkle in your eye, and your rosy cheeks don't exactly hide the truth." Aunt Kristi laughed. "What aren't you telling me?"

"Aunt Kristi, you're like a human lie detector." Her eyes lit up, but Taylor held up her hand. "Most of the time." Taylor laughed. "There isn't anything to tell. I mean, it's only been one day. The co-workers are nice, and we should leave it at that." She downed the rest of her water and stood up.

Aunt Kristi grimaced. "I am disappointed that you aren't going to tell me what you're hiding from me. But if that's the way you want it." She huffed and looked away.

Taylor sunk back down to her chair, and her Aunt grinned. Taylor shook her head. Her Aunt tended to get Taylor to talk, even if she didn't want to. But, in this case, Taylor wasn't eager to hide something. She was looking forward to getting something off her chest. It didn't sit well with her on how the workday ended, how she and Anne went from laughter to an icy silence.

"There is this one woman."

"I knew it," her Aunt said with a gleam. "Doctors and nurses always date each other. Am I right? Do tell."

Taylor laughed. "First of all, you can't know if it's something special after a few hours in the same space. Secondly, we ate lunch together, having a good time. Or so I thought. She then rushes off, like someone had lit a fire under her butt." Taylor shook her head. "I have no idea, but it was the strangest thing. Then she was almost cold when she saw me in the afternoon, and when I was grabbing my things from the break room, I saw her again. Nothing in that interaction said she even enjoyed getting to know me. So, whatever. Maybe that's why I'm single. I just don't get women." Taylor frowned. "I know that came out weird, but you know what I mean."

Aunt Kristi nodded. "Quite well. But you said it yourself; it's only been a day. Maybe she's shy and reserved."

"Not her," Taylor argued.

"It's hard to judge a person when you hardly know them. It's possible she just had a lot on her mind. Or some people are different. Your forever love doesn't need to be found on the first day, Taylor." Aunt Kristi stood up and walked over to her, taking the glass from her hand and kissing the top of her head. "Give it in time. Don't cut anyone out of the equation. You never know. Good night!"

"Night, Aunt Kristi." Those words played in Taylor's mind as she stared at the fireplace, then leaned back to watch the glow. It was true that Hailey said Anne was one of the sweetest people she knew. She didn't see Hailey as someone who would intentionally lie. Maybe Anne had a lot on her mind. Taylor got lost in the glow of the fire. She could stick around a few more minutes. Now, she hardly felt tired.

CHAPTER EIGHT

HOUSEHOLD VISITORS

Anne

The house was eerily quiet as Anne peeked into her spare room. Lily and Rose were asleep peacefully as if Melanie hadn't pulled them from the only home they knew. Anne was glad Melanie had agreed to come to the house, even though Anne spent the night with Melanie hashing over things.

He said it was a mistake. The affair is over. Anne rolled her eyes at that one. Josh had been caught. It didn't matter what he said. Anne wasn't about to believe him. She didn't understand why Melanie quickly let it go. She knew why, at least based on the one-word answer she usually got from her sister. *Love.* Was Melanie sure about that? Anne had been in love once, but it felt like forever ago. She couldn't imagine giving up herself and her beliefs for another person. But then again, abuse was a cycle.

True, he never hit Melanie. Or so she always tried to convince Anne. But there were other kinds of abuse; her sister and nieces needed and deserved better.

Anne rounded the corner, and Melanie sat at the table, a coffee cup in her hand. She looked up when Anne's slippers padded on the kitchen tile. Her brown eyes looked worried. Anne could tell Melanie hadn't been sleeping; bags were under her eyes. She looked exhausted. Melanie was always the girlie girl in the family. She loved makeup and clothes. Melanie wore no makeup tonight, and Anne could see her roots peeking out of her blonde hair. She looked like a shell of her former self.

"Just made a fresh pot. Help yourself."

"Don't mind if I do." Anne grabbed her mug and poured herself a cup. "Checked in on the kids, and they're sleeping like two snug bugs in a rug."

Melanie laughed. "It's been a long time since you said that."

Anne looked over at her sister, and she had the brightest smile. It felt like ages since she had seen that smile, and she had forgotten how much she missed it. "You know, sis, you and the kids can stay here as long as you want." She slid into the seat across from her and sipped her coffee. Melanie's face fell. She nodded but glanced down at her mug. "Okay, if staying here doesn't cut it, I can put you up in a hotel." After all, she wasn't going to get her house paid off this month anyway. What were a few hundred dollars spent at the hotel? If it meant her sister and nieces would be safe, she was all for it.

"Anne, I appreciate the offer. But I think we're going to head home tomorrow. If the kids were awake, we might even make it tonight." She smirked. "I was a little rash earlier."

Anne frowned, leaning back in her chair. "Did you hear from him? Is that why the sudden change of tune?"

"No!" Melanie argued. "He's my husband and the girl's father. What's running going to do? Absolutely nothing."

"Show me your phone." Anne held out her hand and waited. Melanie's jaw dropped. "If there's nothing on your phone from Josh, there's nothing to hide."

"With all due respect, Anne, I'm thirty-two and way too old to have my sister think she can control my life." She dropped her gaze, and Anne slammed her hand down on the table.

"Dammit, Mel. What did he say this time? How many tears do you have to cry before you realize that you're just being a doormat to your husband?" Anne didn't mean to sound so harsh, but watching her sister fall for Josh's same old tricks was frustrating.

"That's not fair." Melanie shook her head. "You're not married. You wouldn't understand."

Anne huffed and dropped her gaze to the table. She could stare at the wooden furniture for hours, and those words wouldn't hurt any less. But if that's what Melanie felt about it, then why sulk? She had made up her mind. *You know you don't feel that way. If she walks out that door and Josh takes his anger out on her, then you're going to be sorry you ever let her go.* "I may not be married, but I saw the pain in our mother's eyes, and I'm sure you did, too."

Melanie looked away from her. Her eyes darkening. Anne shook her head and stared at her coffee. If only her sister would understand that Josh was always going to be the man he was. He wouldn't change, and nothing could make that happen.

"I can't make you stay." The words came out, barely above a

whisper. She bit down on her lip, fearing that tears would soon follow. Josh wasn't worth her tears, but her sister and nieces were. She reached for her coffee as Melanie looked at Anne.

"I know you don't get it. Hell, there are times when I don't, either. I don't want to rush back to him." She pushed the phone toward Anne. "3287."

"Huh?"

"My passcode. It's 3287." Anne reluctantly grabbed the phone and put in the code. Instantly, Josh's message came up.

JOSH:

Baby, I'm sorry. We need to work through this. If you want me to see a counselor, I will.

"He's never offered to see a counselor before. That's a first step that could be our breakthrough." Anne slowly nodded, pushing the phone back toward her. "You don't believe him. Typical."

"Mel," Anne started. "I want to believe him. It would give me no greater pleasure than knowing he got some help and was the father your girls need and the husband you deserve. But I worry about you guys. You forget that I have seen horrible family situations at the hospital. Dads that abuse their kids and broken families. I don't want you in the midst of that."

"I get that, but I promise you, if we go back and things don't change, I will get us out of there. I'll be able to protect the girls. I know that I will."

If only Anne could believe that. But it was her sister's life, and arguing for her to stay could only drive a wedge between them. "Be careful."

Melanie smiled. "I always am." The smile never faded as she took another sip of her coffee. She licked her lips, then sighed. "So, what's going on with you? Anything new lately?"

Anne snickered, taking a drink of her coffee and nearly spitting it out. She didn't want to tell her sister about the accident when Mel had her own crisis brewing.

"My online shop is booming," Anne began. Anne knew she needed to drop the topic, and this was a nice detour. She made small, knitted items, from keychains to stuffed animals, and sold them online. It started as a hobby and slowly turned into another avenue of income, allowing her the opportunity to help with her mortgage and other finances. Anne never thought it would go anywhere, but she was pleasantly surprised by the reputation her online shop had earned. Getting noticed by reviews was sometimes a challenging goal to achieve. Now, she was finally starting to gain some recognition.

"That's great. What's popular these days?" Melanie asked, sipping on her coffee.

"Well, you know anything from *Mandalorian* is popular. People still request Baby Yoda." Anne was glad to have the reprieve from bringing up her biggest drama.

"That's great! I know the girls love the unicorns you made last year." Anne smiled. Lily was six. Rose was five. They were practically twins in Anne's eyes. Melanie and Josh wasted no time before they announced their second pregnancy. Back then, Josh was still a loser, but because he helped bring Lily and Rose into their lives, Anne pushed past his flaws. Now, it seemed there were too many to ignore. "Anything else going on?" Melanie asked.

There was no dodging that question. Anne had to tell the truth. "Your sister was in a little fender bender this morning."

"What?" Melanie stared. "Obviously, you're not hurt, right? But why didn't you tell me? Who's fault was it?"

"Well, I'm not hurt. It wasn't my fault." Anne sighed. "And the person fled the scene, so I'll have to pay for it out-of-pocket." Melanie reached out and touched Anne's hand, finding reason now to console Anne, but Anne didn't want the attention solely directed at her. Her sister was in a precarious situation and needed someone to always be on her side. "It's fine. It's just that when everything is going perfectly, and then it changes overnight, and you feel like everything you've worked toward is getting done for?"

Melanie's eyes widened. "I think you lost me."

"I guess I lost myself, too. I was about to make my last mortgage payment. I had parties planned, and I was super excited. Then this happened. Now, who knows how much this will cost me?"

"That totally sucks. Sorry, Anne."

Anne glanced at her coffee, then downed the last droplets. Perhaps it was her own naivety. She couldn't expect everything to go off without a hitch. Now was the time to survey the damage. No one else could help her out.

CHAPTER NINE

THE NEW TRAINER

Taylor

When the elevator doors opened, Taylor spotted Anne at the nurse's station. Taylor didn't know whether to approach her or avoid her. Unfortunately, the decision wasn't all hers. Anne looked up and offered a brief smile. Taylor sighed. Maybe she was in a bad mood the past couple of days. Yesterday, during her fourteen-hour shift, she had talked to Anne twice. Both times were because Anne needed a computer, and Taylor just happened to be sitting in front of the only free one. She wasn't gruff about it, but she felt none of the sparks during lunch two days ago.

"Good morning, Anne."

"Good morning. We are going to have a busy day today. Hailey called in sick; I'm guessing morning sickness. You're with me."

The air rushed out of Taylor's lungs. She had a strong urge to apologize to Anne. Maybe that would help. Yet, apologizing felt weird. Everyone had to learn sometimes. She feared that Anne and she wouldn't have the same working relationship she had with Hailey the two days before.

Anne continued, "We're down one nurse. It's going to get a tad hectic." Already, they had shared more conversation than they had in the last twenty-four hours; this was going to be awkward.

"Just put me where you need me." Taylor hoped she didn't seem anxious. Anne continued with a smile and nodded.

"Follow me. Our first patient is Willow. She's a frequent flyer around this ward. She has leukemia. She's been sick and moved to this department for follow-up. If things don't improve here, she will be transferred to a Cancer facility specializing in Children and cancer. The poor girl. She's been through a lot."

Taylor could hear the sadness in Anne's voice. She spoke from the heart, and Taylor could practically feel the pain oozing from Anne. Hailey had mentioned Anne had a big heart and was fabulous with the patients. Taylor experienced that from the first second Anne spoke, relieving Taylor's fears. Everyone could have a bad day, even two.

"Good morning, Willow. How are you feeling today?"

"Sick." She rubbed her stomach and frowned. "Can I get a Jell-O?"

"Absolutely. I'm going to get some vitals, and we'll grab that right away for you. Willow, this is Taylor. She's going to be assisting me today."

Willow gave a slight wave. "Hey, Willow. We're going to get you all better." Taylor grinned at the little girl, but from the corner of her eye, she saw Anne staring at her. Taylor shrugged it off. "What kind of Jell-O would you like when we're done?"

"Strawberry!" Her eyes lit up, and Anne hurried to the side of her, grabbing a thermometer as she passed the cart. Taylor stood there awkwardly. Hailey would tell her what to do, but Anne seemed focused on the patient. She understood, though, because it was just the two different work personalities. If she wanted to make it, she would have to be sure to understand the nuances of the hospital staff. After all, that, too, was part of a nurse's duty.

"Would you like me to grab the BP?" Taylor asked, reaching for the cuff.

"No, I got it. Just observe right now." Her tone cut through like a knife, and Taylor frowned, withdrawing her hand as if someone had just slapped her.

A lump slowly formed in her throat. Was Anne moody? For the rest of the visit with Willow, Taylor didn't even attempt to assist. Anne didn't seem like she needed or wanted the help. If that's how she felt, then Taylor would back off, but she made a mental note for future patients. Anne had excellent bedside manner, though. Anyone could see that. She knelt at her eye level and talked to her more than she even acknowledged Willow's parents. They were huddled on a couch, watching, observing. Taylor saw her mother's red, puffy eyes, and Taylor's heart went out to them. She bit down on her lip, hoping she wouldn't start crying. That was one thing Taylor hadn't considered: her inability to control her emotions. Yet, she needed to work through that because the patients weren't there to console her.

"We're all set in here. We'll grab you your Jell-O and be right back."

"Thank you, Anne." Willow's mother said. Anne turned to her and nodded, then turned back around and swiftly moved toward the door. Once they were both outside the door, Anne stopped and turned to Taylor.

"Are you nuts?"

Taylor cowered back, frowning. "Excuse me." Anne grabbed her arm and pulled her away from Willow's room, not stopping until they reached the nurse's station. "You can't seriously tell me that you thought it was a good idea to tell a little girl with cancer that she was going to get all better, right? Did your brain glitch? Because no one would think that was a good idea."

Taylor's eyes furrowed, and she thought back to the encounter with Willow. "Oh." She covered her mouth. "I wasn't thinking."

"That's painfully clear, but you need to start thinking because we have patients that die every year in this ward, who we would give our own breath to have saved. Many of those patients are Willow's age or even younger. Don't let that happen again." The last sentence stuck in Taylor.

"I'm sorry," Taylor mumbled. "It won't." She looked away, wary that a tear might fall. Anne was seething. Taylor didn't dare look in her direction. It'd only been two days, but Anne acted like she shouldn't mess up. Things were bound to happen, but maybe Taylor was destined to fail.

"Take this to Willow. She's waiting." Taylor turned back, and she had the Jell-O cup. There wasn't an ounce of a smile on Anne's face. Taylor grabbed it and dropped her head as if Anne scolded her as if she were a child. There had to be a way for her to show Anne she wasn't a complete failure.

She entered Willow's room, and Willow looked up, her eyes bright and expecting. "Here you go, Willow."

"Thank you!"

Taylor peeled back the top and handed over the Jell-O and spoon. She glanced over at her parents; her dad had snaked his arm around the mom's shoulder, protecting her. It was a noble sight, indeed.

"You let us know if you need anything. The doctor will check in on you in an hour or so."

"Thank you!" Her dad replied. Her mom appeared like she was ready to break. Taylor nodded and then left the room. When she returned to the nurse's station, Anne glanced up but immediately looked back down at the computer. "I can't imagine watching your child go through something like this."

"And for so long," Anne mumbled.

"Does Willow have any siblings?"

Anne sighed and looked away from the computer. Her eyes were still dark and hazy. Yet, there was still a vulnerability in them as Anne spoke. "Two brothers and a sister. The sister is older. The brothers are younger. They're staying with their grandparents while her parents can be here. The mom stepped away from her job. From what I understand, the dad's job is in peril. Their lives could be uprooted even more."

"So sad," Taylor whispered.

"Unfortunately, it's what we face around here. We need to get on to the next patient. Follow me." And again, they were off. Throughout the rest of the morning, when it came to Anne and the patients, she was phenomenal. Taylor watched her with curiosity. Hailey was right. As much as Anne loved her job and the patients she helped, the patients loved her just as much. Even the new patients seemed to have this connection with her and feel at ease.

While it was amazing to experience, Taylor couldn't help but notice that Anne was avoiding her. One screw-up, and it was like Taylor was dead to Anne. It was heart-wrenching because Taylor wanted to be there and learn from Anne.

The last patient of the morning was twelve-year-old Simon, and he needed labs drawn as he was getting ready to remove a benign tumor from his leg. Anne and Taylor entered the room, just like they had with so many patients earlier in the day. Only this time, something was different.

After Anne finished taking his vitals, she turned to Taylor. "Would you like to draw the labs?"

Taylor stared at her; her jaw dropped, beads of sweat popping up on her forehead. She glanced at Simon, who frowned and grabbed onto the bed, not looking interested in any mention of a blood draw. Then, he turned to his mom, who didn't notice Taylor's hesitation.

"Sure!" Taylor's voice cracked. The last time she had poked a patient was when she was doing her clinicals, and it wasn't a twelve-year-old boy. Instead, a fifty-eight-year-old woman didn't seem phased by getting her blood drawn. She had enough experience. During her clinicals, though, she had done several. She got some of the even tougher sticks, with which her teachers struggled. There was nothing to be concerned about except why Anne was suddenly putting her in this position. After barely two words to one another, when she wasn't introducing Taylor, this seemed like a sudden stretch.

She took a stride of confidence and walked over to the tubes Anne had already laid out before her. Feeling all eyes on her, she worked on getting everything set up. When it came to putting it in his arm, though, Taylor's mind blanked. She stared at the needle and then his arm. She had already disinfected the arm, but her mind was jumbled. Taylor released a breath and moved in. She felt again for the vein, swabbed the area with an alcohol pad one last time, and just went with it. There was no holding back, and it was a clean stick. One tube was taken, followed by another. She removed the tourniquet, pulled the needle out, and took a swab to his arm, but there wasn't a drop of blood.

"Let me know when you're done." He squeezed his eyes shut.

"I'm done." He opened his eyes and looked at his arm.

"I didn't even feel that."

Taylor breathed a sigh of relief. "I'm always happy to hear that." Taylor's words were cheery, but she was jumping for joy inside.

"We are all through here," Anne piped in. "The doctor has one more patient and will then be checking in to see if you have any questions on the forthcoming surgery. Let us know if you need anything."

They left the room, and Taylor finally released the pent-up sigh. "You did a good job in there."

Taylor stopped and turned to Anne. Those words filled her with more emotions than she had anticipated. "Excuse me." She turned and quickly moved to the restroom. When the door slammed behind her, she fell against the sink and tears flowed. After a morning where Anne didn't give her any acknowledgment other than to scold her, she needed that small compliment.

She covered her face, shaking her head. But what if the blood draw had gone wrong? She would never hear the end of it and question her self-worth as a nurse.

She grabbed a paper towel and covered her face, trying to soak up all the tears. She needed more confirmation than she liked to admit. After a few minutes of standing there, gawking at her reflection in the mirror, her phone vibrated in her pocket. She reached for it and stared at the message.

> AUNT KRISTI:
>
> Double shift at the restaurant today. I need to get the electricity paid for. Will you stop on the way home? Write a check, and I'll give you the cash to put back in your account.

Taylor groaned. It wasn't the first time Kristi expected to cover the household expenses, but her aunt eventually paid her back. Yet, there wasn't much in her bank account, so she hoped she had enough to cover.

Taylor heard a noise at the door, and she quickly pocketed her phone. Anne popped around the corner. "Sorry to interrupt, but," Her words trailed off. "Have you been crying?"

Taylor sighed. She didn't want anyone to think less of her, but she could already feel the condescending stares. "No, I'm good. Just caught in a coughing fit."

Anne shrugged. "You're wanted in HR. They said you have to take a test. I think it's just some basic stuff. But they said ASAP."

"Alright then! Thank you for the message. I'll head right there."

Anne left the bathroom and turned back to her reflection.

She grabbed her phone again and pulled up her bank account. After making the payment, she looked at just having a couple of dollars left in her account. There weren't any other options.

TAYLOR:

Yep. I'm on it.

She had to do what she had to do, but she couldn't wait until her first paycheck. Two weeks wouldn't come quickly enough.

CHAPTER TEN

SEEING RED

Anne

The cafeteria was empty as Anne entered the room and looked around at their food options for the day. What she needed was a salad; what she wanted were a burger and fries. She groaned as the salad won. The week felt excruciating. She'd been busy at work. To top it off, she couldn't get anyone to fix her car. It wasn't due to a lack of trying. Every place she called was slammed with customers.

Anne headed toward an empty booth after she paid for her salad and water. The less she had to converse with anyone, the better. This week had put her in a foul mood. It wasn't like her, but it was hard to find a way out of it when every time she perked up, she encountered another blunder. For starters, it still bothered her that Melanie forgave Josh so easily and was willing to take the girls back to their house. Josh promised they could start couples counseling. But Anne had yet to see Josh follow through on a promise. Anne wanted her sister to understand that Josh would say what he could to get them back in his grasp. Anyone could see that except for the one person who needed to.

As she reached the booth, she spotted Taylor two tables away. That was another thing altogether. On the first day, they had a good chat at lunch. She was even mildly intrigued to learn more about the new resident. But then her life blew up. Now, she was stuck worrying about Melanie. She took her aggression out on the co-workers she knew the least, a.k.a Taylor. It'd been two days of being forced into working together. Hailey was still out sick, and there was concern over whether she could return.

Taylor did make some stupid judgment calls; telling Willow she would get all better was at the top of the list. But overall, Anne saw some potential in her. She was young, vibrant, and had the same drive Anne felt at that age. Anne could see that in her. She also noticed something else. Taylor had her emotions at the forefront at all times. She walked in on her crying and never once believed the story that she was in a coughing fit. Those were real emotions Anne saw in Taylor's eyes. She had been there before. At the start of her nursing residency, she wasn't nearly as poised as Taylor was.

"Mind if I sit here?"

Taylor looked up away from her phone. "Um yeah, sure, if you want." She wasn't the confident individual that Anne saw on the first day. Was that because of Anne's gruff tendencies? Taylor's mistakes made Anne frustrated, which she took out on Taylor. She knew this wasn't the best way to welcome a new hire, but she wanted to push Taylor to live up to her potential.

"Thank you!"

Taylor dropped her phone to the table, and Anne's eyes went to it. Taylor touched the phone, switching it to silent.

"You're not eating?" Anne asked. "You need to keep your strength up, especially for a fourteen-hour shift."

"I had a banana. I'm good."

Anne arched an eyebrow. She wanted to scowl and tell Taylor that just a banana wouldn't suffice, but she backed off and dug into her salad. Anne could feel Taylor watching her as she ate. "So," Anne began. "I owe you an apology."

Taylor scoffed. Anne fought the urge to reach across, grab hold of her, and tell her to stop being so nervous. She wasn't there to chastise her or fight her. She swallowed and took another bite of her salad.

"It's been a rough week. It started badly and only went downhill from there. So, if I offended you anyway, jumped on your case for Willow, or treated you poorly the last few days, know it wasn't personal. I shouldn't have been like that because it's no way to treat a new team member."

Taylor gawked at Anne. This time, Anne fidgeted from one side to the other. When the blonde's eyes were on her, she felt like Taylor could see right through her. The feeling was confusing, awkward, and even a bit exhilarating. While she was the senior nurse to Taylor, she was also intrigued by her. Anne had yet to decipher whether it was her looks or her personality, but with Taylor staring at her that way, she felt it was something she'd never experienced.

She laughed slightly. "Will you say something? Anything? Please."

Taylor dropped her gaze and slowly nodded. "Apology accepted. Although, I don't think it was warranted. You were right to talk to me about Willow. It was a blunder that I should have never made. And I totally get having a bad week. I've been there. So, consider it forgotten." Her smile widened, and Anne couldn't help but respond with the same. Already, Anne could tell that Taylor had a forgiving, loving spirit, which would make her perfect for pediatrics.

Anne dug into her salad again and then took a swig of water, finally relaxing. Taylor focused on Anne's salad again, almost as if she was salivating over it. When Anne caught her looking, Taylor put on a smile.

"Your salad looks delicious. I'll have to remember that for the next time."

"You still have thirty minutes in your lunch. I'm sure the banana won't hold you over."

"No, I'm stuffed. Really." Yet, Taylor's actions told otherwise. Was it a financial thing? Taylor had just been working there for four days. She wouldn't be getting paid for another week and a half. Anne didn't know her finances, but she knew her own. It was a rough road until she started making regular pay. Even then, she had moments where she still scrambled to make ends meet.

"Excuse me. I'll be right back." She got up from the table and went over to the salads. She grabbed one and then a water and went to pay for it. When she got back to the table, Taylor stared at her.

"What's this? I said I was stuffed."

Anne shrugged. "Just thought you could try it. That way, the next time, you'll know if it's something you want to buy. Just eat what you want." She sat down and went back to her salad."

"At least let me pay for it." Taylor was slow to reach into her purse, but Anne reached out and touched her hand. Taylor hesitated, and Anne smiled at her.

"Consider it the rest of my apology." She winked, then withdrew her hand.

"Thank you," Taylor mumbled. For someone who wasn't hungry, she started eating the salad with the enthusiasm of someone starving. Anne tried to tear her eyes away, but there was a piece of Taylor's story Anne didn't know. Maybe one day, she could understand Taylor a little more.

Anne's apology lessened the tension between them. The rest of the work day flew by. Anne allowed Taylor to take on more responsibilities with the patients. Without Hailey, it made for some heavier workloads, but having Taylor there did help once Anne allowed Taylor to work solo for a bit. When the shift was over, Taylor finalized the documentation, and Anne watched over her shoulder to ensure Taylor didn't miss anything.

"Like that?" Taylor asked.

"Yep. Looks great. And our shift is over. It's been a long day. We can head on out." Since Hailey was out, Anne had to cover for her. She didn't mind the extra shifts, but it reminded her she wasn't as young as she once was. "You're doing great, Taylor. If I don't say that enough, just remember that."

Taylor grinned. "Thank you, and I appreciate your allowing me more freedom. And I must say, kudos to you for working with the patients. They absolutely adore you."

Anne snickered. "Thank you!" They stepped onto the elevator and rode it down. "I adore them all. I used to plan these excursions to the courtyard. The children would be able to experience the zoo. For the patients that have to stay here for days, weeks, months," Anne sighed. "They needed to have the same experiences that healthy kids get, you know?"

"That's awesome. I'm sure the kids love it. But you said, used to. You don't anymore?"

Anne nodded, leaning back against the wall of the elevator. "They did until budget cuts decimated the program." Anne rolled her eyes. "They've had to let some staffing go, so they bring on residents, who they can pay less." The doors opened, and Taylor frowned. "Not to say it isn't vital to have new nurses. It's the only way a hospital can grow."

Yet, that comment didn't sit well with Taylor, and Anne felt bad as they clocked out and grabbed their things from their lockers. It wasn't until they were out of the break room that Anne proceeded.

"I didn't say it to make you feel bad. It's not your fault. It's politics, and that sucks."

Taylor shrugged. "I understand. I can also see why it would be frustrating." They remained quiet as they left the hospital. Anne felt a pang of regret for even mentioning it. Just when they were back to being good, she had to screw things up and say the wrong thing. It had to be hurtful to hear.

"I really didn't mean anything by it. I was torn to pieces when they nixed the excursions, and I had to tell the kids that it would never happen again. They were understanding. It was me that went off the rails." Anne forced a smile as Taylor stopped in the parking lot.

"I'm sure it was hard to hear."

Anne sighed and looked down at the car they were standing by. "It is what it is," she muttered. Her eyes skimmed over the front of the car until it landed on the damage. She frowned. Then, she diverted her eyes to the rearview mirror, where a familiar ribbon hung. "Is this your car?"

Taylor nodded. "It's not much, I know. I aim to fix it or get a cheap used car within the year. Gotta have a paycheck for that, though." She laughed.

Anne didn't make a move to laugh. She kept staring. "Um, I gotta go." She backed up, her eyes burning into that fiery red color. She couldn't believe another rug had been pulled out from under her.

"Anne?"

Anne turned on her heel and ran away. Standing in front of her was the one person she wanted to see and ask how she could do it. Anne was at a loss for words. The anger was boiling inside, and she just needed to leave.

CHAPTER ELEVEN

SAYING GOODBYE

Taylor

W*hat happened? What is it now?* Those words floated through Taylor's mind as she tried to shake the image of Anne bolting out of her mind. They were good, then there was conflict, then they were good, and now it was like Taylor had burned Anne, and she wasn't even holding the flame. She had to figure out the root cause, or they would be stuck in awkward silence for another month.

The next day, she took a deep breath and entered the hospital. She had every intent of getting the hard stuff out of the way. When she saw Anne wasn't there, a flood of relief washed over her. They could worry about it later if she could ignore that interaction in the parking lot for a day. She would quickly, if not graciously, accept that. Hailey was back so today would be hopefully uneventful.

"How are you feeling?" Taylor asked.

"Better. This little one just wanted to make my life hell for a few days." She laughed. "I don't hold any grudge because, frankly, as the mother, I get to take revenge once he or she is born." She laughed, shrugging. "My doctor wants me to take it easy, but I'll be here while I'm feeling good. Did I miss anything?"

"Nope. Everything ran pretty smoothly. We missed you, though."

Hailey clutched her chest. "That's sweet. It's when you're gone that people really notice you." She wrapped her arm around Taylor. "I missed you guys and am super glad to be back. I hear you rocked the past few days."

Taylor frowned. "You did. From whom?"

"All of these love letters I received." She scattered them out on the desk. "When your main mentor isn't at the office, the other staff have to keep them in the loop. You got all enthusiastic praise. Kudos to you."

"Oh wow!" Taylor looked down at the papers, and she spotted Anne's immediately. She picked it up and read to herself. *I had the pleasure of working with Taylor over the last few days, and I'm pleasantly surprised. She's a brilliant nurse, and I only expect great things to come in her future.* "Interesting."

"And what about this one?" Hailey arched an eyebrow. "Taylor has great potential. She worked diligently and efficiently with our patients and always kept a smile on her face. She can work my rotation anytime. Signed Dr. Pohler."

Taylor's jaw dropped. "I didn't even notice that he noticed me." She was surprised to see the glowing review from Anne, but it made sense. Anne must have written it before the encounter in the parking lot. But Dr. Pohler, it seemed like everyone had taken notice, even when Taylor expected them to nod and shrug and barely know she was alive. "I'm sure it had something to do with my training."

Hailey shook her head. "I can't take any credit. After all, I trained you and then had to be off. I guess Anne would be the one who gets the credit. Either way, though. I'm proud of you."

"Thank you!" Taylor looked down at the raving reviews, and a knot dropped to the pit of her stomach. As nice as it was, she hoped she could speak with Anne and find out what exactly made her rush off.

"I have to drop these off to HR today. They'll go in your file for work; whenever they need to look at raises and promotions, they'll have all the necessary ammo they need." She put them into a neat pile and pushed them aside. "Today, I think it's safe to say you can work a little on your own. Willow is getting ready to be transported today." She grabbed a packet. "The info is right here. Whenever someone gets moved to a different facility, they will add a yellow sticker to her chart. It looks like, at 2:15, an ambulance is picking her up to transfer her to Tennessee."

"Does Anne know?" Taylor asked. "I know that she really cares about Willow. It would be nice if someone let her know. Seeing that she's off today and all."

"Good thinking. I can text her." She handed the chart over to Taylor. "Check on the family and see how she's doing. Ensure she doesn't need anything; if she does, get it for her. This transition will be rough for her, but we want to make her comfortable."

"I'm on it." Taylor grabbed the chart. She reached her room and took a deep breath before she dared enter. The moment reminded her of earlier in the week when she foolishly told Willow that she would be just fine. She deserved the scolding from Anne, but even that didn't deter a negative review. "Good morning! How are you all doing?"

Willow's mom looked at her, and her eyes were red. It was just Willow and her mom. Willow gave a weak smile. "Hi, Taylor." Her eyes widened as she sat up in her bed.

"Hello, munchkin." She brushed a strand of hair behind Willow's ear and then turned to her mom. "Do you have any questions?" Her mom glanced at Willow and then at Taylor, then back to Willow. "Do you want to talk outside?" Taylor asked. Her mom sighed and nodded. "How would you like a Strawberry Jell-O, milady?"

Willow eagerly nodded, and Taylor squeezed her hand. Taylor escorted her mom outside. With the door closed, her mother collapsed back against the wall. "I'm trying to be so strong for Willow, my other kids…" she hesitated. "And Paul."

"Your husband?" Taylor asked.

"He had to work this morning, or he would have been out of a job. We know traveling back and forth to Tennessee will be inevitable for him. I'll stay there all the time, but I worry that I'll break down in front of her, and I don't want to have that meltdown. But what if she isn't, okay?"

"Ella," Taylor started. "May I call you Ella?" She nodded, and Taylor continued. "I know it's difficult, but you have to have faith that Willow is going to be in the best place for her care. It's hard, I totally get that, but unfortunately, you have to be the strong one for Willow. She's going to look at you for your support." Ella sniffled and looked down at the floor. "I'm not saying that to upset you. But trust in the doctors, and we'll all be here rooting for her to get her health back."

"Thank you, Taylor." Ella leaned in and hugged her. When they parted, there were still a couple of tears in her eyes, but Leona smiled. "I better get back to her."

"I'll grab her Jell-O and be back in." Taylor squeezed Ella's hand, then turned to the nurse's station. As she grabbed the cup from the refrigerator, the phone started ringing. "CAPMED Pediatric Department. This is Taylor. How may I help you?" There was breathing on the line, and Taylor waited. "Hello?" The call went dead, and Taylor frowned. It had to be a wrong number; who else would prank call Pediatrics? Hailey rounded the corner before Taylor stepped away to go back to Willow's room. "Did you text Anne?"

"Yep. She said she'll be here to say goodbye." The phone rang again, and Hailey reached across the counter and grabbed it. "CAPMED Pediatrics' Department. This is Hailey. How may I help you?" Taylor turned and headed to see Willow. "Oh hey, Anne."

Taylor looked over her shoulder at the mention of Anne's name. It couldn't be. Anne wouldn't have blatantly hung up on her, would she? She shook that thought out of her mind and hurried back to Willow's room, telling herself it was a coincidence.

———✦———

As Taylor got up from the table in the cafeteria, her phone started vibrating. Aunt Kristi flashed across the screen.

Taylor gasped. The last thing she wanted was to see a call from her. She always texted. Aunt Kristi only called during emergencies.

"Hello?"

"How's work going? I'm not catching you at a bad time, am I? I would hope that if you couldn't answer the phone, you wouldn't."

"Um, is everything alright? I'm used to texts. Calls, not so much. So, I panicked." Taylor snickered, but only slightly, still fearing the worst.

"I'm sorry, dear. Everything is fine. I will be working late tonight and wasn't sure if I would catch you in the morning. I'm putting some money on the counter. Will you be a dear and pay the rent? You can bank what you need to cover the electricity bill you paid the other day. I just want to make sure they get our rent before we get a nasty letter from the landlords. If you don't mind, that'd be great. If I mail it in, I might not reach them on time, and I would much rather do it in person. Do you mind?"

"Not at all, Aunt Kristi." She tossed the banana peel. She was glad that her aunt mentioned the bill so she didn't have to bring it up. Now, she could replace the funds in her bank by the weekend, and it would be as if it never even happened. "I have to get back to work." She checked her watch. Just in time to see Willow onto the next chapter of her health journey. "Have a good night at work. Love you."

"Love you too, girlie."

Kristi hung up, and Taylor left the cafeteria and went to the elevator. As the doors were closing, she heard a woman. "Hold the door." Taylor reached out and kept the door from closing. She saw Anne hurrying to the elevator. When Anne spotted Taylor, she slowed her stride and looked up one way and down the other, hesitating before walking to the elevator. "Thank you," she mumbled.

She was dressed casually, wearing jeans and a T-shirt. The door closed, and the heavy silence continued. This was Taylor's chance, but she was hesitant to take the step. The fact that Anne barely looked at her told her everything she needed to know. The elevator ticked up the chains slowly, too slowly. Taylor felt anxious like the doors were closing on them, trapping them in this uncomfortable feeling. They had another floor to go, the last hint of a moment, before Taylor sighed.

"Did I do something to upset you?"

Anne laughed, then tossed a look to Taylor. Her lips curved upward in amusement. "I don't want to talk about it."

Taylor frowned. "Clearly, I did. I saw the review you gave. That wasn't made up. We were talking fine, and then, bam, nothing." The doors dinged and opened, and Taylor reached out to hold them open. "If I did something, I would much rather like to know what it is."

Anne stared straight ahead, Taylor watching her from the side. After what felt like an eternity, Anne crossed her arms. "Today, I'm saying goodbye to a little girl who means a lot to me. I don't know when I'll see her again. I would prefer not to have to deal with this, too. If that's too much to ask, then I'm sorry. But now is not the time." Anne hissed. Taylor dropped her arm and allowed Anne to exit first.

It was true that something was bothering Anne, but they weren't getting anywhere at that moment. As Anne stormed off to Willow's room, Taylor went to the desk to see where Hailey needed her. Those words weighed heavily on Taylor's mind. Whatever she did was something that Anne found unforgivable.

What could have happened between the hospital and the parking lot was beyond her.

"Did I miss anything while I was on lunch?" Taylor had to force herself to stop thinking about Anne. Anne touched her hand when they were in the cafeteria the last time together. She felt a spark like there was this kinetic energy between them. It struck her so hard and now they were back to being enemies. How would she ever understand?

"We got a new patient straight from the ER. Matthew Sullivan. He goes by Sully. He's five and has flu-like symptoms. Will you start an IV on him? He's dehydrated, and I have three other crises I'm dealing with. His doc is Dr. Pohler, and since you guys are pals, now, I'm sure he'll be pleased."

Taylor groaned. "I feel you're teasing me." She tried to smile, but her heart was in the room with Willow and Anne. "I'll take care of it." Taylor glanced at her watch and grimaced. There was a strong likelihood that with this patient, she would miss the moment Willow left and never get a chance to say goodbye. "Hailey," she began. "Will you grab me before Willow gets transferred? I'd like to say my goodbyes. I know I don't know her as well as everyone else, but I feel we've formed a bond in this short time."

"Absolutely. You do the IV, and I'll make sure I get you before she leaves. He's in room 1140."

Taylor smiled, at least she would have her moment, however small. She went to the drug and supply closet, grabbed everything she needed to start his IV, and then pushed the cart toward the room. A guy was standing beside his bed. He didn't look much more than eighteen. Taylor smiled. "Mr. Sullivan?"

"Um yeah," the guy stepped back from the bed. "Well, I'm

the younger Sullivan. My parents were working, and my brother didn't feel well. I hope I did the right thing. We couldn't reach them, and he needed emergency care. I hope I did the right thing."

"Trust me." Taylor touched his arm. "This is always the right thing." She thought back to her teen years when she had to care for Gavin. It wasn't an easy job, but at least Sully had a figure who could care for him. "And you are Sully, is that correct?"

"Hi!" He gave a small, meek greeting, before closing his eyes.

"He's always such an energetic kid." His brother replied. Taylor turned to his brother, and she saw the wariness in his eyes.

"What's your name?" Taylor asked.

"Trevor."

"Trevor, my name is Taylor, and together, we're going to help your brother so he doesn't feel so icky. Got that?" He nodded, his eyes filled with relief. "I'm going to get him hooked up to an IV."

"What's that for?" he asked.

"It's just so Sully gets hydrated. The worst thing that can happen is that he is dehydrated." Taylor knelt beside him as she remembered Anne doing with the other kids. "Would you like a Jell-O after this is done?"

He nodded, his eyes sparkling.

"Okay, give me a second, and we'll have you all hooked up in no time." She ruffled up his hair, and he already had pinker cheeks. "How'd you get the name, Sully?" Taylor asked as she prepped him.

"My brother," he whispered.

Taylor looked over and saw Trevor had tears in his eyes. "I'd say you have a pretty cool brother." She turned back to him, and he wore a small smile. Trevor watched her every move as Taylor felt his eyes on her. He was a brave young boy as she inserted the catheter and connected the tubing to the IV bag. When Taylor turned to Trevor, he had his hands clasped in prayer. Sully needed a brother like that. "Would you like a Jell-O?" Taylor asked.

"No, thank you!" He continued to pray.

The door flung open, and a woman rushed into the room. "My boys," she cried.

"Mom!" Trevor jumped up and they embraced. The room immediately felt lighter. Taylor left the room, feeling relieved to have experienced it. She also felt a bit sad to recognize the true love of a mother at that moment. Their mother was always too high to care.

She went to the nurse's station, grabbed a Jell-O and spoon, and headed back to see Sully when Willow's door opened. Hailey motioned for Taylor, and Taylor pocketed the Jell-O and hurried over to the room. She entered it, seeing Anne talking to Willow's parents. She hesitated, not wanting to interrupt, but Willow was lying on the bed, and her face lit up.

"Taylor!" she called. Anne turned and met Taylor's stare. Taylor snuck over to the bed and knelt beside her.

"You're going to get lots of medicine at the new hospital, and we look forward to the day you come back here and are big and strong. You got that?" In the back of her mind, she wondered if Anne was displeased, but she didn't promise Willow she would be back there. Besides, everyone needed to carry some faith.

Willow eagerly nodded. "Thank you, Taylor." She held out her arms, and Taylor hugged her. She felt her breath on Taylor's neck and didn't want to let go. Eventually, she had no choice and pulled back from the embrace. "Will you write to me?"

Taylor glanced over to Anne and her parents. How could she respond to that? Would her parents accept that? "We'll leave the address of where we're staying when we're in Tennessee. We'll make sure to get the letters to her."

"Then I absolutely will." She rubbed her thumb under Willow's chin. "Chin-up. We'll all be thinking of you."

"Thank you, Taylor." Taylor felt tears stinging the back of her eyes.

"I have to get going, but take care." She dropped her hand and turned on her heel, hurrying out the door before everyone saw her crying.

"Taylor?" Taylor turned around and Anne stood at the door. "I heard you were the one that said I should be notified about Willow's transport today. Thank you!"

"That's alright. You would have done it, as well."

Anne shrugged, then turned around and went back into the room, refusing to acknowledge their previous issues. Taylor reached her hand in her pocket and felt for the Jell-O, then hurried to Sully's room, where he was probably curious about what took her so long. Maybe she wouldn't know why Anne was so irritated with her. Perhaps Anne was just quirky. Either way, she had to accept it and see if there was any way they could work around the misunderstandings.

CHAPTER TWELVE

TRUTH REVEALED

Anne

Anne clocked out and headed to her locker. The day wasn't as bad as she thought. With Hailey there, she didn't have to bother being in close quarters with Taylor, and she could try to ignore the fact that Taylor hit her car, fled the scene, and subsequently delayed her mortgage. If it meant being the bigger person, then so be it. Bringing more drama into the hospital was not going to help anyone. Besides, she already knew that Taylor didn't live a life of luxury. She wished she knew why Taylor felt the need to rush off. Things would have been so much better if she had owned up to it and not rushed off like a child.

Anne's phone rang, and she grabbed it, spotting Melanie's number. "Hey, Mel. Perfect timing. I just got off work."

"I have a huge favor to ask." Anne waited, holding the

phone to her ear to see if she heard anything that sounded like tears. To her relief, she didn't.

"Anything. What's going on?"

"Well, I feel like Josh, and I need a night alone. No kids. No distractions. Maybe that will show him we're where he wants to be."

Anne rolled her eyes. If it took that, it was clear he wasn't the right man. "Of course, I'll watch them. I'm off tomorrow, so bring them over at whatever time works for you."

"Thank you, Sis. I appreciate you."

"Not a problem. I love you. Talk tomorrow." She disconnected the call and slammed her locker shut. She left the break room and headed to the front door. She had just stepped outside when she spotted Taylor. She mentally groaned. She almost made it to her day off without an awkward interaction. Taylor gave a simple nod.

"Have a good weekend!" she called.

A crack of thunder sounded, and Anne looked up at the dark skies. She glanced at Taylor.

"You too!" Anne called, then sprinkles started, followed by a downpour. She ran to her car, wishing she had grabbed the umbrella from her locker. If she had only known, she reached her car and unlocked it with her fob, but not before her hair was drenched. "Good times," Anne mumbled. She looked out her window and saw Taylor running toward her car. "What now?" Anne mumbled. The rain started to dissipate as fast as it came. Sure, it would wait until she was already in the car. That was typical. Anne rolled her window down as Taylor approached her.

"I'm sorry to bother you." Taylor breathlessly leaned against the car. "My car won't start. You wouldn't be able to give me a jump, would you?" She clutched her hands together, a pitiful look clouding over her face. Anne looked up in the sky and saw several clouds had disappeared; they might have a few minutes before another blast of rain appeared.

"Where are you parked?" Anne mumbled.

Taylor motioned, and She took in a breath and exhaled. "Get in," Anne replied. If she was going to do the noble thing, she had to start it right. Taylor looked relieved as Anne unlocked the door for her to get in the passenger side. She backed out of the spot and drove to where Taylor had pointed. The car was eerily quiet, with only a few instances where Taylor would motion with her finger to show the direction to go. Before Anne reached the car, she frowned. "How'd you know where I was parked?"

Taylor dropped her gaze to her hands. "I watched you walk to your car."

So, she's a stalker; that's intriguing. Anne bit down on her tongue and closed in on Taylor's car. The spot across from her was open to allow easy access. She parked, and they both got out of the car. Anne spotted the mangled bumper, and her heart raced again. *Let it go. In the end, you'll feel better, and everyone can rest easy.*

"Do you have cables?" Anne asked.

"Um, I don't know. Possibly?" Taylor hurried to her trunk and dug through it as Anne tapped her foot, waiting for her to come out with her hand clutched around the jumper cables. She sighed. "I'm not finding anything."

"I think I have some." Anne went to her trunk and spotted her mangled-up bumper, just waiting for her to get it fixed. She shook her head. It was what it was. She reached for the cables and was about to close the trunk when she heard Taylor beside her.

"Shit!" Anne glanced at her; Taylor's eyes focused on the bumper. Her jaw dropped, and Anne waited for her to acknowledge it one step further. She looked up, her eyes darkening. "It was you."

Anne scowled, unable to handle the anguish running through her mind. "Yep, it was me, and it was you. You just left me there like nothing ever mattered. I don't get it. How could someone do that to someone else? Someone they don't even know? You didn't even check to see if I was okay, and you work in healthcare!"

Taylor's eyes dropped back down to the bumper. "So, you know it was me?" Taylor asked, her gaze dropping. When? How?"

"A couple of days ago. I saw the ribbon in your hair, and the dent in your bumper looks just like mine."

Taylor released a gasp. "When we were in the parking lot, you rushed off." She covered her face and shook her head. "I didn't mean to rush off like that. It was in the spur of the moment. I felt bad the minute I did it. I regretted it but never expected I'd find the person. I'm sorry, Anne. I'm so sorry."

"You're sorry? That's not doing a bit of good for me, now is it? I had my own problems. I needed that money, and now I'm stuck getting this fixed."

Taylor's brow furrowed. "We'll go to a shop right now." Taylor reached into her purse and withdrew her wallet. She opened it up, and Anne stared at the wad of cash inside. "I'll use a credit card. If that will improve things between us, I'll do it."

"Are you kidding me? You have a wad of cash just sitting there, and you're trying to give me the guilt trip?"

"What?" Taylor balked. "You don't understand!"

"I think I understand quite clearly," Anne huffed. "It is what it is. A lot of good going to a shop will do. I've called around. I'm on a waiting list for every shop in town. Don't you think I tried? Do you think I like this mangled-up bumper? The answer is no, but there's not a damn thing I can do about it." Anne crossed her arms, the car suddenly a distant memory. "I'm outta here."

"You're just going to leave me?" Taylor argued. "Stranded?" Anne sighed and returned to her car, jumper cables still in hand. "I have an idea. I know someone, and I'm sure I can get you in, probably even tonight."

"Oh yeah, right." Anne snickered. "I've tried everyone. Are you not understanding?"

Taylor shook her head. "Please, jumpstart my car. I'll prove it to you."

Anne knew that Taylor was grasping at straws, but at the moment, she had to take advantage of it and hope that something good could come out of it, even if it ultimately bit her in the ass.

ANNE PACED BACK AND FORTH AS TAYLOR STOOD AT THE DESK, talking to the man who owned the shop: *Joe's Auto Body*. That was one place she hadn't tried. She couldn't even find a listing for him, but the parking lot seemed packed with cars. The shop was unlisted thanks to a recent name change. Anne just hoped that it wasn't another letdown. After several minutes, Taylor came back to her. Why Taylor asked her to wait by the door was beyond her, but if Taylor kept this promise and fixed her vehicle, she would be back on track to making her last house payment.

"I have good news, and I have bad news," she began.

"Let me guess, the bad news is there's a month turnaround, so it's back to the drawing board. At least you tried, right?" Anne held out her hand and tilted her head. "Give me the keys, and I'll just plan on one of the shops."

"Well, can't exactly do that. They're pulling your car in now. He said it could take twenty-four hours to fix, then another twenty-four hours for the paint to dry. But I have everything entered, and he knows I'm covering the costs."

Anne's jaw dropped. "I don't understand. His parking lot is packed. I checked the reviews, and they are nothing but high praise. And we're looking at the weekend."

Taylor shrugged. "He reworked his schedule."

Anne scrunched her nose, still confused but trying not to argue too much. She was one step closer to having her vehicle repaired, and unless Taylor let her down, she was getting it fully paid, like it should have been from the start. Seeing the money in Taylor's wallet did nothing but cinch the idea that Taylor had the means to get the job done and had only been playing the sympathy card.

"So, the bad news is I must get an Uber for the next few days. No biggie."

Taylor shook her head. "Not the bad news I was referring to. "Turns out my car is in dire need of a battery. He has to order one, and it won't be here until the morning."

"Oh," Anne muttered. "So, basically, we're both currently stranded."

"Appears that way." Taylor reached into her pocket and finally pulled out her phone. "I can call my aunt to pick me up. I can order you an Uber."

"Yeah, seeing you have all that money," Anne grumbled.

Taylor sighed. "Anne, it's not what you think."

Anne rolled her eyes, "I think you're a spoiled rich kid who's never had to take responsibility a day in her life, so you fled the scene of the accident. Who's Joe? Your Dad? Are you a body shop heiress?"

Taylor's mouth hung open, unable to reply.

Anne waved away Taylor's words. "I can get my own Uber."

Anne grabbed her phone and pulled up the app. Not exactly how she expected to spend her Friday night, as she fiddled with the app, Taylor called up her aunt. Anne didn't intend to listen to the conversation, but she was right there, and it was hard to ignore.

"Hey, Gavin. What are you doing answering Aunt Kristi's phone? Ugh. Are you serious? When do you expect her?" Anne looked up to Taylor as Taylor turned her back away from her. "I need to be picked up. It's a long story. I forgot she works tonight. I'll see what I can do. I'll keep in touch. Bye." Taylor whirled around, and Anne quickly looked down so it wasn't obvious she had been listening to every word. "Well, it looks like I need to call one, too."

"Well, the closest ride is half an hour away. There's a Cubs game tonight." Anne slipped her phone back into her pocket. She shrugged. "My house is only about a mile up the road. I might head on out and take my chances before it rains."

"Alrighty then. I'll see if I can get that Uber. I don't mind waiting a bit." Taylor sat down in a chair, and Anne sighed.

"Or you could come with me. I have plenty of room. You can stay over in the spare bedroom and come get your car in the morning."

"Even after everything I put you through?" Taylor's eyes widened.

"Guess I'm just in a generous mood unless you'd rather stick it out here. It's your choice, but make it."

"A mile isn't so bad. I'm in." Taylor jumped up, and they left the auto body shop. They were quiet on the first part of the trip. The sky had darkened some, but that was due to the continuous impending rain. The walk was slow. Anne didn't mind.

As they rounded a curb, Anne spoke up. "So, plan on telling me how you got Joe to take in my car tonight?"

Taylor snickered. "Well, it's rather simple."

"Ex-boyfriend?" Anne interrupted. "I mean, he looks a bit older, but maybe you like the balding type."

She glanced over at Taylor, whose face was eerily pale. Taylor then burst into laughter. It was interesting to see her laughing when Anne ignored her in silence. It felt good to make her laugh.

"Not hardly," Taylor remarked. "He isn't quite my type. But he does have a crush on my aunt. She won't appreciate that I said she would go out with him, but I'm sure she'll understand it's for a good cause."

Anne snickered. "Interesting. I hope your aunt is the forgiving type."

"She can be," Taylor mumbled. Anne motioned toward a street, and they turned. At those words, a loud crack of thunder sounded. "Uh oh!" Taylor mumbled. They both looked into the sky just as big drops started to fall.

"We don't have too much further," Anne yelled. "Follow me." She ran as fast as her legs would carry her, with Taylor falling in closely behind. The rain continued to fall harder, and Anne felt the large pelts hitting the back of her neck as she focused ahead, not on what Taylor was doing. "My house is up here," Anne yelled. She ran up the walkway, thoroughly drenched, and fumbled with her key until the door was unlocked. She pushed through, and Taylor stumbled in after her.

"We are soaked!" Taylor said, coughing through the water that had covered her face.

Anne looked at her and then chuckled. "I should have grabbed an umbrella from the car."

"Now you think of that," Taylor said, laughing. Again, the radiant sound of her laughter echoed in Anne's ears, gently coming through the foyer and catching Anne off balance.

"If you follow me, I'll get you something to change into. Anything would beat these wet clothes." Anne hurried up the stairs, with Taylor padding behind her. She glanced over her shoulder and saw the awe on Taylor's face.

"You have a nice place," Taylor cooed.

"Thank you!" Anne mumbled. "Wait right here." She rushed into her room and dug around in her dresser until she had a t-shirt and lounge pants. She took it back out to Taylor and handed it over. "There's a bathroom down the hall. Feel free to change in there."

Taylor grabbed the items, and Anne waited until she disappeared into the bathroom. Anne returned to her room, pulled out her clothes, and quickly dressed in something more comfortable. By the time she was in the hallway, Taylor was still behind the closed door, so she went back downstairs to the living room. Anne worked on the fire, cooking up a lovely flame, when she heard shuffling coming down the stairs. She turned as Taylor entered the room. The t-shirt was extra-large compared to Taylor's thin frame. The lounge pants cupped her butt, hugging it and then slightly squeezing it. Anne's mouth hung agape as she gawked.

"Nice fire," Taylor replied, moving further into the living room. Anne turned away, glaring straight into the flames. It would be a long night.

CHAPTER THIRTEEN

WHISKERS IS MISSING

Taylor

Things were awkward between them as they sat by the fire, Taylor staring aimlessly around the living room. "I'm sorry I couldn't muster up anything better than chicken. I'm sure you're more used to the glamorous meals."

"What? The chicken is great. You didn't even have to go to that bother. I certainly would have accepted a cold hot dog."

Anne snickered. "I'm sure." She rolled her eyes and dropped her gaze to her plate.

Taylor frowned; this was the second time Anne had insinuated that she was somehow too good for her, acting like she wasn't grateful for anything Anne had in the kitchen. It'd been a long day, and frankly, anything would have been acceptable. Anne acted like she was royalty or something. She looked down at her chicken and stabbed her fork into the meat before popping it into her mouth.

"It's quite delicious."

Anne stared at Taylor before shrugging and looking back down at her food. Again, awkwardness ensued. At least until another twenty minutes went by. Then Anne looked up and gawked, sending shivers down Taylor's spine. The way she stared at her, she wondered if she had horns growing from her head. Taylor nervously looked down. She didn't sense anything wrong. Outside of the elephant in the room, their cars were at the shop, and soon, she could hope the awkwardness was behind them.

"Why'd you do it?" Anne asked suddenly.

Taylor's jaw dropped, and then she snapped her mouth closed. She didn't have to inquire about what Anne was talking about. She knew.

"Why does anyone do something stupid? I was scared. I bolted." She shrugged. "It's like asking why bees sting. Or why does water flow down a waterfall? Hell, if I know."

"The latter two, you can search for the answer and most likely find one. But for why you ran from an accident, I guess you should search within your soul because I haven't a clue.

"Anne, I know you will probably never understand it, but you live in this fabulous place."

"A place I've worked hard to maintain," Anne quickly interrupted.

"I get that. Please let me finish." Anne didn't make another move to jump in as Taylor continued. "I have never had that luxury. I don't have the finer things. When I get a paycheck, I'll be living paycheck to paycheck. I don't have car insurance. Did I plan on bolting? No. Did I see any other way out? Not exactly."

"You are giving out this sob story, but I saw the wad of cash. Remember? That doesn't look like someone who has to fear living paycheck to paycheck."

Taylor shook her head. "And that's where you don't get it. As I've been trying to explain, that money isn't mine. My aunt needed me to pay the rent. I didn't get a chance to before my evening went to shit. She works two jobs to keep food on the table so my brother and I can stay with her. We aren't wealthy. I'm not the enemy."

Taylor's phone rang, and even though Anne stared at her, she reached for her phone and spotted Gavin's name.

"Hello?"

"Sis? Where are you? I've been worried sick. Sirens have been up and down this road, and I've tried calling you three times." She checked her phone and grimaced.

"Sorry. I didn't hear it. I meant to call you, but I'm staying at a co-worker's tonight."

"You are? Is everything alright?"

"It's a long story. I'll explain it tomorrow when I see you. You get some rest, and I'll call you in the morning. Love you."

"Love you, too."

Taylor hung up the call, and she looked back to meet Anne's gaze. "My brother. He heard sirens and was worried." Anne locked her gaze on Taylor's, making Taylor feel a few more nerves. She stood up from the couch and walked over to the shelves that housed Anne's DVD and Blu-Ray collection. "Wow, you sure have a ton of movies."

"Yeah, my sister will come over periodically, and we'll have movie nights. As you can see, there's a whole mess of Disney movies reserved for my nieces, and then when they fall asleep, we'll watch something else."

Taylor pulled out a movie and smiled as she looked over at Anne. *Labyrinth* is a great movie. It's easily my top choice. I blame David Bowie."

Anne slowly nodded. "Ugh, same! I used to love the soundtrack when I was a little kid." Taylor looked up, and their gaze met once more. She swallowed as that spark greeted her again, then returned to the movies. She replaced the movie, returned to the coffee table, and picked up her plate.

"It's getting late. I should help by washing the dishes. You get some sleep."

"You don't need to bother with that," Anne argued as Taylor reached for Anne's plate.

"It's the least I could do. You were nice enough to make us dinner. I know my way around a sink." She laughed, trying to make it lighthearted, but her chest caved in. She was exhausted, mentally more than physically. She went to the kitchen and started digging around the sink to find the stuff to wash the dishes, oblivious that Anne had made her way to the kitchen.

"I'm sorry," Anne replied. Taylor looked over her shoulder. "I apologize," Anne replied, moving closer to her. "I shouldn't have just assumed you were rich and trying to stiff me with the bill. After all, you put your card on file and made this all happen. I appreciate it."

Taylor shrugged. "You wouldn't have needed repairs if it wasn't for my carelessness. I was distracted, mainly because I was excited about my new job. And nervous. So, that's what happens when you're careless."

"Accidents happen," Anne commented.

Taylor arched an eyebrow. "Most people don't run. That's the cowardly thing to do."

"You were scared. Heck, I'm sure more people run than we even know."

"What are you doing?" Taylor whirled around and stood her stance, staring at Anne. "I'm trying to admit my fault in the whole thing, and you're trying to make me feel better. Why?"

Anne shrugged. "I was once young, too. We all make mistakes."

"Some with a higher price to pay," Taylor mumbled.

Anne reached for a towel and began drying the dishes that Taylor had already washed. They tag-teamed it until the dishes and kitchen were clean.

"But you're right. We should get to bed."

"Right. Should I make a bed on the couch?" Taylor knew this would be when things got more awkward. But Anne shook her head and motioned for Taylor to follow her. They went up the stairs, and she directed her to the spare bedroom.

"If you need me. You know where to find me." Anne started to disappear into her room.

"Anne? I am sorry, and I hope this will at least make things easier at work." Anne nodded. "We'll get there. Goodnight." She disappeared into her room, and Taylor considered those words. They were already one step closer.

TAYLOR SHIFTED IN BED, THEN FINALLY OPENED HER EYES. THE bedding was lush. The bed felt like a layer of clouds, but she couldn't even will herself to sleep. Sure, she could expect a hefty credit card bill, but at least she would have her dignity and smile, relieved that the truth was out there. How could they keep a working relationship going if there was the truth on Anne's side, with Taylor oblivious to their connection?

Taylor heard a noise, and she glanced over at the bedroom door. A light shone underneath the doorway. "Whiskers? Where are you?"

Taylor frowned, holding her breath and waiting.

"Whiskers! Come out, come out, wherever you are."

Taylor tossed the covers back, now intrigued. She moved to the door and flung it open, peeking her head into the hallway.

"Whiskers!" Anne came out of the bathroom, and her face flushed. "Sorry. Did I wake you?"

"That's alright. Do you have someone else living here who is named Whiskers?" Anne's cheeks reddened, and she shrugged.

"My cat. I haven't seen him all night." She frowned, opening another door, shaking her head, and closing it. "It's not like him. You didn't happen to see a little fur ball running around here, did you? He's knee-high and gray, with white feet."

"I didn't know you had a cat, so I'm sorry to say I haven't seen him. I can help you look, though?"

"You don't have to do that. I'm sure he's just hiding somewhere. You can go back to bed. I'll keep looking and eventually have to give up and hope he'll come out when he's good and ready. The storm earlier probably startled him." She shrugged. "It's no biggie."

Yet, her eyes looked panicked. Taylor could have returned to the room, shrugged it off, and shut her eyes, but she couldn't. Not when Anne seemed beside herself, her eyes filled with worry.

"Where's his favorite hiding spots?" Taylor asked.

"Under the bed, in closets, on the refrigerator." Taylor arched an eyebrow, and Anne laughed. "He doesn't hide well there but thinks he's invisible. But really…"

"It's fine. You take the downstairs, and I'll take the upstairs. We'll find Whiskers if it's the last thing we do." Anne gave a gracious smile and hurried down the stairs. "Oh, Whiskers! Where are you, Rascal?"

Taylor looked under the bed, and Whiskers wasn't hiding there. Before leaving the spare, she checked the closets and did not leave a single area untouched. Most likely touching the same place at least twice. Anne rounded the corner when she got downstairs, hope filling her eyes but quickly failing.

"I've looked everywhere. I even ran the can opener, which usually makes him sprint." Her eyebrows furrowed.

"He couldn't have gone anywhere, Anne. Does he go outside?"

"Never!" Anne shook her head. "He's always been an indoor cat." A loud crack of thunder sounded, and Anne's eyes went wide. "There was once, right after I rescued him. He got outside. He was gone for five hours, and I never thought I'd see him again."

"But you did. He knew where his home was. That's a promising thing, right?" Anne didn't even respond. She walked over to the window and stared aimlessly outside. "Maybe we should check outside, just in case."

Anne hurried to the front door and flung it open as Taylor

went back through the kitchen. She had spotted a back patio. They would cover more area if they separated. When she was younger, Taylor once had a kitten, and she had gotten out. They weren't lucky enough to get her back, as a car came by and swerved, unable to miss her. That experience wrecked her long enough that she couldn't imagine what it would do to Anne, even if she was an adult and could handle disappointment.

"Whiskers!" she called out. "Where are you, kitty?"

Meow. She glanced around, fearful that maybe she had dreamt the sound of a cat. She held her breath and waited. *Meow.* That was definitely a cat. But where?

CHAPTER FOURTEEN

HEATED MOMENT ENTERTAINED

Anne

The rain was past them, but Anne still couldn't understand where Whiskers could be. He had never run off to the point where she couldn't find him. Other than those five hours a year ago. Even then, she didn't feel the dread and panic she felt now. Whiskers was a cat that liked to snuggle and held. He was way too skittish to be off by himself. Or so she thought.

"Whiskers?" she called. "Where are you?"

She shook her head. It was useless. Taylor was out helping her, but at what cost? They were both missing out on sleep, and she couldn't expect this to go on for the whole night. Anne entered the house with a feeling of defeat. Why should she be surprised? When it rains, it pours. She understood the cliche now.

"Anne?" Taylor called out.

"Yeah? No luck here." Anne headed to the kitchen, where Taylor's voice echoed. "We've looked everywhere, and you might as well…" Her words trailed off when she saw Whiskers nuzzling against Taylor's chest.

"I know there's a possibility I just brought a feral cat into your house." Taylor grinned. "I'm going out on a limb that this is—."

"Whiskers," Anne finished. She rushed over to Taylor and pulled the cat out of her arms. "Where have you been, my silly boy?"

"I found him under the porch. He probably got outside, and when the rain came, he looked for a place to stay dry."

Anne nuzzled her lips against his fur. "I've been a bit distracted lately. I probably didn't notice him run past me. I never realized how attached you can get to a pet until that pet is no longer here." Anne kissed the top of his head and then looked at Taylor. "Guess it's a good thing you were here."

"Nah, you would have found him soon enough. But, I'm glad I could get him back where he needed to be." On cue, Whiskers meowed, jumped out of Anne's arms, and hurried over to his food.

Anne laughed. "He's probably been out there all day. I'm sure he's starving. But I'll say it again. Thank you."

Taylor shrugged. "It's my pleasure. No need to say thanks." Taylor looked over to Whiskers as he ate, and a soft smile glistened on her lips. "He seems like a sweet cat. I can see why you'd grow so attached."

"I hope he feels the same way," Anne started with a smile. She heaved a sigh, and there was a long hesitation. Whiskers had been found, and they could go back to their rooms and try to get some sleep. However, she was on her second wind, and sleep wasn't on her agenda. "Would you like some coffee? The adrenaline kicked in, and I don't think I could sleep, even if I wanted to."

"Coffee sounds good," Taylor agreed. Whiskers meowed, and Anne looked down to where he stood at Taylor's feet.

"I think you just gained a friend for life." Taylor quirked up an eyebrow. "Whiskers, I mean. He's probably grateful for how you saved him."

A redness popped onto Taylor's cheeks, and Anne quickly looked away. She shouldn't notice her blushing, even though that was a sight she had already seen a couple of times. It punched her in the gut every time.

"I was glad to do it." Taylor picked Whiskers up in her arms and bounced him a few times as if he were a baby. Anne laughed under her breath.

"You make yourself at home in the living room. I'll make the coffee and be in shortly."

Ten minutes later, Anne had two mugs, a sugar container, and creamer lined up on a tray to present to her. When she reached the living room, she stopped short of entering. Taylor sat on the couch, Whiskers in her lap, slowly rubbing below her chin. On the other hand, she was holding one of Anne's knitted creations, and Anne couldn't tell if she was conversing with Whiskers or the doll Anne had knitted the night before. Either way, Anne didn't want to interrupt. She moved in further to hear her talking, and she smiled. The conversation, directed to Whiskers, was like someone talking to a new friend.

"You're such a good kitty, Whiskers. And so cute, too. If I

had a cat, I'd want him to be just like you." Taylor nuzzled her lips into his neck, and Anne heard the loud purring from the other side of the room. "That's right, boy, such a sweetheart." She turned, her cheeks flushed. "And I'm embarrassed."

Anne laughed. "Don't be embarrassed. Whiskers is used to praise. We talk a lot. He's probably surprised to get such attention from a stranger, though. That'd be a new one. I didn't know if you wanted sugar or cream in your coffee."

"I usually take it black." She held up the doll. "Cute doll? Did you make this?"

"I dabble in knitting and crocheting," Anne replied.

She handed the mug over to Taylor. "Black coffee? You're hardcore," Anne said, impressed, changing the subject.

Taylor placed the doll back on the coffee table and grabbed the mug. "Well," Taylor began, then shook her head. "Never mind."

Anne arched an eyebrow. "You're leaving me just hanging here? Not cool," she teased, pouring some of the creamer into her mug and gently stirring it before taking a seat on the couch next to Taylor.

"Maybe for another time." Taylor gave a weak smile, then sipped on her coffee and nodded. "Simply the best. Thank you!" She scratched Whiskers until he jumped and scurried out of the living room. "Must've exceeded my welcome."

Anne laughed. "No, he's a pig and probably left to get more food. I doubt it had anything to do with you." Anne sipped on her coffee, and it was nice to sit in the living room, not have to reach for conversation, and even enjoy the solitude. If Anne listened hard enough, she could hear the gentle sprinkle of rain tapping against the window.

"Your crocheted doll looks a bit more than just dabbling. Then again, I don't have a creative bone in my body." Taylor laughed.

"Doubt that," Anne commented. "Everyone has some kind of creativity. It's just acting on it that requires strength. Knitting isn't so hard. I'm sure you could even learn if you had the patience."

"Patience…not always my cup of tea," Taylor smirked, sipping her coffee. She glanced around the living room, and Anne saw a hint of jealousy in her stare. "You have a beautiful home, Anne," Taylor began after several minutes of taking in that stillness.

"Thank you! It'd always been a dream of mine to own a home, not have to rent from someone or hold a thirty-year mortgage. It's been a long time coming, but I'm just getting to the point where this will soon be all mine."

"It's quite impressive. You're still so young."

"A few nights of only eating Ramen and drinking water never hurt anyway." Anne snickered, taking another sip of her coffee. And again, that silence hit her, but not in an overpowering way. She didn't need to stress over the conversation when there might not be some. She sipped on her coffee and watched Taylor doing the same. Yet, she noticed that Taylor's eyes dimmed slightly. "What about you?" Anne asked. "I imagine you have a nice place. You dress nice and all."

"Well, scrubs are all the rage," Taylor laughed loudly, her eyes lit up a smidge. "Let's just say I don't have a place like this."

"And we'll leave it for another time?" Anne inquired.

"Something like that. Can't show all my cards, right?" She quirked up her lips. Anne didn't pry, but it was clear that Taylor was reserved and wanted to keep up that wall. Anne couldn't object when they barely spoke twelve hours earlier. "This coffee was delicious. Glad you suggested it."

"I was going to make a cup for myself, so I figured you might as well join me."

Taylor nodded. "I appreciate it. I'll help you wash up, and I should be getting to bed."

"Yeah, me too. You don't need to help me. I'll just put it in the sink and take care of it in the morning. We both need to get some sleep." Taylor's jaw dropped, and her mouth was agape. Her eyes were wide, inquisitive, her lips curved into a smile, and she laughed, then looked down. "You know what I mean. You in your bed. Me in mine."

Taylor vigorously nodded in response. "Of course. Nothing else crossed my mind."

Anne grimaced. It sure crossed her mind, and she didn't even know why. One minute, she was ready to have this woman's head on a platter for damaging her car; the next, she would smother her with compliments or kisses if she had her way.

She discarded the tray into the sink and met Taylor in the foyer. She reached for the railing at the exact moment as Taylor, their hands touching, and Anne quickly pulled back. A spark had hit her, and she had to step back and allow Taylor ample room to get upstairs.

"I apologize," Anne mumbled.

"No worries."

Taylor was cool and nonchalant, while Anne stood back red-faced and confused. They reached the top of the steps, and Taylor turned to Anne. "Thanks again for everything." Her words trailed off.

"Well, thank you for finding Whiskers." Anne reached for her door, glancing over her shoulder, and saw Taylor awkwardly gawking at her. There was this tension and pull between them, right? She wasn't feeling something one-sided, was she?"

"Anne," Taylor started. Anne whirled around, ready to give her full attention to that one mention of her name. Taylor shrugged. "Goodnight."

A breath escaped Anne. "Yeah, goodnight, Taylor." Anne reached for the door.

"Anne?" She turned around once more, baffled by the call of her name. "I can't go to sleep without doing something," Taylor whispered. She had already closed the gap, snaked her hand around Anne's neck, and pulled her to her. Her lips crashed against Anne's with a million watts of electricity crashing through her. Taylor's tongue dipped in and met Anne's, and Anne stood there, confused and anxious. Until she fully let that kiss embrace her, she grabbed Taylor's waist and pulled her closer. The kiss kept her thirsty for more. Her heart raced, and she envisioned pulling Taylor into her bedroom and allowing the heat to ignite up her room. After all, it'd been ages. Unfortunately, the kiss ended, and Taylor's eyes darted to hers. "I shouldn't have done that." Taylor gasped.

"Taylor," Anne argued. "I didn't exactly push you away."

Taylor shook her head. "I'm sorry. My emotions got the better of me. Goodnight." She turned on her heel, and the moment passed. Every part of Anne wanted to rush after her, but she stayed back and allowed Taylor to disappear into the spare room. They would talk in the morning and resolve so much. She wasn't sorry that Taylor had kissed her. The truth was, she wanted more.

AT WHAT COST?

Anne stepped out of her bedroom. She didn't get much sleep as she thought of Taylor just down the hall. So many times, she wanted to go to her and tell her she wasn't sorry the kiss had happened. Sure, it was unexpected, but was unexpected always a bad thing? She didn't think so. But the fact that Taylor seemed confused, she didn't make that move. If Taylor regretted making a move, then Taylor would need to communicate that.

Anne would support her. Taylor was young; who knows how long she'd been out? Anne looked to the spare room, and the door was open. Taylor was probably already up and ready for some breakfast. It did take Anne a little longer to get dressed, as she was fighting with thoughts traipsing through her mind. Anne went downstairs and first checked the living room. Taylor wasn't there.

"Taylor?" Anne rounded the kitchen corner, and still, she was nowhere. Maybe she was still upstairs, and Anne should have started there. She hurried back up the stairs and cautiously peeked her head in the door. "Taylor? Are you in here?" Silence. Anne frowned, stepping into the spare room. She looked around the room, the bed fully made, as immaculate as Anne had it before she had the visitor. Her eyes landed on the pillow, where a paper sat. Anne picked it up and started to read.

Anne -

Words can't express how sorry I am for so many things. You know what they are, but the truth is, the kiss has me a bit rattled. I feel like I startled or confused you. It's the last thing I want to do. I woke up early so it wouldn't be awkward. I will grab my car and hope that my embarrassment has dissipated Monday morning.

I'm sorry, Anne!
Please forgive me!
Taylor

Anne sunk into the bed. If she had known that Taylor would take it this hard, she would have forced her to have a conversation the night before. Anne reached for her phone and pulled up Taylor's number. At least she had the mind to get the number when they were working on the debacle with their cars.

"The number you have called has been disconnected. If you feel this has been an error, please hang up and try again."

Anne stared at her phone, Taylor's name staring back at her. She had entered the contact information. It couldn't be an error. Taylor was upset that she disconnected her number? She tried it again to ensure it wasn't a fluke but got the same recording.

"Ugh!" Anne groaned and stared down at the letter. Her only choice was to wait until Monday morning when they both worked, and she could square away the misunderstanding. Her doorbell sounded, and Anne jumped up from the bed. Or, she could do it right now, and Taylor was coming back to apologize for rushing off. She ran down the stairs and flung the door open. "Tay…" Her words stopped when she saw Melanie and her nieces. "Hey, you guys!" Anne put on a bright smile.

"Expecting someone else?" Melanie asked.

Anne shook her head but figured her face was bright red. "You are here earlier than I would have thought, though." She folded the note and stuffed it into her pocket. If Melanie had seen the letter, she would have had many questions that needed answering.

"What can I say? The kids wanted to get here."

Lily and Rose threw their arms around Anne's legs, and she held them. "And I'm glad to see you all. Put your bags in the living room. I have to wash up the bedding for tonight." She turned to Melanie, and Melanie arched an eyebrow. "What?"

Melanie shrugged. "You look weird."

"Gee, thanks a lot," Anne muttered. She grabbed her sister's arm and pulled her into the living room. She needed just a few minutes with her before she sent her back to her husband. But also, it wouldn't hurt to have a distraction.

CHAPTER FIFTEEN

AWKWARDNESS RETURNS

Taylor

When Taylor went in for the kiss, she had no intention of deepening it. Anne was right; she didn't exactly smack Taylor for kissing her. There was a moment when Taylor believed Anne was enjoying it just as much as she was. She grabbed onto her waist and pulled her to her in a moment of pure passion. She felt it down to her toes. When the sun rose, though, she had to leave. Taylor didn't want to face a morning where Anne would wake up with regret.

Taylor grabbed her phone and looked at it, grimacing. Anne had her phone number, and she'd be lying if she didn't say that she would have hoped Anne would have picked up the phone to call her. The fact that there wasn't one single call told Taylor everything she needed to know.

"Knock, knock." She looked up as Aunt Kristi entered the

room. She smiled at Taylor, then grabbed the corner of Taylor's bed and made herself at home. Well, it was her home, but it wasn't often that she came into Taylor's room and just sat down to talk. Usually, they saved dinner time or the living room to hold conversations. With Aunt Kristi's busy schedule, they didn't allow much more time than that.

"What's up?" Taylor asked.

"I could ask you the same thing. It's the weekend. You're off, and I haven't seen you out of your room much more than an hour at a time. It's like you're hiding from me or something."

Taylor frowned. "Didn't mean to. I'm not hiding; I'm thinking. Besides, I know you're busy. Gavin's been out with friends. Guess I just needed to be somewhere I could think and not be in anyone's way."

"Honey, you're never in my way." Aunt Kristi caressed Taylor's cheek. "Do you have the money I gave you for the rent?" she asked, dropping her hand.

Taylor's mouth hung open, and she slapped her palm over it. "Oh my gosh, it completely slipped my mind." She never wanted to feel like she let her aunt down, but she could feel her aunt's disappointment at that moment. She got up from the bed and grabbed her purse. She opened her wallet and grabbed the cash. "I'm sorry, Aunt Kristi. I can get up early in the morning and drop it off."

She shook her head. "No worries. Barry called me last night and asked. I told him you have been super busy with a new job and forgot to deliver it, but that I would bring it over tonight before I go to work. He's understanding."

"I let you down, though. You asked me to do something simple, and I blanked."

"Taylor, don't be so hard on yourself. If you have other things going on, it's liable to happen. You have done plenty for this family, so don't stress." She hesitated, then smiled. "But, it's clear something is going on. We've always been able to talk, so I would feel better if you could tell me why this escaped your mind. Trouble at work?"

"Not exactly," Taylor mumbled. She looked down at her clenched hands, her heart racing as she relived the kiss again. She sighed. "Friday night, I was leaving work, and I had every intention of taking the money to Barry. Well, my car wouldn't start."

Aunt Kristi nodded. "Gavin mentioned that to me when I got home. So, you stayed at a co-worker's home. That seems reasonable enough. Did something happen?"

"Well, Gavin didn't know the whole story. And frankly, I'm still processing it myself." Taylor pulled her feet up under her butt and stared at her aunt. It turns out my co-worker is the one I had the accident with on Monday." Aunt Kristi's eyes widened. As surprising as that was, the details couldn't flow from Taylor fast enough. "She needed to get her car fixed. Frankly, I wanted to do anything I could to ensure she didn't have to wait another day. She tried everywhere. She did. Everywhere except Joe's Body Shop." Aunt Kristi arched an eyebrow. Taylor shrugged. "He was willing to do it and get me a new battery."

"I see." Aunt Kristi crossed her arms and stared back at Taylor. "He did this, no strings attached?"

"Well, not exactly." Taylor dropped her gaze. "I'm sure you can put it off as long as possible. Once the job is done, if you don't go out on a date, you don't. It's not like he can take back fixing the car."

"Wow!" Aunt Kristi shook her head. "We'll save that conversation for another time, seeing that I'm going to be late getting out of here." She rolled her eyes. "Continue."

"If it wasn't for Anne being one of the head nurses, I would have shrugged my shoulders and just said, oh well. There's nothing I can do. But I had to do something to salvage our relationship. The truth is, Anne, discovered that I was the one who hit her and ran from the accident. She didn't confront me with it, but things have been tense. Once I found out the truth, I had to do something to rectify our working relationship."

"Just your working relationship?"

"Yes, of course. Why do you ask?" Taylor sat up straighter.

Aunt Kristi shrugged. "You light up when you talk about her. I'm just wondering if maybe there's more to this than you're expressing." Taylor's cheeks burned, and she quickly looked away. If she mentioned the kiss, Aunt Kristi would surely see the truth. She swallowed the lump in her throat and shook her head.

"It's complicated."

"Affairs of the heart, usually are." Aunt Kristi reached out and grabbed Taylor's hand. She gave it a slight squeeze. "I'm proud of you for not shirking your responsibilities. I know it's not easy, as we are not rolling in dough right now, but you are doing the right thing." She stood up from her bed and grimaced. "And if I have to go out on a date with Joe to help my niece, then it's what I have to do." She gave Taylor a wink. "I'm heading off to work to drop off this money. Have a good night, love. I'll see you in the morning before you head off to work."

"Thanks, Aunt Kristi. I love you!" She blew Taylor a kiss and then disappeared from her room. Taylor grabbed her phone and stared at it. A simple message would suffice, but Anne wanted to ignore her. She tossed her phone to the side. The kiss meant nothing to Anne, and writing the letter was for the best.

Taylor pulled into the parking lot and parked around her usual spot. She stared up at the front door of the hospital, a knot forming in her gut. If Anne had called, she would have been able to expect how the morning would go. However, with no call came no certainty. Other than that, she believed Anne would be back to ignoring her; that was a tough pill to swallow.

Taylor leaned back in her seat and groaned. She didn't want to have to face the hospital this morning. She wanted to call in sick, but how would that look? The staff would think she was an unreliable employee. Her shift was twelve hours, and she would have to smile and get through it. As difficult as that might seem. Taylor grabbed her water and took a swig.

"You can get through this, Taylor. You have no other choice."

With a deep sigh, Taylor exited the car and headed to the front door, extra careful not to trip on the curb, as she did a week earlier. The automatic door opened, and Taylor was about to enter the opening when she saw Anne. Anne stepped out of a shadow, and Taylor didn't know where her heart lay, but she knew there was a distinct moment when she wanted to bolt.

"Glad I didn't miss you. Can we talk?"

Taylor stepped back, let the automatic doors close, and then moved to the side. She looked around to see if they were alone, and it was just the two of them. There was nothing awkward about that. Or at least in a perfect world, there wouldn't be.

"I have to be in to work in fifteen minutes," Taylor commented.

"So do I." Anne moved past her and went over to the bench. Taylor followed her with her gaze, confused, as if they sat and talked for too long; they would both be late. But at least in good company.

Taylor sat down. Anne made no move to speak until she had. "I thought my letter explained why I left pretty well."

"Well, enough, I suppose." Anne tilted her head. "What I don't get is the need to rush off. I thought we'd want to talk about it. I guess I expected us to talk about it. But no, you rushed off like you were scared or something."

"Or something?" Taylor snickered. "I was scared. But that's beside the point. If you wanted to talk, you could have picked up the phone. You have my number. All you had to do was pick up the phone and say you wanted to talk. Perhaps then this morning wouldn't be so awkward."

Anne opened her mouth and shook her head. "First off, this morning is awkward because you ghosted me Saturday morning. Secondly, when I tried calling, I saw you disconnected your number. That's low. I can't exactly try to make amends when the other person is doing everything in their power to keep the other person at arm's length."

"What?" Taylor squealed, jumping up from the bench. "I never disconnected my phone." Taylor reached into her pocket and pulled it up. It still showed service, so she offered the front screen to Anne. "I wouldn't disconnected my phone just to avoid you. What kind of person do you think I am?" She frowned, then shook her head. "Don't answer that." Taylor had already fled a hit-and-run that made her look pretty flaky. "But I didn't disconnect the line. Heck, my phone is my life. I might do some shady-ass things, but that is not one of them." She shook her head.

Anne furrowed her brow, then pulled out her phone. Taylor watched as she fiddled with her phone, then held it up in front of her. "I dialed this number multiple times. Not once, not twice, but fifteen friggin' times. Each time, I got the same message."

Taylor rolled her eyes and fell to the bench. "Well, maybe you could put the right number in your phone next time. It's 5165, not 5156." She quirked up an eyebrow and stared at Anne. Anne looked at her phone and then sighed. Taylor watched as she typed something, then pocketed her phone. "So, you tried calling me fifteen times?"

"Give or take," Anne mumbled.

Taylor looked at her watch. "If we don't go now, we're both going to be late. Good chat." She turned and headed towards the hospital, not wanting to look behind her but hoping Anne had followed. When they reached the break room, she turned to see that Anne was on her heels, and Taylor smiled. The fact that Anne did attempt to call her lifted her spirits, but that didn't change everything. She still didn't know how Anne felt about the kiss. They discarded their items in their lockers and clocked in, then walked side by side to the elevator. It wasn't awkward, other than the intense silence. When the elevator doors closed and Taylor pushed the button for their floor, Anne turned to her.

"There's still so much we have to resolve."

"Yeah, you're not wrong." Taylor fell back against the elevator wall, and Anne shook her head.

"You ran off without even discussing it. Just because you went in for the kiss doesn't mean I hated it. In fact," Anne took a step toward Taylor. "I would say that I enjoyed it. But clearly, I'm a terrible kisser because you bolted."

"Anne…" Taylor breathlessly gasped. Anne was inches from her, and Taylor's eyes dipped to her lips. If she took one step closer, there'd be no turning back.

The elevator dinged, and Anne stepped back. "Now's not the place or time, but you can't always bolt." She turned and exited the elevator, and Taylor stared after her.

"It's all I know." She released a breath and stepped off the elevator. Cecilia stood behind the desk, pacing back and forth.

She stopped, and her face was flushed. "I'm glad you guys are here. It's going to be a hectic day."

"What's going on?" Anne asked.

"Hailey is on bedrest for the remainder of her pregnancy."

"What?" Taylor asked. "She's got a few months to go."

"We'll make it work," Anne said, not missing a beat.

"I've been trying to get her shifts covered, but you know how that's going." Cecilia shrugged. "It'll be tough, but as you said, Anne, we'll make it work."

"We'll do what we have to do," Anne added.

Taylor leaned against the counter, the wariness already shaking her. But if the rest could handle it, so could she. She just had to be strong and hope that soon Anne and her could finish that conversation. For a minute, it felt like the heat was rising in the elevator. There was no way she misread that, even with the work day ahead.

CHAPTER SIXTEEN

OVER THE EDGE

Anne

Anne stifled a yawn as she stared at the computer. It'd been eight hours, and the shift seemed never-ending. With Cecilia off at meetings most of the day, it was just Taylor and her. She had to admit, she didn't know what she would have done if Taylor hadn't been there. Anne covered her mouth, another yawn escaping. Eight hours left, and she was already dead on her feet.

Anne was well aware that Taylor had it worse. Anne was used to the frenzy of a short-staffed shift. Taylor was only at the beginning of her second week. It would be a struggle for anyone who was in that position. She leaned forward, her eyes narrowing in on the computer screen. She sighed and fell back in the chair, rubbing her weary eyes. It was downtime for at least a few minutes. Taylor had finally been relieved for lunch. Anne could take a break when she returned. Perhaps. She didn't want to leave Taylor alone for an hour. Maybe she could eat at the desk. As she sat there, her mind drifted to Taylor. She was glad it was only a misunderstanding and Taylor didn't intentionally ghost her. She should have known it was a human error. But they still had so much to discuss, starting with that heated kiss — a kiss that Anne had yet to stop thinking about. If something so wild and passionate could abruptly send her in a tailspin, then maybe it was with exploring.

A light shone at the nurse's station, and Anne pushed herself up, grabbed her clipboard, and headed to the room. "You rang?" she asked, rounding the corner. The patient was Peter White, fifteen going on thirty. He had a wide grin.

"Catch." He tossed the football, and she caught it, clutching it to her stomach.

"Great reflexes," he said.

Anne laughed. "Well, I've come to realize this is going to be an everyday occurrence." She tossed the ball back into his grasp, and he shrugged.

"Gotta get my practice in here while I'm recuperating." He looked down at his leg and grimaced. "When did the doc say I can be released?"

Anne tilted her head. "Soon. Very soon. And next year, if you take it easy now, you'll be back on the field. Just give it time."

He rolled his eyes. "That's what all adults say."

Anne smirked. "Because we're all brilliant." She winked. "Not as brilliant as you, though."

He grinned. "I'm bored."

Anne scrunched up her nose. "I could see if the doctor

wants me to order some labs for you. Let's see, how about four tubes?"

"Ha ha! You're so funny."

Anne laughed, straightening up his blanket at the foot of his bed. "I'm sure you didn't call me in here to play catch. However, I'm sure you're amazed by my athleticism."

"You never cease to amaze me." He laughed, a teasing grin playing on his lips. "But nah. May I have a milk?"

"Sure thing. Anything else while I'm out? A magazine, perhaps? Or maybe I can call your school and see if they can send you some homework."

He rolled his eyes. "It's still summer."

Anne snapped her fingers. "Oh, that's right. Well, maybe they'll put together a package for you to start early." She winked and could hear him laughing as she returned to the hall. She snickered and shook her head. Her favorite moments were working with the kids and enjoying the easy banter back and forth. She shared such great memories with all of them. When she got to the nurse's station, Cecilia was back there. She looked up and smiled. "You're back?"

"Yep. I thought you both could use a break. Where's Taylor?"

"I sent her to lunch. We had a lull and weren't sure when you would return to the hospital." Anne reached in and grabbed the milk. "A thirsty kid awaits." Anne held up the carton.

"You can pass that off to them and then go to lunch. I can man the fort until you're both back."

"Sounds good." Anne turned when Cecilia spoke.

"Oh, and I forgot. We got a letter from Willow. You can do

the honors." Anne turned around, and Cecilia held up the letter, unopened.

"Thank you!" Anne slipped it into her pocket and hurried back to Peter's room. "Here you go, Bud."

"Thank you!" He had the TV on and was on to watching a football game, his spirits already looking to have improved.

"Let us know if you need anything else." He waved her away, barely acknowledging her, and Anne smirked. Just like that, she was forgotten. She turned on her heel and headed out of the room, pulling the letter from her pocket and ripping into it as she stepped onto the elevator.

Dear Hospital –

Hello everyone. I am at the new hospital. It's nice. I have already made a new friend. She stays in my room. We are going to be Besties. That's what my mom says. I am really happy, but I miss you. The doctors and nurses seem nice, but it might be a long time before they make me smile. I love you all. Miss you bunches. I can't wait to see you again.

With Love,
Willow

Anne held the letter to her chest as the doors opened, and she stepped off the elevator. It was good to hear from her, as not a day went by when she didn't think of her. Anne knew it'd only been five days, but that was five days too long. When she entered the cafeteria, she spotted Taylor sitting in the corner, phone in hand, with just a bottle of water in front of her. Anne grabbed two chicken club sandwiches and a water bottle, then paid for them.

Anne walked over to the table, and Taylor finally looked up. Her eyes widened. "You left the floor unoccupied?"

Anne shrugged nonchalantly. "The doctors are there." Taylor arched an eyebrow, and Anne laughed. "Cecilia came back and sent me to lunch. This seat taken?"

"Nope. All yours." Taylor pocketed her phone as Anne slid the second sandwich toward her. "What's this?"

"Accidentally bought two." Anne opened her sandwich, and Taylor shook her head, but that didn't stop her from opening it and mumbling thanks. "Guess who we got a letter from?" Anne handed it over to Taylor, and Taylor unfolded it. Her eyes widened when she skimmed it over.

Anne watched as Taylor read through the letter, her face brimming with a smile. When she looked up, there were even a few tears in her eyes. "She sounds good."

"Thought you'd want to see the letter." Taylor nodded and looked down at it, reading it over another time.

"Thank you!" She pushed the letter toward Anne. "And thanks for the sandwich."

"No problem. And since we didn't talk, I can tell you that I got my car back yesterday evening. Joe did a great job. I hope your aunt wasn't too upset with you that you offered her up for bait."

Taylor shrugged. "She understood, actually."

They settled into silence, and the moment wasn't right to

bring up the forbidden kiss. But why call it illicit? There'd been a spark; maybe they needed to let it fly.

A WEEK WENT BY, AND ANNE DIDN'T PUSH THE SUBJECT. It wasn't that she didn't want to. It was more that time had suddenly escaped them. Down a person, they were both working crazy schedules, many times on opposite rotations. Taylor's training transformed into a crash course, but even from the sidelines, Anne could tell she hadn't wavered. Her skills seemed to be at the level of expertise they needed, running on fumes. But since they were short-staffed, it was impossible to have it any other way. It didn't give them much more than a few minutes here and there to throw in a conversation, and when they talked, the kiss always seemed to be shelved. It was inevitable.

Now's not the time. We can naturally get to know one another; who knows where that will lead us.

The problem was, when there was little time for conversation, it didn't exactly form an everlasting bond between two people. As the start of another week arrived, however, they had a moment where they could chat at the beginning of Anne's shift.

As Anne stepped onto the curb to enter the hospital, she caught a side view of Taylor. Her eyes were down, looking at something on her phone.

"Hey you," Anne started. "Your shift was over thirty minutes ago, wasn't it? What are you doing still hanging around?"

Taylor looked up, and her eyes were frantic. She wouldn't

have looked that high-strung, but she was three cups of coffee deep. Anne slid into the seat next to her and immediately focused on what was happening inside Taylor's mind.

"You look stressed," Anne began.

Taylor huffed and fell back against the bench. "I'm more than stressed. I'm exhausted. My legs feel like Jell-O, and I'm ready to fall into a corner with a pint of ice cream and a bottle of wine. That's a great combo, don't you think?"

Anne shrugged. "I don't know. For the right moment, it could be nice. Wanna talk about it?"

Taylor shook her head. "Not sure there's much to talk about. I just got my schedule. It's like a race to see what will fail first: my stamina or my body. These hours are ridiculous. When I started, Hailey said it was probably that they were getting my feet wet. We're going on three weeks, and the two-week schedule just came out. I don't know how much wetter my feet could be."

"May I?" Anne reached for Taylor's phone, and she willingly handed it over. Anne looked over her schedule. It was true. She had a lot of back-to-backs and several sixteen-hour shifts. At this rate, Taylor would be too tired to discuss the kiss. Maybe that wasn't such a bad thing. After all, the kiss would fade from both their minds at some point, and it'd be like it never even happened. *As if.* Anne swallowed and scrunched up her nose. "I'm sure it's an error. Don't get me wrong. They like to schedule the residents a bunch of hours to start for residents to understand the job's expectations."

Taylor arched an eyebrow. "Do you think they feel they still have to worry? I've been busting my ass, Anne." Her tone went up several notches, and she dropped her gaze. "Sorry."

Anne shrugged. "Quite alright, but I didn't get a chance to

finish. They like to schedule the residents for many hours, but this is a tad overkill."

"A tad," Taylor snickered. "Do they want nurses or zombies?" Taylor took her phone and looked over her schedule. "Don't get me wrong. The pay will be phenomenal. It's not like I don't need it, but I also would like some sanity, and social life wouldn't hurt." Anne couldn't fault her there. Anyone would say the same. "It's not just me, Anne. I heard someone talking in the break room, and she said she was on her ninth night straight. Nine nights. That's unbelievable to me."

Anne furrowed her brows at that. Management was usually understanding. Situations happen, and mistakes can occur. The more Anne considered it, the more she was sure that this was a misunderstanding.

"You know, you could say something to scheduling about it. Maybe they have a new person working in the department. It wouldn't hurt to try, would it?"

Taylor gave a weak smile. "I suppose you're right."

"I'm sure of it." Anne stood up and checked her watch. "Let me know if you decide to bring it to their attention. I'll be happy to get Cecilia and Henry Martin on our side. They were both my mentors when I first started. Henry is in the HR department, so he's good to have in our pocket. You can just let me know." Anne backed away. "I better run, though, because I'm going to be late."

"Anne?" Taylor stood up, her eyes almost pleading as she stared at Anne.

"Yeah?"

"Well, we've both been busy. But I was hoping we could talk.

You know it's been over a week since…" Her words trailed off. "You know."

And there it was. Anne nodded. "Sometime soon." She rechecked her watch. "But I have to go." She spun on her heel and hurried into the hospital, away from Taylor's wandering eyes. She groaned. If only they could have had another fifteen minutes, she would have stopped right there and let that conversation take place.

Anne dropped her purse off at her locker in a daze, clocked in, and exited the elevator. When the doors opened, Christal from the emergency room was at the desk, along with Cecilia. Christal left just as Anne reached the desk.

"Hello," Anne greeted Cecilia.

"Hey, so good news. I got the okay to hire a temp. She should be here next week to help you girls out."

"That's great!" Anne sighed. Maybe things would regulate, and Taylor could get a more reasonable schedule. She could hardly wait until Taylor got the news.

CHAPTER SEVENTEEN

KARAOKE NIGHT

Taylor

As Taylor left the hospital, her entire body ached. As tired as she was, she did feel moments of a second and even third wind. Anne spoke with her three days earlier and clarified that Taylor could talk to HR. She still considered it, but for now, she had hours to work and just went with the flow.

She slid into the front seat and sat there momentarily, taking several minutes to do some deep breathing exercises before starting her car. The accident she had the previous month and the accident from her childhood taught her to be a wary driver. Getting behind the wheel wasn't a good idea if she was too exhausted.

Her phone rang, and she dug for it, spotting Gavin's name

across the screen. "Hey, bro. I'm heading home. I thought I would swing through and grab some takeout. What can I get ya?"

"Actually," he hesitated. "First off, I know I usually have an eleven o'clock curfew, but there's a movie marathon playing at the Plex. All the guys are going. And a few chicks." He laughed, and Taylor rolled her eyes. "I was hoping that my sister would be a dear and say it was alright if I went out. Please. Aunt Kristi is working, and I thought the world's best sister would let me have some fun tonight.

"Flattery will get you everywhere." Taylor stifled a yawn. She was too tired even to argue. "What time will you be home?"

"Before I respond, remember it's summer. School will be starting soon, and I'm street-smart."

"What time?" Taylor asked, yawning once more.

"Two? Two-thirty tops."

Taylor laughed. She didn't have to be at work until six the following evening. She would be in bed, passed out when he got home, but he was right. He was usually smart when it came to not getting in trouble. Luckily, he didn't take after their mother that way.

"Okay, I will trust you."

"Thank you, sis. Love you!"

"Love you, too. Just be smart." She hung up the call and slipped her phone back into her purse. If she was going home alone, she might as well stop and grab something to eat. There was no point in making dirty dishes, and she could wake herself up a little more.

Fifteen minutes later, she turned into Bar None. It was twenty-five percent bar, seventy-five percent dive, but they had great burgers and fries. It wasn't too far from her aunt's house. She entered the restaurant and looked around. It was busy for a Thursday night, busy enough to stay out of the way and go unnoticed. The waitress came up and greeted her with a napkin and a smile.

"Welcome to Karaoke night. You going to get up on the mic?"

Taylor laughed. "Not hardly." She looked around. "I was wondering why it was crowded. A lot of singers, I suppose."

"Wannabe-singer," the waitress corrected. "My name is Vicky, and I'll be helping you tonight. What can I get fresh for you?"

"I'll take a bacon burger deluxe with curly fries and a beer."

"Coming up. If you change your mind, put your name in at the bar." She winked and then walked away.

Taylor shook her head. It was never going to happen. Five minutes later, Vicky had the beer back at her table. Taylor took a sip and sighed as a man and woman took the stage. They began singing *I Got You, Babe*, by Sonny and Cher. Taylor watched them as everyone cheered them on. They weren't in tune, but they looked like they were having fun. Before the song ended, Vicky had the rest of her food. She was eating the fries, not recognizing the time, and enjoying as one after another, people piled onto the stage, sang, then left.

Taylor laughed, but the truth was some of the people could sing. It was the ones that made a joke out of it, which made everyone have a good time. "Get you something else to drink?" Vicky asked, popping around the corner, nearly startling the sandwich out of Taylor's hands.

"Sure, I'll take another beer."

Vicky left and was back within two minutes. Taylor took a swig and then finished off her sandwich. What had started as running in to grab a bite to eat had turned into enjoying the music and not wanting to leave. A song started playing, and she immediately recognized it. "Friends in Low Places" by Garth Brooks echoed through the restaurant.

She looked up, and her jaw dropped. Anne and three other women stood on the stage and started bellowing out the tune. She took a long swig of her beer and watched the foursome, with her eyes lingering on Anne for way longer than intended. Anne wore tight jeans that hugged the curve of her ass, and when Anne turned, Taylor got an indulgent view. She swallowed the lump growing in her throat and quickly broke it down with a gulp of beer. Was it hot in there?

Anne twirled around, looking fine, shaking her ass as the crowd went wild. Being older than Taylor, she had a way of moving that would cause every woman in her twenties to stop and stare. Taylor felt the heat radiating through the restaurant and feared she might pass out if it got hotter. Anne turned and looked straight at her, a knowing stare, a lingering glance, and Taylor gave a slight wave. Anne's smile brightened as the song came to an end. Taylor looked down at her basket of food. She could bolt or stick around. Before contemplating all options, she spotted the group headed her way.

"Hey, Taylor." Anne stopped, the other three stopping short, as well.

"Hey! You all sounded great up there." Taylor glanced between the four of them.

Anne turned to the other women. "Girls, this is Taylor. She

works at CAPMED. Taylor, this is Melanie, my sister. Her best friend Josie and Josie's little sister Gwen."

"Do you have to call me the little sister?" Gwen mumbled.

"Well, you are," Josie pointed out, and the four of them laughed.

"It's nice to meet you all."

"Likewise," they spoke in unison. Melanie leaned forward and said something to Anne, and Anne nodded, then the other three skirted away from the table. Melanie and Anne looked alike. They had the same mannerisms, and right now, Melanie was making the same face Anne made when she looked over a file: she was sussing something, or someone, out.

"Was it something I said?" Taylor teased.

Anne laughed. "Nah, they're good. So, are you going to get up there and sing?"

Taylor snickered and shook her head. "I would need a few more of these." She tilted back her beer bottle.

"That can be arranged," Anne motioned for Vicky to come over to the table. "Two beers, please."

"Anne, I really shouldn't," Taylor argued. She knew her limit, and she had just about reached it. One more, and she for sure would max it. "I've had plenty, and I should be getting out of here. It's been a long day at the hospital. I'm beat."

"Just one more. You don't want me drinking alone, do you?" Anne winked and scooted into the booth across from Taylor. "Unless you were saving this spot for someone."

"Nope. Not at all." Taylor took a swig from the beer that Vicky dropped off at the table. "Do you come here often?" Taylor asked.

"Only when Melanie wants to get out of the house." She snickered, taking a sip of her beer. "Long story."

Taylor drank her beer, realizing that the heat had encased her as Anne sat only inches from her. Anne wore a white blouse that revealed her cleavage, and Taylor downed a quarter of the bottle.

"You girls were good up there," Taylor said, the music getting louder as another song started playing.

Anne laughed loudly. "Then you're hard up for talent if you thought that was good."

Taylor kept her eyes on the rim of her beer bottle but felt Anne's gaze on her. She looked up to see if she was right, and sure enough, there were those magnetic eyes. She grabbed her bottle and downed the rest.

"Want another?" Anne asked.

"I wouldn't dare," Taylor mumbled. Her head was hazy, and she could slowly feel the room spinning. She looked up, and Anne had a grin on her lips, obviously not knowing the position Taylor was in. "Anne," Taylor began.

Anne jumped up and grabbed Taylor's hand. "Come with me."

"What?" Taylor asked. Her feet flailed behind her as she stumbled after Anne and right up to the stage. "Anne," she hissed.

"Trust me," Anne said. "You're going to be great."

Taylor felt sick, the room still spinning. Anne said something to the bartender as Taylor stood there awkwardly. Then the song "Summer Nights" from *Grease* started playing. Anne began to sing, and the words blurred on the screen. When it came to Taylor's part, she didn't know where it came from, but she started belting out the tune, and the crowd roared to life. Taylor looked over at Anne, who moved in closer to her and snaked her arm around Taylor. They continued the song, not caring who watched them, but the crowd seemed pleased, and Taylor felt like she was on top of the world.

CHAPTER EIGHTEEN

TIMING AT ITS WORST

Anne

Taylor lit up on that stage. Anne wanted to see her let loose, but she didn't know she had a karaoke star on her hands. By the time the song played on, Taylor was flirting, hanging all over Anne, and acting like they had been doing this for years. Anne felt every word Taylor sang and couldn't tear her eyes away. Taylor was a beauty that only got more beautiful when she opened herself up.

They exited the stage, and Taylor laughed. "Anne, that was great." She fell against her, and Anne turned to steady her to her feet. Anne didn't expect that the last beer she got for Taylor seemed to be the one that took her over her limit. Now, Taylor was slurring her words, and that intoxicating beauty was coming from someone highly intoxicated.

"Taylor, you're drunk." Anne covered her face, feeling slight guilt over the matter.

"Nah, no, I'm not," Taylor argued. "I don't get drunk. I get even." She laughed louder than Anne had ever heard her laugh. Anne grimaced, wrapping her arm around Taylor's waist, then grabbed their purses and awkwardly stumbled toward the door. Once outside, the fresh air washed over her. Maybe that would help to sober Taylor up. "You're beautiful," Taylor moaned. "Do you know that? You're so beautiful." She caressed Anne's cheek, and Anne winced. She'd wanted to hear Taylor say those words but now wasn't the time.

"Come on! I'll get you home." She then frowned. *Home?* She didn't even know where Taylor's home was. She had no choice but to get her back to her house. Once they got to Anne's car, getting her into the passenger seat wasn't easy.

"Kiss me," Taylor breathlessly said. She snaked her hand around Anne's neck and pulled her to her, kissing her hard.

"Taylor," Anne argued. "Not now." Anne felt a gut punch. She wanted the kiss to deepen, not end, but how could she kiss her like that when Taylor was drunk and wouldn't even remember what happened the next day? "Not this way," Anne helped her into the seat, reaching across to buckle her up.

"Your lips are so soft. I could kiss you forever."

Anne jerked and stared at her. Taylor had a grin on her lips. "In the morning, you won't remember any of this." Taylor closed her eyes, and Anne shut the door behind her. She didn't want to believe that statement, but there was a strong likelihood it was true.

Anne looked around the small parking lot and saw Taylor's car.

She would get her there the next day to pick up her car. At least Anne was there to see that Taylor got home safely. As Anne merged onto the highway, her phone rang, and she looked over to see that Taylor was sleeping, not even moving when the phone rang.

"Answer call. Hello?"

"Hey, sis. So, what's the story with Taylor?" Anne swerved at the mention of Taylor's name. She shot a look towards the passenger seat, but still, her eyes were tightly closed.

"There's no story. Taylor's just a co-worker. That's all."

"Hmmmm. Well, you lit up when you saw her."

"Shhhhh…" Anne sharply replied. "Can't talk now. But is everything alright with you? Is Josh home?"

"He stayed home with the girls while I was out, but then he went out with the guys once I got home." Anne rolled her eyes. She had heard that story way too many times. "I just wanted to check about Taylor. She's cute. If you like her, then go for it."

Taylor moaned in the seat next to her. "Gotta go!" Anne quickly disconnected the Bluetooth and looked where Taylor shifted in her seat. She held her breath, waiting, hopeful that Taylor would fall asleep. Taylor started snoring minutes later. Anne relaxed and drove the rest of the way home. Everything Melanie said, she had to push out of her mind. Sure, there might be something there. She sometimes felt it down in her bones when she looked at Taylor. The sparks always flew, but thinking of that now wasn't going to change the fact that there wasn't anything she could do about it. Taylor was in no position to respond reasonably.

Anne shifted in the chair, attempting to find a comfortable position. She stretched, her neck cracking a few times. "Anne?"

Anne jerked and looked to the bed, where Taylor leaned on her elbows. Taylor looked around the bedroom and then back to Anne.

"You want coffee? You could use some coffee." Anne stood up, but even in the room's darkness, Anne saw Taylor's frown lines.

"What happened?" She groaned and touched her head, then looked up and met Anne's gaze. She released a growl. "Beer, that's what happened." She fell back into bed.

"Do you think you can make your way downstairs? I'll put on a pot of coffee."

"Yeah," she grumbled. Anne didn't wait for her to say anything else as she hurried from the room and straight downstairs to the kitchen. Taylor continued to flirt, and Anne continued to dodge her advances. Even when Taylor pulled her into the bed, it took all Anne's might to crawl off of the bed and keep her distance. If there was an award for perseverance, they both deserved it, but Anne was weakening, and with any more attempts, she might have caved.

Anne heard the shuffling on the steps, and she turned to see Taylor rounding the corner. Taylor dropped her gaze. Her cheeks were flushed. "Just in time. Your coffee is served." Anne poured two cups, and Taylor reached out for the table, steadying herself. Anne had been in that position one too many times. However, she was in her early thirties the last time it happened. "This should heal your headache in no time."

"I'm good," Taylor mumbled, falling into the chair and

reaching for the mug. Anne scooted it closer to Taylor when it was clear that Taylor's depth perception was off. "Thank you." Taylor grabbed the mug and took a sip. She winced and then looked up, making eye contact with Anne. Anne gave her a consoling smile as she took a sip. "Usually, I never get too drunk to drive." Her eyes widened. "My car?"

"It's at Bar None, as it should be. Later this morning, I'll drive you there, and you can grab it. I didn't think you could drive home safely. I didn't want to overstep, but you were clearly under the influence." A vision of Taylor desperately placing the moves on Anne, only to get stopped in her tracks, attempted to wander into Anne's mind. Taylor's cheeks turned red, and she dropped her gaze.

"Do I even want to know?" she asked.

"Depends. What do you remember?"

"What did I do?" Taylor asked, still wide-eyed.

Anne smirked. "What do you remember?"

Taylor sighed. "The last thing I remember is singing with you."

Anne looked down and shrugged. "That's pretty much all that happened. However, it's a shame that you don't recall the crowd cheering you on."

"Are you sure they weren't boos?" Taylor asked.

Anne laughed. "You were a star up there." Taylor closed her eyes, opened them, and looked at her watch. "After you drink your coffee, you should lie down more. No need to rush off and get your car at this hour."

Anne took a sip. "Six o'clock. I feel like I've been asleep for forty-eight hours."

"Then I imagine the rest did you good since you've been working so many hours," Anne pointed out.

Taylor tilted her head. "Did you get any rest? I mean, you were sitting in the room. You didn't look all that comfortable."

Anne shrugged. "I can sleep anywhere. I'm fine. Just drink up."

Taylor took a sip, a little longer this time. When she dropped her mug, looking off into the distance. "I never do anything like that. After my…" Her words trailed off, and she clenched her hands together. Anne watched her, mild curiosity piquing her interest. "Water under the bridge. Just know that that's not like me."

"I wasn't judging," Anne remarked. "Besides, you might not remember that I practically forced that last drink upon you. Who knows what would have happened hadn't you taken that last beer on."

Taylor snickered. "Well, my limit is usually one. I recall drinking two myself, and it wasn't a hard sell to get me to go for the last one, that I remember."

"Yeah, I'm not much of a drinker either. I've seen what it can do to people. I don't much care for things that have that kind of effect on a person."

Taylor looked up from her drink. "I feel the same way," Taylor admitted. "My mom had a problem with alcohol and drugs when I was growing up. She changed in ways that hurt not only her but also her family. The fact is, when I was younger, I was in the car with her. She was under the influence, and we got into a nasty accident. One of the reasons I ran from our fender bender was that car wrecks triggered my anxiety. I had nightmares for years. I probably needed therapy, but the hardest thing is admitting you have a problem."

Anne slowly nodded. The heartfelt words that Taylor spoke left Anne hanging on her every word. She liked that Taylor felt comfortable enough to share such a personal story.

"I'm no therapist, but having someone to talk to is never bad. But I don't think your story requires therapy. It just requires understanding and knowledge that people are out there to listen. If you ever wanna talk, I'll listen."

Taylor smiled. "I don't have a lot of friends outside of a few here and there that I went to school with. So, I appreciate that."

"We all could use a few more friends. As you saw last night, my friends consist of my sister and hers." Anne laughed. "I hang out with a few from the hospital now and again, but everyone is so busy with life and their families. It's hard to find the time. But my sister, that's another story." Anne finished her coffee and stood up from the table. "Do you want a second cup?"

"No, I'm good. Thanks." Taylor moved the mug closer to Anne, and Anne turned to wash them in the sink.

"If you ever wanna talk, I'm here, too." Anne looked over her shoulder, and Taylor grinned. She reached up and massaged her temples. "Headache and all."

"I divulge info about my life, and you're bound to think my family is crazy. You might never want to hang out again." Anne smirked and turned, putting the mugs back in the cabinets. She hesitated and turned around, noticing that Taylor hadn't turned away. "My sister is in a rocky marriage. They have two loving daughters, and her spouse is cheating on her. He says it's over, but I see right through it. It's hard to know how to handle that. Being supportive is fine and all, but when he's mentally abusive.

He drinks until he's passed out cold in the living room. There's something genuinely unsettling about him. It's hard to turn the other cheek."

"That's rough." Taylor scrunched up her nose. "I can't even begin to piece together what makes a happy relationship or how a marriage can survive in the long term. I haven't had a serious relationship, and who knows if I'll ever get married."

"You don't believe in marriage?" Anne asked. She knew that many younger lesbians were cynical about getting married, but most of her friends still thought that true love would conquer all. Anne wondered if Taylor was hesitant because of the patriarchal idea of marriage or if she didn't want to be bothered with the paperwork.

"I haven't met a marriage that's worked yet." Taylor shrugged.

Anne nodded, understanding. Yet, even though her dad up and left them for another woman, she still wanted to believe that, ultimately, when two people loved each other, a lasting marriage was inevitable.

"It's hard to argue when you have lived through marriages breaking up. I've been there and done that with my parents. My dad wasn't any better than my brother-in-law is to my sister. So, I get it. Yet, the hopeless romantic in me wants to believe." Anne shook her head. "Let me rephrase that the hopeless romantic in me has to believe that when two people are in love, they will move mountains to be with one another. I know when I find that love, I'll never want it to end."

Taylor's brow furrowed. "You seem so confident."

"When you're talking about love, how can you not?" Anne pushed into the chair. "If we get to bed now, we'll be able to get in a couple of hours. Now that I know you're okay, I'll lie in my bed."

"Sounds good to me." Taylor stood up. The color had returned to her cheeks, and she hesitated. "Thank you for making sure I got home safely."

"I'm glad I was there." Anne started to head out of the kitchen when her arm brushed across Taylor's. She looked up, and their eyes met. Anne smiled and went to look away, but the longing hadn't once wavered. *Dammit! She had almost escaped.*

"We never did talk about that kiss," Taylor began. "Perhaps the moment is gone, and we'll pretend it never happened. Or perhaps…" Before Taylor could finish that sentence, Anne moved in and claimed a kiss. Taylor had initiated so much between them; this was the least she could do. Standing in the kitchen, Anne reached for Taylor's shirt, aching to pull it over her chest, revealing her two breasts. Instead, she just held onto the shirt with one hand. With the other, she moved her hand up the back and rested it on her skin. Her tongue dipped in and claimed a moan from Taylor's mouth. This was where they had to end it. It was disappointing.

CHAPTER NINETEEN

GROWING CHEMISTRY

Taylor

Taylor stared at her phone as she stepped off the elevator. Wrapping up another day at the hospital, she was ready to go home, sleep, and be grateful she had the next day off. Taylor still hadn't said anything to the hospital about her schedule. While she was tired, no doubt, having the extra experience under her belt made her feel accomplished. Besides, did she want to complain less than a month into her career?

As Taylor stepped outside, the summer wind washing over her, she spotted Anne. There was a moment of hesitation where Taylor could have quickly walked past her and pretended she never saw her. But Taylor wanted to talk to her. It'd been two days since the encounter at Bar None and the even more awkward encounter the next morning. What she hadn't confessed to Anne was remembering more than she led on. There wasn't much Taylor had forgotten about that night at Bar None, whether it was the karaoke or her repeated attempts to seduce Anne. It turns out tipsy Taylor was also flirty Taylor. "What are you doing here? It's your day off."

Anne looked up and smiled. "I had to speak with HR about an issue with my bank. All taken care of." Anne started walking beside Taylor. A distinct heaviness was in the air as Taylor's mind returned to the morning at Anne's house-- a morning that felt like a lifetime ago. Still, she wanted more, and she could tell that Anne felt that way, too. "So," Anne continued. "Are you hungry?"

Taylor stopped in the parking lot and turned her head. "I could go for a bite."

"Meet me at the diner?"

Taylor nodded, and Anne hurried off to her car. Taylor looked down at her scrubs and groaned. It wasn't like it was an actual date, but she would have given anything to be out of her scrubs and dressed in regular clothes. There was no time to do anything about that, though. She pulled up the group text for Aunt Kristi and Gavin and shot them a message.

> TAYLOR:
>
> Grabbing a bite to eat with a friend. I'll be home late.

It wasn't entirely false. However, there wasn't a distinction between acquaintances and friendship. She and Anne were friends.

She pushed the thought from her mind and drove to the corner diner. Perhaps they would finally have a few minutes to talk. They had shared two passionate kisses and intimate moments that Taylor remembered vividly. They had to talk about it sometime. If Taylor didn't discuss it, she would surely lose her mind. How could they let something that palpable go undiscussed?

Anne pulled into the parking lot after Taylor got out of her car. Taylor waited for Anne to join her at the door before they entered. Since this wasn't a date, there wasn't any reason for awkwardness. Yet, her palms couldn't stop sweating.

They grabbed a corner booth, and Taylor didn't bother opening the menu. "You know what you want?" Anne asked.

"I usually get the fish basket."

Anne tilted her head. "A woman that knows what she wants is sexy. But if you're saying you have a usual, then you don't escape outside of that box, and you might be missing out on new adventures."

Taylor laughed. "Adventures in eating at the diner? I never considered that. So, what do you suggest?"

"Well, let's see." Anne skimmed through the menu, then returned to the first page and pointed. "Tenderloin basket. It's the best in the world, and ask for it with the gravy. I promise you; you won't be disappointed."

"You say it's the best in the world? How many places have you tried?"

"Twenty. No, wait a minute, I forgot Salt Lake City. So, twenty-one."

Taylor smirked. "You figured that out all in your head. I'm impressed." Anne continued to grin, and the waitress approached them.

"May I start you, ladies, off with something to drink? Or perhaps you're ready to order?"

"I think we're ready." Anne looked at Taylor and motioned for Taylor to take the reins.

"I'll take a water to drink, but I want the tenderloin basket with the gravy." The woman jotted down her notes and then turned to Anne.

"I'll take a fish basket. Water, as well." The woman took the order, then turned and left.

Taylor snickered. "After all that, you ordered what I was planning on?"

Anne shrugged. "I'm used to the tenderloin. It is the best, but I don't think I've tried the fish. I'm taking my advice and thinking outside the box." Taylor considered those words, then looked down at her hands, clenched on top of the table. There was something magnetic about Anne. If they had never worked through the accident, then she would have never been able to see the kind of person Anne was. She would have missed out on a great opportunity. But Anne was a personality that Taylor couldn't just turn away from.

The waitress brought them water, and they waited until the waitress had left before each took a sip. "Do you come to this diner often?"

"Quite often. It's just a hop, skip, and jump from the hospital. It makes for easy access." Anne took another sip, then looked up. "What about you?"

"Not that often. Aunt Kristi is a surprisingly good cook. I don't usually like to spend money if I can avoid it."

"That's smart," Anne replied. The table quieted, and Taylor questioned if that was because she brought up money. They hadn't talked about what it meant for Taylor to spend over a thousand dollars on her credit card. But Taylor didn't think it was necessary to point out those trivial matters when it was her fault, and rightfully so; she should be the one to have to pay for the damage. Besides, that got both cars fixed and could have been much worse. "Speaking of your aunt, though, did she have to go out on a date with that Joe guy."

Taylor guffawed. "Oh yeah, speaking of that…" Her words trailed off as the waitress brought their food. "Thank you!" Once the waitress was gone, she continued. "So, yeah. He called, and Aunt Kristi first attempted to ignore the calls. She's pretty busy, so she has a solid excuse, but he's called every day for the past two weeks."

Anne laughed. "Two weeks? She got him to wait that long?" She shook her head. "Is Joe that bad of a person?"

"I don't think it's that he's a bad person. My aunt has a type. She's been with the bad boys, and Joe rides a motorcycle. She gets the feeling that he's not the settling down type."

"So, your aunt wants to settle down and all?"

Taylor pondered over those words. Her aunt had a fiancée once, and everyone thought they would marry. It shocked everyone when they broke it off because they supposedly fell out of love—everyone except Kristi. "I'd say she's a lot like you," Taylor began. "You know, hopeless romantic and such."

"Far less cynical than you, I see." Anne smiled, then offered a wink when Taylor met her eye. She was cynical, but Anne had vibes that might turn her around.

"Maybe I'm not the cynic you think I am." Taylor tilted her head and grabbed her tenderloin. "This thing is huge."

Anne laughed. "Let's see if you can handle it."

Taylor choked on her bite as she comprehended the innuendo. She chewed so as not to swallow the sandwich in whole. "Delicious," she said as she swallowed.

Anne grinned with pleasure. "I knew you would like it." She took another bite of the fish. "And your recommendation is spot on."

They ate for a few minutes, letting the conversation drop off, but periodically, Taylor would look across the table, checking out what Anne was doing. In many cases, Anne had her eyes directed on Taylor until they both looked away.

"So, when do you work next Saturday?"

"Let me look." Taylor grabbed her phone and pulled up her schedule. "I work seven to seven. I have Sunday off, though, so the weekend won't be too bad. How about you?"

"I'm off, but I'm having a party. Some friends, co-workers, and my sister and nieces will be there. Nothing crazy. We'll have a bonfire, roast marshmallows, and do things like that."

"What's the occasion?" Taylor asked, grabbing two fries and putting them in her mouth.

"Last week, I made my last house payment. My house is free and clear. I vowed I would have a party to celebrate, and I'd love for you to come if you can make it."

"Sounds like fun. I could come after work." Anne nodded, and the conversation died again for a few minutes. "So, your sister…how's she doing? Have you talked to her?"

"Every day. Same ol' same ol'. She knows that she deserves better, but when your heart wants what it wants, it's hard to tell it differently. That's why I try to give her as many nights out as possible."

"Does her husband ever come around?"

Anne laughed. "He knows if he dared to come around, I'd kick him out. So, he stays away, and that's all the better." Anne dipped her fish in tartar sauce and held it there. "But, Taylor, I didn't just come to the hospital for HR. I had to talk to them, but I could have waited until the morning. I was hoping I'd catch up with you."

"You were?" Mildly intrigued, Taylor didn't move a muscle.

"I was. I didn't think I could let another day pass without talking to you about what's happening between us." Taylor clamped down on her lower lip, aching to pinch herself to ensure she wasn't dreaming. "When we kissed, it was highly likely I could just forget about it and move on. If we didn't discuss it, then it could be like it never even happened." She laughed. "And then, kiss number two occurred, and try as I might, I can't move on from it until I know what we're going to call this. I mean, maybe there's chemistry, but that's all. I'll nod and move on. But, if there's something more we should be exploring, then we owe it to ourselves to figure that out." Anne leaned back in her seat, putting the piece of fish in her mouth with a satisfied smile.

"I don't think we should ignore it." Anne grinned and leaned forward, and Taylor shrugged. "I mean, I've been thinking about it, too. And I think that there could be something there. I like being around you, and ever since we could move past the, you know." She looked down at her half-eaten basket. "It just isn't something I'm willing to look away from."

"I'm glad we agree." Anne clapped her hands together. "I was worried that maybe I was reading too much into it, but I'm relieved you feel the same way."

Anne and Taylor were on the same page. Now, all they had

to do was figure out the next steps. They finished their food, and when it came time to pay, they reached for their wallet. It was Taylor who prompted a request. "How about this? We both pay for our own tonight. We can argue over the check when we go on an actual date. But surely, we can do nicer than this."

Anne nodded with enthusiasm. "That's a plan." They tossed money to cover their bills, left the diner, and walked to Taylor's car. When Taylor turned to face Anne, Anne was already inches away. Anne reached for her hand and pulled her to her. With no hesitation, she went in for a kiss.

CHAPTER TWENTY

IT'S MY PARTY

Anne

Anne glanced at her watch once more. She shot a look at the fence and sighed. Taylor said she would be there, yet she was already thirty minutes late. She tried to shrug it off. Taylor would be there. She promised. She took a sip from her water bottle and tossed it in the trash outside the circle of lawn chairs.

"Does anyone want anything to drink?" Anne asked, taking a stand.

"I'll take a beer."

"I'll take a water."

"I'll take a wine cooler."

She nodded and laughed, glancing around the fire pit where everyone had seemingly been enjoying themselves. "Anything else?"

"I'll take another burger. Well done." Her neighbor, Tyler, added. She rolled her eyes, ready to tell him he could grab that himself. But the truth was, she was just grateful that everyone had made it out to her party. She felt loved and couldn't have asked for a better turnout.

She had considered making it two parties, but the truth was that after giving it much thought, she realized just having a bigger party seemed to make more sense. Besides, she had help. Melanie had come over early with Lily and Rose. They prepared the backyard. Then, her neighbors Mark and Aimee offered to come over. Aimee was a part-time DJ and said she would bring her music. Mark had a knack for grilling. Everything seemed to come together.

"As long as my memory doesn't fail me, your orders will be coming right up." Anne snickered.

"I'll help you," Cecilia commented, joining Anne in her journey to ensure she could fulfill everyone's wishes.

"Mark, will you put a couple of burgers on?" Anne asked, passing him to get to the coolers. "Well done for Tyler."

"Coming right up!" Mark turned from her, and Anne reached down to open the coolers.

"By the way, I heard from Hailey," Cecilia began. "I've been meaning to catch up with you. She's still on bed rest, but the doctors state she's improving. It doesn't look like she'll be coming back before her maternity leave is up, but I think we all figured that would be the case."

"Yeah. No surprise there." Anne frowned. "Was it two beers and a water?"

"No, your sister wanted a wine cooler," Cecilia commented.

"That's right. I'm glad you came along to help." Anne

laughed, reaching into the cooler and pulling out a wine cooler." She looked over to where her nieces were playing games with Mark and Aimee's kids, and she reached in and grabbed four juice boxes.

"Let me help you here." Cecilia laughed. "I'm more than just the person that remembers the orders. I can deliver them, too."

Anne smiled. "Take this over to the circle, and I'll take the juice boxes to the kids and grab Tyler's burger."

"Teamwork makes the dream work." Cecilia winked and then hurried over to the circle. Anne sighed as she headed off to the table where the kids were.

"Who wants a drink?"

In unison, they all cried out. "Me!"

Anne gave them each a box and helped her nieces stick the straw through the hole. Mark and Aimee's kids, Ethan and Rory, were a bit older, at eight and seven, but she liked how they instantly took her nieces in and played games with them. That way, no one was feeling left out.

"Need anything else?" she asked. Anne ruffled Lilly and Rose's hair, and they looked up and grinned.

"We're good," Lily commented.

"Alright then. Holler if you need anything." Anne left the kids and went over to get Tyler's burger.

"Just in time," Mark commented, putting it on the bun and handing it over.

"Thank you, and you really should be taking a break. Have you eaten anything?" He shrugged, and Anne arched an eyebrow. "Precisely why I feared if you helped out, I would be taking advantage of you."

"You're not! I'm happy to be here." He smirked. "But I'll take a few minutes and make myself a burger. Does anyone need any hot dogs?"

"Nope. It looks like they have that covered over by the fire pit. Take this chance to rest. Promise me?"

He nodded. "Yes, Mother."

She playfully punched him, then turned to the fire pit. "Tyler? What do you want on this burger of yours?"

He laughed and stood up. "I was just coming to get it. I was only teasing. You didn't have to get it for me."

"Sure, you were." Anne laughed.

Tyler was only twenty-one. His parents had him at an older age, and when they hit retirement, they decided to move to Florida. Tyler inherited the house that was already fully paid off. Anne vowed that she would be sure to be there if he needed anything. Inviting him to the party was a no-brainer when he had no family in the area.

Anne's phone started ringing as Tyler grabbed the plate from her. She saw Taylor's name, and her face fell. Anne moved away from the crowd and answered the call. "Hello?"

"Hey, Anne. I just thought I'd check about tonight. I'm just now leaving the hospital, and I know it's late. So, if everyone is going to be leaving shortly, then I might as well not come. Right?"

Anne looked over to the fire pit, where Melanie and a few nurses were dancing to Aimee's playlist. "I don't think anyone is planning on leaving anytime soon. So, unless you don't want to come…" Anne held her breath. She didn't want to hear Taylor mumble that she would prefer to go home. She had been waiting all night to see her, a confusing situation.

"No, I'd like to come if the offer still stands." Taylor released a breath that washed through the phone. Anne smiled.

"Then it's settled. I'll see you soon." She disconnected the call and turned back to Melanie and her friends. Taylor was the only person missing from the group; she couldn't wait until Taylor arrived.

ANNE CONTINUED TO WATCH FOR TAYLOR LIKE A HAWK. SHE tried not to be too engrossed in waiting for another person, so she brought her eyes numerous times back to the circle. She sipped on her water some and just waited.

"I want to believe Josh will change," Melanie said. "But seeing is believing, right?"

"You have to do what's right for you, Melanie. Josh will only change if he wants to. The sooner you remember that, the happier you will be." Tisha, a co-worker who happened to work in the psych department, said the exact things Anne had said numerous times to her sister. Yet, it was always easier to take news from someone else. And if Tisha could provide that to Melanie, then Anne wouldn't complain. She was surprised Melanie felt open enough to discuss her marriage, but it made sense, given Tisha's expertise.

Anne checked her watch for the millionth time that night. Taylor should be there at any moment. Or so she expected. She turned toward the gate, and that's when she saw her. Taylor gave a slight wave and smile.

"Where'd you get these chips, Anne?" Cecilia asked. "I've

never had this flavor before. They were kimchi-flavored chips from a Korean market.

"Will you excuse me?" Anne jumped up and hurried toward Taylor, completely ignoring Cecilia's question. "Come here." Anne motioned for Taylor to follow her, and they went through the house's backdoor. "I didn't think you would ever get here." Anne turned to her and pulled her into her arms. She kissed her, the kiss taking Anne's breath away.

"That's some greeting," Taylor breathlessly exclaimed, breaking from the kiss.

"Too forward?" Anne teased.

"Not hardly. Too perfect," Taylor whispered. She moved in and pressed her lips against Anne's. They hungrily kissed, their tongues swerving through a fiery greeting. Anne had one thought: it wasn't going outside and rejoining the party. As far as she was concerned, she was ready for a party for two. Her tongue swooped in and claimed a moan from Taylor. She groaned and pulled back. Anne stared into Taylor's eyes, and a sparkle shone from her eyes. Taylor laughed and lowered her gaze.

"Anne?"

Anne whirled when she heard Melanie's voice. Melanie gave an awkward wave to Taylor, then turned to Anne. "Um, yeah?" Anne asked. Two seconds earlier, Melanie would have caught them entangled in one another's arms.

"It's getting late. I think I should be getting the girls home."

"Of course." Anne shot a look at Taylor, then quickly moved to follow Melanie into the backyard.

Melanie tilted her head. "Please tell me I interrupted something," Melanie hissed.

Anne felt her cheeks burning, and if it hadn't been dark outside, everyone would have noticed the embarrassment coursing through Anne's blood. "I plead the fifth," Anne whispered.

Melanie giggled and rolled her eyes. "Girls, we're going to have to leave."

"Do we have to?" Rose asked, clasping her hands together. "We're having so much fun."

Melanie shook her head and looked over to Anne. Anne shrugged. "Maybe you guys can come back sometime and play."

"Alright," Rose groaned, standing to her feet.

"Give me a hug." Anne opened her arms and hugged each of them; then they said their goodbyes to the neighbor kids. "Goodbye." She leaned in and kissed Melanie's cheek. "Call me if you need anything."

"I always do." Melanie grinned, and Anne walked them over to the fence and watched them leave. She waved when her nieces turned around and looked in her direction. They got in the car, and her sister drove away. Anne turned and spotted Taylor with the rest of the group. She was in a conversation with Tisha, Cecilia, and Kara from the hospital. Anne watched them until Cecilia and Tisha left the group and headed toward Anne.

"I have to be at a meeting out of town early in the morning. So, I should head out," Cecilia replied.

"And Cecilia is my ride," Tisha added.

"Thank you both for coming." Anne hugged them both.

"Congrats again on getting your mortgage paid off," Cecilia commented. "That's a huge accomplishment."

"You should be proud," Tisha added.

Anne couldn't control her grin. "Thank you! You guys drive

safe, and I'll see you both later!" Anne waved, and they left through the gate. Kara started dancing with Tyler, leaving Taylor alone in the circle. She reached for a stick and then looked around, her eyes catching Anne's. She blushed.

"I'll confess. I've never made a S'mores before."

Anne's jaw dropped. "Is that so? Well then, I think you need a good teacher, and trust me, I have loads of experience." Taylor watched her as she showed her how to toast the marshmallows and then melt the chocolate over the fire. "Then you place them between the graham crackers and have a delicious masterpiece. Just don't burn yourself."

Taylor popped a piece into her mouth and sighed. Anne smiled and looked away so Taylor wouldn't see the heat radiating on her cheeks.

"You're right, Anne, this is amazing." Taylor's amazement had Anne raising her eyes to indulge in the satisfaction on Taylor's face. The intimate moment had passed, but it wouldn't for long. They could reconvene once everyone was gone. Anne was ready to get back to sharing some sweet moments.

CHAPTER TWENTY-ONE

SEXUAL TENSION RELEASED

Taylor

As the last guests left, Anne stayed outside to say goodbye to them, and Taylor kept to the kitchen. She had plenty of experience with cleaning since she spent her childhood cleaning up after her mother. Taylor heard Anne outside yelling goodbye to her neighbors. When Anne returned to the kitchen, Taylor washed the last dish and dried the counter from the water left behind.

Anne cleared her throat. "I didn't mean for you to get stuck cleaning up. You're a guest."

Taylor shrugged. "It was fun." She tossed the towel to the side and turned to Anne. "I know I got here late, but the whole night was a blast."

"Is that so?" Anne moved in closer to her. "What part was your favorite?"

Taylor scrunched up her nose in thought, then smirked. "Learning to make S'mores from a pro."

Anne leaned back against the table, and Taylor followed her eyes to meet Anne's. "Do I have experience camping? You could say that. My sister and I used to set up tents in the backyard. A million stars would be in the sky, and we would be crouched in a tent, reading to each other and making S'mores." She then shrugged. "But it wasn't just camping outdoors. I recall many adventures at campgrounds with my parents before my dad, you know." Anne sighed. "Camping was a favorite pastime of mine. What about you?"

"What? Camping? Didn't you see my mad fire skills out there?" Taylor giggled. "It's hard to go camping when you're living on the streets."

Anne frowned. "I'm sorry."

Taylor shook her head. "Don't say you're sorry. I'm a firm believer that your past helps dictate your future. Someone would take the rims off a tire a few times and use those for a fire pit. That would be when it was below zero." Anne's eyes widened, and Taylor laughed. "Don't look so serious. That was a long time ago. I've come a long way." She moved closer to where Anne stood and reached for Anne's hands. She intertwined her fingers with Anne's and ran her thumb slowly across her palm. "You know what?" Taylor whispered.

In her mind, a million thoughts raced. What funny or clever thing would she say, something riveting to mark the way to a compelling conversation?

"What?" Anne's breath released, and Taylor's mind went blank.

Taylor dropped her lips into a grin. "The house is so quiet and inviting. No one's here. It's just you and me."

Anne nodded. "And so, it is…just you and me."

"Wanna make out?" Taylor asked all inhibitions lost. She pulled Anne closer, and Anne's lips collided with hers. There was a moan, but Taylor couldn't catch if it were her or Anne. Anne slid her tongue between Taylor's lips, thrashing her wildly around Taylor's. After several minutes of heated kissing in the kitchen, Taylor pushed Anne back against the table. She reached her hand down, cupping Anne's ass in her palm, and held her, aching for so much more at that moment.

Anne seemed to read Taylor's mind, slipping her hand under Taylor's shirt and riding it up, revealing Taylor's breasts. Taylor broke from the kiss and stepped back, staring longingly into Anne's eyes. Anne grabbed Taylor's shirt and pulled it up and over her head, then tossed it to the side, with their eyes never wavering.

"May I?" Anne asked, reaching for the front clasp of Taylor's bra. If she didn't rip it off, Taylor would do the honors herself. She nodded, feeling the heat of Anne's gaze bore holes through her body. Anne flicked her wrist, and Taylor's bra opened. Taylor slipped out of her bra, and Anne moved in and captured Taylor's left breast into her mouth.

"Yes," Taylor cried. Her core throbbed as Anne sucked on her left nipple. If Anne didn't indulge quicker, she would come right there in the kitchen. Taylor arched her back and relished the feel of Anne's tongue flicking with pleasure against her nipple. She swiftly moved to her right breast, and again, a guttural groan shuddered through Taylor's body. "Ugh…" Taylor cried. Anne kissed her way around Taylor's areola, sending shivers through Taylor's spine. Taylor grabbed hold of Anne's hair and squeezed her fingers through her hair, enjoying the greed that Anne displayed between Taylor's two breasts.

Anne bit down slightly, just enough to cause Taylor to shudder, before releasing Taylor's left breast from her mouth. She looked up, and Taylor couldn't control the urge. She grabbed Anne's blouse and pulled it open, breaking a button or two in the process. Anne's mouth hung open, and Taylor laughed, slipping her tongue back in to capture another moan. Taylor was about to give her the ride of her life, and Anne seemed to be full throttle ahead.

TAYLOR SQUIRMED BENEATH ANNE AS SHE FLICKED HER TONGUE inside of her. "Oh, God," Taylor groaned, moving her body in time to Anne's thrusts. She closed her eyes and attempted to relax. It'd been a while since she had a workout in this capacity, and Anne knew how to make her body sing. Her stomach churned, and she thrust her hips harder. Anne greeted every move with pleasure. "Anne," Taylor whimpered, her mind going numb, her body slowly convulsing. She held onto the bed and cried as another orgasm raked over her.

Anne crashed against her, giggling as she hiked up Taylor's naked body. She looked down into Taylor's eyes and then kissed Taylor's lips. The alarm started going off, and Taylor groaned.

"Not now," she moaned between kisses.

Anne pushed herself up and longingly gazed directly into Taylor's soul. "Duty calls, and believe me, I don't want to leave."

She rolled off of Taylor and stood to her feet. They were wrapped up in each other's arms for two days straight. Taylor hadn't even gone home to grab a change of clothes. Having Sunday off gave them plenty of time to explore each other in Anne's bedroom. She just hoped that when she got home, her aunt and brother didn't have too many questions to ask.

Taylor watched Anne's naked form as she stood next to the bed. Anne smirked and shook her finger. "What?" Taylor asked.

"You're oogling."

Taylor pouted her lips. "You don't like that?"

"On the contrary…" Anne moved in closer to her lips. "I love it, but it won't get me out of here any quicker. I can't be late for work."

Taylor snickered. "Well, you are taking a shower, right?"

Anne tossed a look over her shoulder. "I think I better. I can't be smelling like sex at work, can I?" She reached for Taylor's hand and pulled her up off the bed. Taylor laughed as they hurried into the bathroom, and Anne started to shower. Taylor cupped Anne's firm ass into her palm and kissed her neck as they waited for the shower to be warm, and then Anne pulled her into the shower after her.

Taylor closed the sliding door behind them and pressed Anne against the wall, the shower water cascading over them. They hungrily kissed one another, neither caring that the water could turn cold before anyone could shower. Taylor massaged Anne's breasts in her hands as the kiss lingered, tweaking the nipples as her thumbs approached them.

"Taylor," Anne gasped. "Work."

Taylor smirked, parting from the kiss. She grabbed the washcloth, lathered it up, and then fell to her knees to face Anne's femininity. Taylor ran the cloth up one leg and down the other, then moved her hand between Anne's thighs. As she caressed Anne's mound, Anne jerked. Slowly, Taylor moved in and out of her, washing her most sensitive spot.

Anne melted into Taylor's grasp, and once Anne was thoroughly cleaned, Anne did the same to Taylor. Taylor closed her eyes and enjoyed the intimacy that ignited in the bathroom. Taylor could get used to this. She felt warm, hopeful, and renewed. Taylor always dreamed of a place like Anne now owned, free and clear. As the feeling hit her, it brought a smile to her lips, but maybe it wasn't a place like this that Taylor desired. Perhaps it was the security and love that went with it.

Getting out of the shower left her feeling a sense of dread. She longed to spend another night wrapped up in Anne's arms, but Anne had to work at seven, and Taylor had to work at five.

"I'll see you when I get in?" Taylor asked as they walked to Anne's car.

"I get off at four," Anne said, groaning. "What time do you get off? Maybe we can have a nightcap or something."

"I work twelve hours. I won't be off until tomorrow morning." Taylor dropped her gaze, missing her already.

"Meet me for breakfast tomorrow? Five thirty at the diner?" There was a continued twinkle in Anne's eyes, and Taylor could never turn away from that.

"I'll be there." Taylor moved in and planted a sweet kiss on Anne's lips. It was a kiss that would have to last them. She parted and waved to her, then hurried to her car. Once inside, she looked over as Anne backed out of the driveway and drove away from her. She grabbed her phone and looked down at it, noticing several missed calls and texts.

AT WHAT COST?

GAVIN:
> Sis, you better be having a good weekend because Aunt Kristi has lost her mind.

GAVIN:
> She said she doesn't care what anyone says. She's not going out with Joe on Saturday.

AUNT KRISTI:
> I must've been out of my mind for agreeing.

AUNT KRISTI:
> This guy has gone mad. He sent me flowers. Flowers. We haven't even gone out.

AUNT KRISTI:
> I'm not doing it.

Her phone flooded with messages once she typed in her passcode, including three missed calls from Gavin. She didn't want interruptions. With the heat that carried between them, could anyone blame her? She smirked and tossed her phone into the passenger seat. It was too early to deal with it now. She was confident she would have her aunt convinced when she had to go to work. After all, once she heard about Taylor's satisfying weekend, Aunt Kristi would be ready for anything.

CHAPTER TWENTY-TWO

HARD TO CONCENTRATE

Anne

Whenever Anne sat down or took two minutes to think, her mind immediately went to Taylor. Spending the weekend together was unexpected, but it was one of Anne's best weekends in a long time. She felt her cheeks warm as she thought of Taylor, the instant heat Taylor brought to her body, and the gentleness of Taylor's caresses. One could say simple pleasure, but to Anne, it was magical.

"Earth to Anne." Anne jerked to find Cecilia at the desk. She could feel the warmth of her cheeks and knew she had been daydreaming way too long.

"Hey, CC." Anne gave a bright smile, but her heart never ceased pounding.

"You were off in some fantasy world, I imagine. Anything you want to talk about?"

Anne blushed, quickly looking down at her computer. "I'm just daydreaming. You know, of what I will spend my money on now that I don't have the mortgage." It sounded logical. Anne nodded with relief. She could pull that off with a snap of her fingers. Cecilia wouldn't think anything of it. Or would she?

"I don't know, looked more like a person in love sitting there." Cecilia snickered and sank into the seat next to her. Anne quickly looked down. *Love?* Now, that would be moving way too fast. This was nothing more than a fun, flirty fling. That's all. *Never mind that the thought of Taylor makes my heart clamor in my chest.* She quickly cleared her throat, removing the knot that lodged inside, choking her.

"I don't really have the time to meet someone right now. With my sister and…" She cut herself off. Cecilia had always been a great confidante, but even now, she didn't feel like divulging too much in that situation. "There's just no time. I'm daydreaming about finally going on vacation, that's all."

"You're still young, Anne. Just don't miss out on opportunities of finding love." Cecilia pulled up the computer, and Anne considered those words. Even if what she felt was the path where love was possible, she wasn't about to get into those murky waters. "We're admitting a three-year-old for some tests. ER just paged me." Cecilia changed the subject, which was a great relief to Anne.

"Oh no. Nothing serious, I hope." Anne went into nurse mode.

"She's experiencing stomach pains. We're putting her across the hall, making maneuvering easier for staff. They'll be doing a

CT and X-ray scan of her abdomen this afternoon and plan on keeping her overnight for observation until Dr. Carr can see her tomorrow. Will you prep the room?"

"Absolutely!" Anne got up, grateful for the opportunity to concentrate on something else. Anne went to the room and was immediately hit by nostalgia. The room had been vacant since Willow transferred to her new hospital. Being back in the room, she gave it a once over. Willow was always there to bring a smile to her face, and aside from that letter they received, Anne hadn't gotten much info from Willow's family. She knew she was receiving treatment and responding well, but that was the extent of her knowledge. She just might've found the push to get her to write a letter to the seven-year-old.

Anne looked through cabinets, pulling out some extra bedding and prepping the room so they could bring her in and get her settled. She returned to the nurse's station and looked down at the information sent to them. She would need fluids and lab work done as well. Anne could take care of both things before she arrived on the floor. She had finished grabbing the tubes for blood work just as the elevator doors opened, and two orderlies wheeled her into the room.

"Savannah?" Anne asked, looking down at the three-year-old. She instantly looked scared, shooting a look at the woman beside her bed. The woman nodded, then reached over and squeezed the little girl's hand.

"My name is Vie," the woman said. "This is my daughter, Savannah, and she's freaking a little." She whispered the last words. The two men helped Savannah into the bed, and when they were out of the way, Anne moved in closer to her, kneeling to her level.

"I know you're frightened, but you can be sure I'm going to take great care of you. My name is Anne." She reached out and took hold of Savannah's hand, squeezing it slightly. A small smile appeared on her lips. "Now, let's do everything possible to make you feel better. Shall we?"

Next came the hard part: starting an IV on a three-year-old and drawing her labs, but her mom was there to assist. There was little apprehension from Savannah. When she finished the labs, the girl turned to her mom. "I'm hungry."

Anne looked over to Vie, and Anne gave a weak smile. "I'm sure you're hungry," Anne said, kneeling to the little girl again. "Unfortunately, we have to wait until the tests are done. Hopefully, it won't be long. Okay?"

"Okay."

"Good girl." Anne squeezed her hand, then turned and motioned to the door. "Vie, may I speak with you for a moment?"

She followed Anne out to the hallway, where Anne could speak to her more freely. "Is it bad?" she asked.

"No. Well, I'm not sure. We can't give her anything to eat in case she needs surgery. I know that sounds scary, but it might not be; this could be absolutely nothing. We have to go in prepared. We will get her something to eat as soon as we can."

"I understand."

Anne hesitated. "Are you alone? Will your husband or partner be joining us?"

"Probably not. We're separated, and he has other priorities." She shrugged. "It is what it is, but I appreciate you being so good to her. She's all I have."

Anne squeezed Vie's shoulder. "She's in good hands, and so

are you." Anne smiled at her, then released her grip. "I'm going to go get her information loaded in and her bloodwork taken down to the labs. That way, we can figure this all out. If you need anything, you can just pull that lever by the bed."

"Thank you, Anne." She turned and disappeared into the room. Anne returned to the computer and entered the information, then started to take the blood to the basement, where the lab would work it. Cecilia came around the corner and waved Anne down.

"Two-year-old Jax fell off his bike and has a fractured ulna. He's headed up here and putting him in room 1012. Will you prep it?"

"Sure thing," Anne said.

Cecilia sighed, "Looks like the afternoon is turning into a crazy one."

Anne nodded and rushed off to the other room. It was hectic and possibly draining, but she enjoyed working with the toddlers the most. There were moments when she reached adulthood when she considered adopting a toddler. Then, the dreams drifted far from her. But now, she realized how maybe the dream hadn't entirely dissipated in her mind, especially if she had someone, such as Taylor, in her life.

Anne sighed, forcing the image from her mind. She took this too far and had too much going on to dwell on craziness. Even if the thought suddenly made her giddy.

CHAPTER TWENTY-THREE

MUCH NEEDED VISITOR

Taylor

Taylor felt the yawn coming on, and she patted her mouth. She leaned forward and stared at the computer, her eyes dipping to the time. "Ugh, two o'clock," she moaned. She still had three hours until Tessa would be there to relieve her, and she felt like her eyes were closing. She leaned back in the seat and stretched out, staring absently in front of her. "Wake up. Wake up. Wake up." She pushed herself up and began pacing. It was a slow night. She didn't mind it, but she was ready to fall once midnight hit. She continued to pace and checked her watch. Now, 2:02. She would never get to five o'clock with such moments.

She stopped pacing and leaned against the desk. To be where Anne was at that moment would indeed send exhilarating shocks through her body. She grinned, the image beckoning her to cave and settle into the erotic fantasy. The last thing she needed to do when, at any moment, an emergency could call on her, and she'd be left in a puddle of ecstasy.

Taylor moved around the ward, peering into rooms, many with parents asleep on the couch or chairs. After making her rounds, she returned to the desk twenty minutes later. She slumped in her chair and stared aimlessly at the computer. On the one hand, she was relieved tonight was slow. But she needed to stay awake. As she sat there, her eyes went to the room Willow once occupied. It now had a three-year-old. She didn't have to assist her much, but it did remind her of when Willow was there. She wondered what she was up to and if the hospital was treating her well. Taylor had promised to send a letter but hadn't had time. Taylor looked around the desk until she found a notebook. She sat there momentarily, thinking of everything she wanted to say, then began to write.

Twenty minutes into the letter, she heard the elevator spring to life. Taylor pushed the notepad away and glanced at her watch. It was just before three. Hearing the elevator at that time of night wasn't a thrilling moment. After all, it could only mean one thing: an emergency. The doors opened, and her jaw dropped.

"Anne? What are you doing here?"

Anne smirked, stepping off of the elevator. "I was in the neighborhood and thought maybe you could use some company."

Taylor snickered. "Neighborhood? At three o'clock? Are you trying to cruise the hospital?"

Anne moved in closer. "There's only one lady on my mind." She winked, swooped in, and kissed Taylor, taking her breath away. To say that those words caught her off guard was an understatement. She bit her lip, pulling back from the kiss. "Don't fret; chances of anyone catching us this time of night are slim to none."

Taylor blushed, looking down at her hands. Anne came to liven up her work schedule, and it surely would do that, but she was there to work. If they got caught, their jobs would be on the line. She looked up, scrunching up her nose in thought. "We're at work. It feels kind of dirty."

Anne smiled. "I'll admit, I never thought you'd shy away from PDA." She moved past Taylor and walked over to the nurse's station. "It makes me appreciate you all the more if I'm being honest. You're not the type that would go for a quickie in the supply closet—duly noted. I'm disappointed, but I can surely understand your concerns. I respect them." Taylor turned on her heel and stared at Anne. When she talked, it made her want to forget all her inhibitions, wrong or otherwise.

"What brought you here, Anne? Outside of being in the neighborhood, of course."

The smile never wavered from Anne's face. "Truthfully?"

"I'd appreciate the truth." Taylor stepped up to the counter, mere inches from Anne.

"I couldn't sleep. My mind kept returning to you, and I know how rough these mornings can be." She looked around and shrugged. "This is about as lively as it gets, I recall. So, I took a chance. I got dressed, jumped in my car, and here I am. The rest is history."

Taylor brushed her hand along Anne's cheek, and Anne's grin widened. Just one passionate kiss wouldn't hurt anyone. The kids were all nestled in their beds. The parents were out like a light, and she didn't have to do vitals for another hour. She moved in and pressed her lips to Anne's. Her tongue swiftly dove between Anne's lips, and her hand rested on Anne's heart. It thudded with every second that passed.

"I wanted you," Anne breathlessly spoke between kisses. "I couldn't resist rushing to the hospital."

If words caused a spark, Taylor was on fire. Her hand moved from Anne's heart and slipped beneath the buttons of her blouse, resting leisurely along Anne's breast.

"What if someone wakes up?" Taylor whispered.

"Easy enough." Anne winked and reached for Taylor's hand, pulling her after her. Taylor laughed until they entered the supply closet, and Anne pressed her against the door. Her lips eagerly sought her out.

"Anne!" Taylor gasped. "Now I won't know if someone needs me."

Anne turned and pointed to the wall, where the call lights for each room were conveniently displayed. Taylor laughed. She had forgotten that. In the heat of the moment, Taylor panicked. She swept her hand along Anne's neck and pulled her to her, melting into the kiss. Their tongues were back in a tangled mess, easily maneuvering one another. Anne slid her hands down Taylor's body, resting delicately on her pants. Taylor gasped as she gently pulled them down, taking her underwear along with them.

She didn't hesitate for a moment. She tossed her head back

and groaned, Anne's warm breath resting on her inner thighs. *Do it already. She* wanted to cry. Her body tightened, clutched onto Anne's shoulders, and braced herself for the intimate connection. Her jaw dropped, and Anne's tongue eased into her.

"God," Taylor cried, bearing down and trying not to disrupt the smooth entrance. A beep sounded, and Taylor jerked from their intimate tryst. "Shit!" Taylor cried.

"It's okay," Anne said. She met Taylor's frantic stare. Taylor shook her head, yanking up her underwear and pants and glancing over at Anne, the moment quickly gone.

"It's not okay." She glanced up to where the light flashed on the screen and shook her head again. "I'm supposed to be readily available, and now…this." She rushed out of the supply closet, straightening her clothes as she hurried to Savannah's room. When she entered the room, she halted, hoping to calm her racing heart. Vie leaned over her daughter, and Savannah was wailing. "What's wrong?" Taylor asked, almost breathless from the moment that happened minutes ago across the hall.

Vie turned to her. "She woke up crying. She's so hot." Vie backed away from the bed as Taylor moved in. She felt her head and nearly pulled back from the heat. Taylor grabbed her stethoscope and leaned in to check her heart. Savannah wiggled underneath her, wailing and trying to reach for her mother's arms.

"I know, sweetheart," Taylor cooed. Her heart was racing, but most likely from the fever. She grabbed the thermometer and held it to her head. *One hundred and four.* Savannah's heart wasn't the only one racing. "We have to get the fever down. The doctor isn't in for a few more hours." She fought the urge to pace as Vie rushed back to the other side of Savannah's bed. *Think Taylor, think.* "I'll be right back." Taylor ran from the room where Anne was doing the pacing. She stopped when Taylor got to the hallway.

"I didn't want to come in and take over. Everything alright?"

Taylor shook her head. "Her fever is 104. She's boiling. I'll page Doctor Newsome. She's on a break, but it's an emergency."

"Shhhhh..." Anne reached out and touched Taylor's hand. "You've got this. She has a fever. What does she need?"

"She needs Tylenol, but if she has to have surgery..."

"Think about it, Taylor." Anne's voice was calm and soothing. "If she has a fever..." Her words trailed off.

"Combined with the abdominal pain, she could have appendicitis. We'll have to operate." Anne nodded. Taylor sighed, relieved Anne was there for her.

"I paged Doctor Newsome," Anne said with a nod.

Just then, Doctor Newsome burst through the door, "Alright, what do we have here?"

"Three-year-old came in this afternoon with acute abdominal pain. We gave her abdominal X-rays, but now she has a fever," Taylor explained.

Doctor Newsome nodded and pressed a palm to Savannah's forehead, "She's burning up. Don't administer Tylenol orally; give her a suppository if needed." Doctor Newsome explained.

"Wait twenty minutes and see if the cold compress works," Anne added.

Doctor Newsome clapped her on the shoulder, "Good call, Anne."

"While Taylor worked around to get the cold compress and go back to Savannah's room, she left Anne behind.

"Just in case the doc decides surgery is necessary, we're going to try the cold compress." She pressed it against Savannah's forehead as Savannah quieted down some. "If after twenty minutes she still has a fever, we're going to give her the Tylenol. If it is appendicitis, we need to get her fever down. What's most important is relieving the fever; the sooner, the better."

Vie nodded, and her face wasn't nearly the frantic mess Taylor had initially found her. Savannah nodded back to sleep as Taylor stayed by Vie's side and waited twenty minutes together. When she returned to check on her, the fever had broken. Savannah was in a puddle of sweat and resting comfortably.

"She might not be out of the woods, but she's peaceful right now. Her fever broke. We'll recheck her in thirty minutes. I'll be right outside the door; don't hesitate to ring for me."

To her surprise, Vie leaned in and hugged her. "Thank you! I was so worried."

Taylor mustered up a smile. Vie wasn't the only one. "I'll be back soon." She left the room and looked around as Anne had vanished, or so she thought. Anne came out of another room, and their eyes met. "Everything alright with Samuel?"

She nodded. "He just wanted a glass of water. I got him taken care of. No worries. How are things?"

"The cold compress worked. I don't know what I would have done if you and Doctor Newsome weren't there."

Anne waved away Taylor's words. "You would have figured it out. This was your real first challenge, and many more will come. Believe me." Anne backed away from the desk. "I should probably head out and leave you to it."

Taylor widened her eyes. "Do you have to? I would prefer if you stayed." Anne stepped back in and nodded, leaving Taylor to sigh. It wasn't right to put all this work on one person, and it was true that before then, the morning had dragged on, but anything could happen. Emergencies happened constantly; it was far too much for one person to handle. Taylor needed to talk to HR before any other issues arose.

CHAPTER TWENTY-FOUR

WORLDS COLLIDING

Anne

"I appreciate you being here for me this morning." Anne walked Taylor out to her just after six thirty—an hour and a half after her scheduled shift was supposed to end. "I'm telling you, I was glad to be here." Anne reached out and touched her arm. She saw the fear in Taylor's eyes. It was a new experience for her, and when Taylor asked, there was no way Anne would have been able to abandon her. "Luckily, Savannah seems to be doing much better. Dr. Newsome's scheduling her surgery for this afternoon."

Taylor rolled her eyes. "Not hardly. I would have been panicking in the corner if it was just me." Anne didn't believe so. Taylor didn't have the confidence in herself that Anne assumed she would have. But Anne knew that it just came with experience, and soon Taylor would be riding the waves of knowledge.

Taylor sighed. "We didn't even get that breakfast date."

"There will be other mornings. Trust me." Anne looked toward the hospital. She didn't want to say their goodbyes, but time was ticking, and she only had thirty minutes to get changed and get back to the Pediatrics floor. "I hate to bolt, but…"

"You have to get changed. I appreciate you, Anne. More than you'll know." Anne shook her head as Taylor leaned in and gave her a soft and gentle kiss. Passion was great, but the sweet and intimate moments really jolted Anne to life. "I hope we can see each other soon."

"I hope so, too." Anne stepped away from the car as Taylor got in and backed out of her spot. Anne waved, then walked back to the hospital and went to the break room, where she had an extra set of scrubs tucked away in her locker. As she dressed, she thought of Taylor. They had started going hot and heavy in the supply closet, only for things to get stopped so suddenly. It left her craving more, but the rest of the morning didn't seem right to try to start where they had left off.

When Cecilia arrived at five, she seemed confused about what Anne was doing there. Luckily, the ER paged her, sparing Anne. Yet, she knew the inevitable would occur, and to her unfortunate dismay, it happened sooner than she would have hoped.

When the elevator doors opened, Cecilia sat at the nurse's station and looked up. Anne did her best to play it off, moving to the computer and signing in with her credentials. She could look down all she wanted, but it didn't stop the eyes from boring holes into her. She turned, and just as she felt Cecilia's gaze.

"Do you need something?"

"Well, yeah. For starters, I'd like to know what brought you into the hospital early this morning. I checked the schedule and rechecked it, only to find that my eyes hadn't deceived me. You weren't scheduled until now. And there's the fact that you were in regular clothes, but now you're in scrubs, so clearly, you didn't misread your schedule. I feel that some explanation is warranted. Don't you?"

Not if I can help it. The truth is that I was in the neighborhood this morning. You know how it is when you're new, alone, and working the graveyard shift. I wanted to check on Taylor and see how she was doing."

"What time did you get here?" She arched an eyebrow, and Anne quickly looked away. "We have cameras, you know. It would be easy enough to find out."

"What does it matter?" Anne asked, sighing. "If it was midnight or five o'clock in the morning. Neither makes much difference."

"I want to know why you were roaming the streets to get here before I did. That's all." Cecilia threw up her hands.

"It was about three," Anne huffed. "My sister…" She hesitated. She was a horrible liar, and the truth would eventually come out. "I was just worried. Taylor is getting a lot of hours, and I wanted to ensure she was handling it. I couldn't sleep, so I came here. That's all there is to it. Besides, it's a good thing I was here because our newest resident needed assistance."

"Oh yeah? Why's that?"

Anne proceeded to tell her about Savannah as Cecilia nodded and listened. "Luckily, she's improved this morning, but Taylor is still fresh here. I just guided her along the way."

"Well, that's fine and all, but you can't work off the clock. Put in your hours, and I'll mark them for approval."

"Cecilia, that's not necessary. I was happy to be here."

"I'm not arguing this." Cecilia stood up from the desk. "I have to go to a meeting, but give me your hours, and you'll get paid for them."

Anne rolled her eyes but didn't comment on it. She didn't stop by with the intent of making a profit from it. Besides, the added attention she got from Taylor more than made up for lack of sleep and monetary value. But, if Cecilia insisted, there wasn't much sense in arguing. Anne turned back to her computer and pulled up the calendar when she spotted the notebook shoved into the back. Anne grabbed it and only saw Willow's name before tearing the page off and stuffing it in her pocket. She instantly recognized Taylor's writing and was intrigued to read the letter, but for now, she needed to get her day started, or at least the second part of it.

Dear Willow –

It's two o'clock in the morning. I'm at the hospital, staring at your room and thinking about you. I hope that you are getting the care that you deserve. I know we haven't known each other for long, but know that you are an extraordinary girl, and I wish only the best for you. If I ever have kids, I hope they're just as sweet as you are.

I trust that you're getting the best care in

Tennessee. Are you getting plenty of Jell-O? Strawberry's your favorite, right? When you come back here, I will make sure you have a whole case of strawberry. Would you like that? I hope that you're able to make it back here soon. We all miss you. But we want you to get all better before you get back here. So, stay strong. Be well.

That's where the letter had ended. Whether Taylor had wanted to add more and got interrupted, or if it was just her missing signature, the note just fell off, hanging out in the open for someone to complete it. Anne folded it and put it back into her pocket. The next time she saw Taylor, she would surely give it to her. It was hers to finish, but it reminded Anne of Taylor's sweetness. Anne wrote to Willow last night. Maybe they could send them off together. It almost made Anne smile when Taylor mentioned Willow. It wasn't out of the realm of possibilities that Taylor wanted kids. It was just one more thing that Anne liked about her.

The door to the break room opened, and in walked two women. Anne recognized them both. "Hey, Anne," Hannah spoke. She'd been working in the ER for just over two years. Anne didn't know her well, but she knew of her, and they were always cordial to one another.

"Hey, Hannah, Trista. How are you both?"

"No complaints," Hannah said.

"Well, I might have a few." Trista laughed and tilted her head back and forth. A pop sounded, and Anne smiled. Trista was a new one. Having been there only a few months, but also from the ER.

Trista and Hannah sat across Anne as Anne dug in her pocket and pulled out her phone. She went to her text messages and skimmed through them to find Taylor's name.

> **ANNE:**
> Thinking of you. I hope you're getting plenty of rest.

Before hitting send, her mind went to Trista and Hannah's conversation. "That's right, can you believe it? I mean, never in a million years did I think a newbie would have the nerve to call out HR." Anne glanced in their direction, trying not to eavesdrop but suddenly intrigued by the conversation.

Hannah's gaze met hers, and Hannah's cheeks reddened. "I didn't mean to gossip, Anne. I'm sure you know more about it than I do."

Anne furrowed her brow. "Know more about what?"

"Taylor. She's in your department, right?" Anne nodded. "Rumor has it, she went to HR this morning and complained about her schedule. I guess she made a pretty big stink about it."

Anne shook her head. "Don't believe everything you hear." Anne knew that she had walked Taylor out to her car. There wasn't any time to stop at HR. She knew that Taylor had considered it, but she never brought it up again. She told Taylor that she would help her make a move if Taylor decided to proceed. It was all just a misunderstanding. *Probably.*

"I don't know," Hannah replied. "Someone spoke with Clarissa from HR, and she said she could hear her talking behind closed doors."

"You know what they say about rumors," Anne offered. Yet, she grew more curious about whether they were simply rumors or something more. Anne looked down at the message, just hanging there for her to send. She deleted it and put her phone back into her pocket. If the rumors were true, she would have wished Taylor would have said something to her first. But what if Taylor was right and something shady was happening in scheduling? It wouldn't be the first time the hospital tried to cut corners and work on a staff shortage.

"Anne? Are you alright?"

Anne jerked her attention to Hannah, and she smiled. "Yeah, I'm good." She got up and waved. "See you, ladies, later." She hurried from the break room so they couldn't question the wheels running through her mind, but the gears hadn't stopped turning, and Anne didn't know if she should be angry with Taylor or HR.

CHAPTER TWENTY-FIVE

BURNING THREAT

Taylor

Taylor stepped into Savannah's room two days later. This time, Vie had a smile on her face and looked up, a rush of relief cascading over her features. "And how's the patient this morning?"

"Much improved," Vie said. "She's recovering like a champ." Vie ruffled her daughter's hair, and the color had returned to Savannah's cheeks.

"I'm so happy that you are both doing so well. Do you want anything, Savannah? An applesauce? Jell-O? Maybe some pudding?"

"I want it all." The little girl giggled. After her surgery to remove her appendix, her appetite improved significantly, which was a great sign.

"Coming right up." Taylor patted her knee and then left the

room to retrieve the snacks. Hospital life had proven quickly to be Taylor's thing. She adored the kids and was falling into a groove. Yet, her exhaustion was overwhelming at times. She braced through a yawn and reached into the refrigerator. When she came up, she saw Cecilia approaching her.

"Hey, Taylor. You should head to lunch. You're wanted in Henry Martin's office when you're done."

Taylor frowned. "Henry Martin?" The name sounded vaguely familiar, but she couldn't quite place it or why the man would want to see her.

"He's on the Board of Directors. He handles hospital complaints." She shrugged. "I'm sure it's nothing to fret over. But he's expecting you at one."

Taylor frowned. "Alrighty then. Where can I find his office?"

"It's outside the cafeteria. You can't miss the nameplate. We'll cover for you." Taylor nodded and then went back to Savannah's room. It was daunting nonetheless. If only she could place this Henry's name. She was sure she had heard of him before.

"Here you go. Let the nurses know if you need anything else. I'm headed to lunch, and we'll be back later." Taylor smiled at Savannah and her mom, but the thought of meeting this Henry had her nerves running rampant.

As Taylor stepped off the elevator at the cafeteria, she glanced over to the wall of offices. Sure enough, there was Henry's name. She fought the urge to bust through his door and demand answers now. What good would that do her? *It might help ease my nerves.* Taylor grabbed her phone and pulled up Anne's name. It'd been two days of peace. She had texted Anne and even called her twice, but Anne seemed too busy to pick up the phone. Or she was avoiding her. That last thought had her laughing. What reason would she have to avoid her?

She stopped outside of the cafeteria and dialed the number. It went straight to voicemail. "Hey, Anne. I thought I'd try giving you another call. I hope you're doing well. I'm thinking of you and wish we could get together soon. Call me." She disconnected the call and looked over to Henry's office. *Henry Martin.* The thoughts trickled in, and she knew where she had heard his name. Anne mentioned it a couple of times when they had their conversations. He was a mentor to her when she first started alongside Cecilia. But Cecilia stuck around the department while Henry flourished and made a name for himself at the hospital.

Anne seemed to like him. If he was there to speak with her, there wasn't a reason to believe it was bad. Taylor stepped into the cafeteria and looked around. She loved many things about CAPMED so far, but the cafeteria food wasn't one of them. It was good enough, but her mind latched on the patients in the pediatric department and Anne. She never anticipated finding a girlfriend when she started her work there.

She felt her cheeks warm and never anticipated calling Anne her girlfriend. They'd only known each other for a month. But there she was, not imagining her life without having met Anne. A text sounded on the phone.

ANNE:

> Been busy the past couple of days.
> More drama with Mel. Catch up later.

It wasn't the loving message she'd hoped for. Part of her expected Anne to ask her out on another date. Yet, it was a response. It had nothing to do with her and more to do with Melanie. She could relate to that, as she had her own family situations to deal with, so it was a text that she could understand.

TAYLOR:

> I hope all is well with Mel and the girls. I look forward to catching up.

Taylor grabbed a salad and water and took it to her favorite booth. However, her stomach wasn't in the mood to eat. Her thoughts returned to Henry and why he wanted to meet. There were a million reasons, but none that she found to be all that thrilling. Taylor wasn't the type to get herself into trouble, and she feared that maybe a patient had complained. She had never had an experience with a patient or their parents that worried her. But when Cecelia brought up Henry, she put her guard up. An hour later, she only took two nibbles of her salad, and her water went untouched. "That was a waste of money," she mumbled. But there wasn't any way to force the food down. She went to Henry's office and tried desperately not to appear so shaken. She knocked, with a gruff voice coming from the other side.

"Come in!" She peered around the door cautiously.

"Hello, Mr. Martin. I'm Taylor, and I hear you wanted to see me. If now isn't a good time, I can come back." *Please don't make me come back. I'm scared to death and want some answers.*

"Now is about as good a time as any. Have a seat."

He was older than Taylor envisioned. He looked close to retirement age, with his gray hair pronounced and his wrinkles not hidden. Taylor grabbed the seat across from him. She turned at the closed door, wishing she had left it open. Now, she was stuck in this enclosure, expecting the worst.

"I called you into my office today to discuss the recent accusations you've made."

Taylor frowned. "Accusations? You mean the truth?"

He arched an eyebrow. "You're new, so I will pretend you didn't just say that. You see, Taylor, residents are a dime a dozen. There are a thousand more where you came from, and all of them would be eager to be in your position. We chose you because of your high marks and references, but I can assure you that no one would bat an eye to let you go, seeing that you're not happy."

Taylor's mouth went dry. She wished she had kept her water at hand.

"It's not that I'm not happy, Mr. Martin. And from what I can tell, I do a…" Her words stalled as she realized she was about to go off on this man who could literally hold her life in his hands. She released a breath. *Breathe in. Breathe out. Whatever you do, don't cry.* "I do a good job, Mr. Martin. I take pride in my work, and I want to be here. But hospital regulations are put forward for a reason. The hours that I'm working are unheard of. My schedule would cause anybody to break."

His face clouded. "Not anyone," he replied with a huff. "Maybe you're not as strong as you've perceived yourself on your application."

Taylor's jaw dropped. Tears threatened to fall. She worked long and hard to prove herself, only to have Henry Martin act like she didn't deserve to be there. And no one would speak to her that way and get away with it. Yet, she couldn't get the words out. She looked down at her clenched fists.

"If a resident can suck it up and stick it out, they will surely get better hours and higher seniority. If they can't, there's not much to do about it, at least on my end. If you want to get there, you must suffer the consequences. You don't get stronger by playing the victim." He looked down at his computer. "Now, I'm busy, and you should get back to work."

Taylor felt like Henry slapped her. She was in shock as she closed the door behind her and couldn't believe her day had resulted in a meeting like this. The anger welled up inside of her. Yet, she was frightened. How could she experience both emotions at once and not know which feeling would ultimately win?

CHAPTER TWENTY-SIX

EXPLOSIVE ARGUMENT

Anne

Anne tossed a crocheted turtle and started on her next one. A pile of animals rested on the couch beside her, and she sighed. What else to do on her day off? She had been crocheting starting at six and hadn't stopped to breathe. Even when she ate lunch, she continued to crochet. Was it because her online store was booming? Partly. But mostly because she was thinking about Taylor when she wasn't crocheting. And while she wanted to believe things were great with her, she knew that wasn't true. It was just after six, meaning she spent twelve hours crocheting. There was no doubt why she had a pile of creatures staring back at her. At least it would mean the paying customers wouldn't have to worry about waiting for their orders.

Crocheting was Anne's therapy, and it had helped today to

keep her hands busy. She stifled a yawn and went back to crocheting a frog keychain. She was nearly finishing it thirty minutes later when a knock was on her door.

"Wait right here, little froggy." She said as she headed to the door and opened it. "Taylor!" she gasped. She was the last person she expected standing there. Her face fell. "What's wrong?" Tears cascaded down Taylor's cheeks. As frustrated as she was about how things went down, she didn't want to see her upset. She reached for her hand, pulled her into the foyer, and closed the door behind them.

"Do you have a few minutes to talk?" Taylor asked between sobs. "I know you're busy with Melanie and all." She hesitated and looked past Anne. "Is she here?"

"Um, no." Anne stammered. She felt a pang of regret as she recognized how this would seem. She had sent the text on a whim, not even realizing what she was saying until it was too late. She needed space. She barely had time to think between work and Taylor's constant texts and calls. However, she also didn't want to seem like a cold-hearted bitch and not answer the phone when Taylor kept on it. "She's home now," she said, lying once more but feeling the angst coursing through her veins. "I have some time."

They walked into the living room, and Taylor glanced at the mountain of crocheted animals. Anne felt her cheeks burning, knowing that, again, the truth could come out that she had lied to Taylor. If things ever quieted down, Anne would have to straighten it out. For now, she couldn't backpedal.

"I've been working on these all week. Here, let me move it out of the way." She grabbed them in her arms, tossed them to the floor, and then turned to Taylor. "Sit down. Would you like something to drink?"

Taylor shook her head. "I'm good."

She obviously wasn't good, but Anne felt she was about to find out why. They sat on the couch, and there were several minutes of awkwardness. To go from the minutes they spent in the supply closet to suddenly not knowing what to say to one another, ate Anne up inside. She wanted to reach out and touch Taylor's hand, ask for her to look at her, plead with her to come clean. Only then could they make things right again.

"I don't know where to start," Taylor began.

Anne released a breath. "The beginning is always great." The space between them was too long, but Anne stayed in her corner of the couch while Taylor stayed in hers.

"Right…" Taylor released a breath. "The beginning. I spoke with HR about the scheduling."

"Yeah, I heard," Anne mumbled.

Taylor glanced up, meeting her gaze. "You did?" Anne nodded. "Now I'm thinking, as much as I'm glad I said something, maybe it was the worst decision I could have made."

Anne looked down at the couch; so many thoughts were playing in her mind, but she didn't know where to start. Taylor continued.

"I wanted to see if I was making a bigger deal out of it than I should. I thought if I said something, I could resolve many things, but now… I'm not so sure."

Anne looked up and shook her head. "Taylor, I told you to talk to me if you decided to go to HR. I said I would help you through it. Some strong personalities are in there; they don't take kindly to people trying to tell them what to do. I tried to warn you. You didn't even get me involved."

"I thought I could handle it alone," Taylor replied. She sobbed again, and a tear trickled down her cheeks. Her face was red and splotchy, and Anne felt bad for her, but she still couldn't reach out to touch her. "Today, I got called into Henry Martin's office."

Anne nodded. "Henry is a good man. That's not the worst thing that could happen."

Taylor's jaw dropped. "He practically threatened me. He said if I didn't want to work, he would find another resident from the thousands of applications they have. He was anything but pleasant to me."

Anne frowned. "I'm sure you just misunderstood. That doesn't sound like Henry."

"Misunderstood?" Taylor stood up from the couch. "He said residents are a dime a dozen, and there's a thousand more when I came from." The tears were thick in Taylor's eyes. The emotions were real. Anne could feel them, but the Henry she knew wouldn't be so cold and heartless. She couldn't believe that Henry would go down that road.

"You're emotional. Sometimes, our emotions cloud our conversations. Are you sure he said it like that? I mean, you could have easily misinterpreted things. I know that sometimes I take things the wrong way when I get overwhelmed."

"Are you taking his side? Do you not trust me? He said it that way, exactly. Clearly, you don't know your mentor like you think you do. He said I'm weak. Maybe that's how you feel about me, too."

Anne stood up and stared at Taylor. Her mind raced as she

considered those words. "I know him very well, Taylor. And what you're saying doesn't sound like him. But then again, maybe he's different with new hires. I don't know. But I know you need to take a deep breath and stay calm. He's probably trying a new tough-love approach. I know he's had some problems with residents before. Maybe you just need to push yourself a little harder." Anne felt the fiery rage burning through her.

"Push harder? I push plenty hard. I'm a damn good worker, Anne. I never thought you'd take the hospital's side over mine."

"Taylor, I'm not," Anne argued.

"That's exactly what you're doing. Correct me if I'm wrong, but you said that the hospital stopped you from doing things for financial reasons. Don't you see how this could all be interconnected? I'm not crazy, Anne."

Anne stared at Taylor. She saw the tears flashing in Taylor's eyes, and there was a moment when she wanted to rush to Taylor and apologize, but she stayed her ground. Taylor shook her head and hurried past Anne. Anne stood there, stunned, and waited for the door to slam behind Taylor. Just as she expected, the sound came, and Taylor was gone. Anne sank into the sofa cushion and stared straight ahead. Henry wouldn't say things like that. He just wouldn't. She had to trust her gut, even though her heart just left the house.

CHAPTER TWENTY-SEVEN

RASH DECISIONS

Taylor

Taylor didn't know how she made it to work the next morning. She spent the entire night crying, wallowing in pity, shaken to the core by Anne's dismissal of how Henry treated Taylor. It was one thing for Anne not to take her calls or texts, but it was a different story when Anne acted like she was making it all up. Everything Taylor spoke when it came to Henry, Anne made an excuse for him.

She beat her hands against the steering wheel, tears stinging her eyes again. A notification sounded on her phone, and she quickly glanced at it. There was a moment when Taylor had hoped the notification would be from Anne, telling Taylor she was sorry she didn't believe her. Then again, she hoped it would come as a phone call. Instead, it was an ad for Viagra. She rolled her eyes and tossed the phone to the side.

She glanced down at her clock. It was just after eight o'clock. She still had an hour before she had to be at work. She was there so soon because she couldn't sleep. She didn't want to be in a place that could abuse their power and then laugh about it afterward. She groaned and stared straight ahead. If the money wasn't so good, she would have called in and quit in the middle of the night. She didn't need this stress, and she didn't need to work in a place that brought her only anger and dismay.

Another notification sounded, and she grabbed her phone again, instantly filling herself with regret. "Dammit," she groaned, tossing her phone to the side. Another ad, just for clothing, this time. But wishing and hoping it would be Anne was only killing her inside. Anne had made her choice when she stuck up for the hospital. She wanted someone who would stand by her side, not the big tycoons who could prey on the little people.

Taylor was used to mistreatment. However, this wasn't the same mistreatment she experienced growing up. Her mother had a sharp tongue that could reach out and strangle a person with just a few words. She saw the rude people around her, mainly because they were all in the same boat. Homelessness was brutal, and everyone had to find ways to survive; some struggled longer than others. Yet, those people always came around. There wasn't any redeeming grace from these superiors at the hospital. They had you locked in a place where you were desperate to be. After all, what good was an education without a career?

Taylor flicked away a tear; what she wouldn't give for her biggest problem to be the handful of assholes she encountered as a teen. At least then, she had the love and support of her younger brother. But she was there for Gavin, fighting for him, being the strong woman she needed to be. She resented Henry for saying she was weak because she was anything but. She'd be damned if she allowed Henry to see her cowering in a corner, doing nothing about it. She vowed to be strong and stick up for herself like she stuck up for Gavin. Taylor grabbed her phone again, this time not for notification but to check her schedule, which would surely be online now. As she stared at the schedule, the tears stalled on her cheeks. She couldn't even believe it. While she figured arguing with HR would give her a lessened schedule, she was looking at even more harsh hours. With a schedule like this, she would collapse by day ten.

She pulled up Gavin's name and busied herself, typing a message.

> TAYLOR:
>
> Hey, Gavin. Remember what we always say to abusive assholes?

She pocketed her phone and got out of the car. They might think that she's some weakling they can walk all over, but they had another thing coming. She had worked too hard in school to cry in the hallway. No man or woman was going to be the death of her career. She entered the HR office, where Clarissa looked up, her eyes wide at the sight of Taylor.

"Hey, Taylor."

"Clarissa." Taylor grabbed her badge from her purse and tossed it onto the desk. "You can tell anyone you want to know that yesterday was my last day. I quit." She spun on her heels and stormed towards the door.

"Taylor!" Clarissa called out. Taylor hesitated at the door

and turned to face Clarissa. "You can't just quit like that. You have to give a formal resignation. That means it has to come in writing."

Taylor released a breath. "Alright. Do you have a piece of paper?"

Clarissa arched an eyebrow but handed her a sheet of paper as Taylor fished a pen from her person. She only added two words to the piece of paper. *I quit.* Then, Taylor signed the papers and pushed them toward her. "That should suffice, don't you think?" She waited for no response and stormed out of the office. It wasn't until she had exited the hall that she took a moment to breathe.

On the one hand, she felt crushed; on the other, relieved. Tears started to rush back to her when she stepped outside, taking in a whiff of the air. She would never see the kids again, and that feeling overwhelmed her, clenching at her chest.

A notification on her phone sounded, and she fumbled for it and read Gavin's reply: *We say, screw you.*

He was exactly right, and it was necessary as much as it hurt. If Taylor ever wanted to get her life back, she had to tell the administration what she thought of them, and that was the right step.

CHAPTER TWENTY-EIGHT

FAMILY EMERGENCY

Anne

Anne stared at the television; the reality dating show continued to play, but she rolled her eyes. "Love, it's such a waste of time." She turned off the show and leaned back against the couch. Her eyes drew to the cat she had crocheted, still sitting on the coffee table where she had left it. She had made it for Taylor, a replica of Whiskers. At this point, Taylor would probably never get it. She picked it up and stared at it as Whiskers hopped onto the couch and meowed.

Anne rubbed behind her ears and loudly purred, rubbing her head against Anne's hand. "She's not coming back. We both have to get used to that." Whiskers crawled into Anne's lap and lay there, getting all comfy and ignoring Anne's dire tone.

Anne tossed the cat she crocheted across the room and closed her eyes as I landed somewhere in the living room. She thought maybe Taylor was someone she could fall for. She was opening her heart to love with Taylor. The notion confused her but also excited her. But now, they weren't even on speaking terms, and there was little hope that would change.

Anne had no idea that Taylor could be so immature, though. That was a red flag. So, maybe it was a good thing that Taylor stormed out of the house and never returned. She at least got a chance to see the person that Taylor was. Taylor said that Henry called her weak, and by the looks of things, Taylor wasn't as strong as Taylor thought. She quit her job on a whim. And for what? To prove a point? Talk about immature. She couldn't just forget her responsibilities and leave without a word. Maybe that was what bothered Anne the most; Taylor never said goodbye.

"Stop thinking of her!" Anne fumed, jolting Whiskers out of her lap. "Sorry, buddy," she mumbled.

She fell back against the couch and stared at the ceiling. She watched TV so she wouldn't have to think about Taylor, but the TV only brought shows that made her think about her. It was a never-ending circle that continued to revolve. She jumped up from the couch and hurried upstairs. Perhaps sleep was the only thing that would soothe her. She changed into a t-shirt and lounge pants and fell into bed, her phone in her hand.

As she lay there, she pulled up pictures that she had taken of Taylor. She was so beautiful and independent. When Anne first got to know her, she believed that Taylor was this angel who could only breathe light into any situation. But now that this darkness had clouded around them, she knew it was only a mirage.

"Why didn't you say goodbye?" Anne whispered. It was true. That notion hurt her more than anything. She knew they had argued less than fifteen hours earlier, but the courtesy was to tell her. She wouldn't have bolted if the situation had been reversed. She tossed her phone down and leaned over to shut off her light. It was just after nine, but the sooner she got to sleep, the sooner she could stop thinking about Taylor.

How wrong she was. Her dreams immediately went to the woman she wanted to push out of her mind. Only it was her intimate fantasies that fell over her night.

Taylor's breath was like molten lava as they kissed, her tongue swooping against Anne's, wildly dancing, tasting like peach cobbler, only better. "I love you," Taylor whispered between kisses. Those words left Anne reeling with intensity. She couldn't stop the exact words from flowing out of her mouth. Why would she? She was in love with this woman, and their differences couldn't interfere with those three words.

Taylor straddled Anne, pressing her bare chest against Anne's. Anne just wanted to taste her nipples once more. As Taylor pushed herself up from Anne, Anne latched onto one nipple and then the next. She tasted so sweet. While she pampered each breast, she felt Taylor slipping her fingers down Anne's panties. Anne jerked, groaning, and Taylor moved her fingers in, pleasuring Anne with her touch.

"Yes, Taylor," Anne cried, breaking from Taylor's breasts to thrust her hips up and meet Taylor's fingers. She bit down on her tongue and anxiously rocked back and forth. "Don't stop. Just don't stop."

"Anne, the phone's ringing."

"What? Don't stop!" Anne's thrusts turned frantic as she begged each finger to slide into her.

"Anne! The phone!"

Anne jerked from her sleep. "Taylor?"

There was sobbing echoing on the other end. Anne quickly came out of her deep sleep. "Anne?"

"Mel? What's going on? Why are you crying?" Anne whipped her eyes and shook her head, clearing the image in her dreams.

"I was in a car accident. It's pretty bad. The car's totaled." She sniffled again. "CAPMED…please, can you?" The words came out broken, but Anne tossed the covers back and sprang out of bed.

"I'm on my way." Her head was fuzzy, but she had to get to her sister. She wasn't in her right mind. But something was wrong, and Anne needed to be by her side.

Anne paced back and forth, waiting for her turn at the ER. She checked her watch, then paced again. It'd been an hour since she had gotten the call from Melanie. So many thoughts were running through her mind about what had happened; if the girls were with her, how did it happen? Who's fault was it? She couldn't stop long enough even to think. Her head was a mess.

"Anne?" Anne rushed over to the desk, glad to finally get called. "You can go in now. E-7."

"Thank you!" Anne hurried through the double doors and went straight for the ER bed. She pulled back the current, and Melanie looked up and started crying. "Mel." Anne rushed to her and held her in her arms.

"I just can't believe it. I wanted to think Josh would change, but it's impossible. He's a dirty rat, and I was the fool to always fall for it."

"Oh, Mel." Anne rubbed her hand along her hair. "What happened? Where are the girls? Whose fault was it?" Every question she had in the lobby came flooding back to her."

"It was awful." Melanie covered her face. The kids are with Josh's Mom and Dad. We were going to have a romantic night in. Or, so I thought. I went to the room to change into something sexy, and a text popped up on his phone. The man is clueless because he shouldn't have left his phone out, but he did. It was from a woman. I'm pretty sure it's the same one he'd been screwing. She talked about all these dirty things they would do together, and I confronted him."

"Oh, Mel. I'm sorry." Anne sat on the edge of the bed.

She shook her head. "Don't be sorry. I should have realized the guy I was married to. You tried to warn me, and I ignored you because I was in love. He confessed everything, though. He told me he felt he was in love with her and wanted to marry her one day." She started crying again. "I burst into tears and tore out of the house. I wasn't seeing where I was going. The tears blurred my vision, and I missed a red light. I tore through it, and a car hit me."

"Are you alright? I mean physically. You have some bruises, but is that all?"

"They ran some tests, and I'm waiting for the results, but I'm in some pain. Mostly, I feel stupid. How could I be so dumb?"

"It's okay, Mel. You're not stupid. You were in love," Anne did her best to soothe her sister. Even though Anne was far from Josh's biggest fan, Melanie didn't need to be chastised right now. Anne slowly realized that she couldn't make Melanie leave. Mel had to come to her conclusion by herself.

"I still am," Melanie admitted. Anne ran her hand down her

sister's bed railing. "But I know that the girls and I deserve better."

Anne loved hearing those words coming from her. It was the first time Mel admitted that. "You do deserve better." Anne quickly added.

The curtain fell back, and Dr. Newsome appeared. "Anne? What are you doing here?"

"This is my sister." Anne then tilted her head. "What about you? A far cry from Pediatrics."

"Gotta go where the need arises, right?" She rolled her eyes. "I'll be here all week, but I hope to return to our home next week." She then turned to Melanie. "All tests returned and confirmed that it's just bruises and cuts. I do want to keep you overnight for observation, though. That way, if anything comes up within twenty-four hours, you'll be here but moved to an observation floor. I'll set that up and send the nurse back here to see you in a minute. How's the pain on a scale of one to ten?"

"About a seven," Melanie commented. Anne suspected the pain was mainly in Melanie's heart, but she didn't divulge that.

"We'll get you some pain meds to help manage the pain. See you in a bit." She left the room, and Anne turned to Melanie.

"It could have been a lot worse. Do you know how the person in the other car is doing?"

"They walked away from it, didn't even have to come to the hospital." Anne sighed with relief. The last thing they needed was any more heartache.

"I'm glad you're leaving him this time. No one deserves to be mistreated." Those words danced around Anne's mind. Taylor came to her mind. She forced her to exit her mind because thinking about her helped no one.

"I'm going to call the girls and see how they're doing." Melanie reached for her phone. "But I don't want them to know about the accident."

"I think that's smart. I'll give you some alone time." Anne slipped out of her room and fell back against the wall. She was relieved that Melanie only had some bruises and would completely heal. Even more so, she was glad Melanie would finally do herself a favor and escape the situation with Josh. She was on the road to a better life, and Anne would be by her side the whole way.

CHAPTER TWENTY-NINE

WORSE THAN SHE KNEW

Taylor

Taylor entered the house after a night at her friend Hannah's birthday celebration. She had considered not going, but staying at home and dwelling on her life wouldn't change the fact that she was out of a job. She didn't regret the decision because working at a place she didn't feel respected wasn't worth it.

"You're home early." Aunt Kristi looked up from the living room when Taylor entered the room.

"I only had one drink. I'm glad I went, but I kept thinking about work, or the lack thereof. I wasn't the best of company." She shrugged, then tilted her head. "You're all dolled up."

"Dolled up? This old thing." Aunt Kristi shrugged, but she looked great. She wore a tight-fitting black velvet dress, a flared skirt, and a sweetheart neckline. A bold red lip replaced her usual soft pink lip gloss. She wore her hair in an elegant twist.

Taylor squinted, "Hold up. Is that highlighter? Since when do you spring for a blush that isn't Mary Kay?"

"Since I felt like I needed a bit of a change. It's nothing. I'm just going out with a friend."

"You're wearing heels!"

"Well, my flats didn't go with this dress."

Taylor arched an eyebrow. "Aunt Kristi, be real with me. Is it a guy friend?"

Aunt Kristi rolled her eyes. "Well, you'll find out soon enough. It's Joe."

"Joe?" Taylor laughed. "I thought you had a date with him on Saturday. You're a night early."

"He has to work tomorrow at the shop. He called. I was going to blow him off, but I guess I realized I work so hard. Getting drinks with someone or dinner isn't the worst idea. I doubt it will be a late night. I have to work in the morning, and it's Joe." She shivered, but Taylor could only smile. She sure had a smile on her face for someone who appeared like she was dreading it. If things worked out, she could say she had a hand making it work.

"Well, I hope you both have fun," Taylor said, sinking into the couch.

Aunt Kristi frowned. "I feel bad leaving you here alone tonight. Gavin is out with friends, and after your week, I feel like you could use someone to hang with. I could call and cancel with him."

"Don't you dare!" Taylor shook her head. "I'll be fine." She'd be fine if she could get Anne out of her mind or

CAPMED. Neither seemed likely, but she wouldn't want Aunt Kristi to stick around when Taylor felt this heaviness in her heart. She wouldn't feel right pulling Aunt Kristi down into her depression pit. "I'll be fine alone. It will give me time to think. At the party, it reminded me how tight the money would be. They were splurging at this party, which I think is great, but I need a job. The sooner, the better."

"We'll manage to get by. You honestly had to do what was right for you."

That's why Taylor appreciated her aunt and brother so much. They were there to be her support system. It wouldn't be easy, but they wouldn't abandon her, unlike some people. A chill fell over her just thinking about her fight with Anne. Or rather, the moment she rushed out on her. She didn't want to hear Anne making excuses for what CAPMED did. There was no excuse for their behavior.

A knock sounded on the door, and Kristi groaned. "That's him."

"Aunt Kristi, go out and have a good time. I understand you're wary of getting together, but Joe may surprise you. Just remember that he does have a good heart, and you don't get out nearly enough."

Aunt Kristi made a face. "But it's Joe."

Taylor laughed. "People have a way of surprising you. Don't sell him short. You never know."

"If you say so." She turned and headed toward the door, but she looked like someone being escorted to a funeral, not a first date. Taylor attempted to listen in on the conversation, but all she heard was some mumbles, and then Aunt Kristi appeared around the corner. Her eyes were wide, a bouquet in her hands. "Will you put these in water?"

"They're gorgeous," Taylor replied, rushing over to them. She peeked her head around the corner. "Hello, Joe."

"Taylor." He nodded, and her aunt made another face when she pulled back.

Taylor laughed. "You kids, have a great night." She patted her aunt on the shoulder, then added the flowers in the kitchen to a vase. She stared at them as they soaked in the water. She thought she had met someone that she would have showered with roses. Now she was home alone and didn't even know where Anne was.

Taylor returned to the living room and pulled her laptop closer. She could get through the night and find some jobs to apply to by the time her aunt or Gavin got home. However, it wasn't the job listings she found. Instead, Taylor ended up at Anne's online shop. She stared at the various creations, complete with a new listing. It was a replica of Whiskers. Taylor pulled it into her cart and stared at it for a moment. Anne would know that Taylor was still thinking about her if she purchased it, and she couldn't fathom answering. Taylor closed out of the shop, stopping herself just in time. Besides, she didn't have the money to spend on frivolous things. She could barely put food on the table.

Taylor then started to pull up Indeed for job listings when her eyes went to a previous site she had visited many times before. She nibbled on her lower lip and then went with it. Taylor searched Reddit: Nurses with toxic experiences at **CAPMED**. She held her breath. There was little chance it would find anything, but it popped up. Taylor stared at the list, then pulled the laptop to her lap and started to read through them. One after another, there were cases where nurses had issues while working at CAPMED.

I was so stressed that it took a toll on my body and health. The best thing I could have done was switch departments. I never looked back – Maddie.

All they care about is money; frankly, it's not a place where anyone should work. – anonymous

Taylor looked up after reading over thirty experiences that were much like hers. She wasn't crazy, but how could this information help her? Talking to someone who experienced the same could be helpful.

Someone should form a support group for those facing the same issues. I was a new resident, only a month in, and they treated me like garbage. My superior called me weak for complaining about my schedule when they scheduled me for back-to-back twelve-hour days. Quitting was the only thing that could help my sanity. I'm looking for another job, but I know I will get through this. – Taylor

Taylor stared at her message. Maybe she shouldn't sign her name, but the longer she considered it, the better she felt about that one decision. Taylor checked the box, stating they could email her if anyone wanted to chat and that the website helped her move to where she needed to be. She pulled up the job listings, a smile back on her lips.

CHAPTER THIRTY

FEELING THE PAIN

Anne

Anne woke up already exhausted. It'd been a rough couple of days. She stayed in the hospital with Melanie until she was released the next night, and they both went to pick up the girls. Melanie didn't tell Josh's parents about the mistress or their separation. The girls didn't even question when Anne returned them to her place. Melanie and Anne spent all night talking about Josh and how it wouldn't be easy on her or the kids. However, Anne knew that they would somehow make it work.

Anne told Melanie she and the girls could stay at her place for as long as Melanie needed. It beat the alternative, Melanie thinking they should go back and work through the problems because there was no going back.

But now Anne had to be to work early, and she was still tired from the previous days. She sat at the table, drank her coffee, and pulled up her schedule for the following week. Anne shook her head. She knew that things were going to be rough for everyone. After all, they were down a nurse, but Taylor was right; this was ridiculous, and something had to change, or she would be the next one to falter.

"Anne, are you sure that us being here isn't going to be a burden on you?"

Anne backed out of the schedule and looked to find Melanie in her kitchen. "Are you crazy? I'll be happy to have you guys here." She then got up from her place at the table. The truth was, with her work schedule, she wouldn't be there much, so someone should appreciate the house. "Want some coffee?"

"That'd be great!" Melanie slumped down in the kitchen chair as Anne turned to the coffee. "If things get hectic around here and you change your mind, we will find other arrangements. The truth is, I'm hoping Josh realizes the house was mine, to begin with, and gets out of there. But I can't go back until I know he's gone."

"Trust me. You guys aren't a burden being here, and you will remain here until you are ready to go back; that's an order." Melanie smiled.

"Have I ever told you how I'm glad you're my sister?"

"I trust we've both said that at some point." Anne turned back to the coffee and poured Melanie a cup. She took it to her, then clapped her hands together. "I'm going to be at work much of the day today. You can call me anytime you need me."

"We'll be fine," Melanie replied, sipping her coffee.

"Alright, then. I have to go finish getting ready." Anne patted Melanie's shoulder and then left the kitchen. When she got upstairs, she heard talking coming from the spare room. She peeked in the door and saw Lily and Rose sitting on the bed, speaking in hushed tones. Lily looked up and smiled.

"HI, Aunt Anne."

"Hey, sweeties. What are you both doing up here? There's cereal and French toast sticks. I'm sure your mommy will be happy to make you something."

"Just talking," Lily replied softly. "Is Mommy and Daddy getting a divorce?"

"What do you know about divorce?" Anne asked, taking a seat on the edge of the bed.

"My friend's parents are divorced. She moved."

Anne gave a weak smile. They were both too young to have to worry about such matters. "I don't know what will happen, but what I do know is your mommy could use a hug. Do you want to go give her the biggest hugs you can?"

Lily and Rose nodded, jumped from the bed, and rushed out. She heard their feet on the steps and got up from the bed. She wished she could protect them from the world's sadness, but they would have to find out about it eventually.

Anne went into her room and looked around for her hair tie. She opened her dresser drawer and reached to the back, and her hand landed on some paper. Anne pulled them out and stared at Taylor and Anne's letters to Willow. In the hurriedness of the week, she had forgotten all about them, stuffed them in the back, and went about her day. But they needed to be mailed, and since Taylor wasn't there, Anne would take care of them. She stuffed them in her pocket and grabbed the hair tie by her bed. Anne pulled her hair into a ponytail and then left the room. She would be late if she didn't get out of there.

When Anne got down to the kitchen, Melanie had both girls seated, and she was speaking to them. She looked up and smiled at Anne. Anne grabbed her purse and keys and left the house without a word.

As she drew closer, she saw that it was cutting it close and that she'd make it on time, but for the first time, she didn't even care. She had something else she needed to do before clocking in for her shift. She didn't hesitate to go to Henry's office when she got to the hospital. What struck her, mostly, was the look he gave her when she busted through his door.

"I'm assuming this is about Taylor."

Anne frowned. "What? No. Not really? Why would I be here because of her?" If that wasn't an awkward statement, Anne didn't know what was. But there was no way Henry knew about their connection and that date. Hell, Anne wasn't even sure if she could call it that.

"Well, those in the same department usually become close. Just figured that you would have something to say." He shrugged. "So, how can I help you?"

"Well, this isn't about Taylor, but it could be." Anne pulled up her schedule in front of him. "Look at this, Henry. You can't tell me that this is normal scheduling."

He glanced, but only briefly, then shrugged. "Anne, I'm sure you know that hiring new staff is expensive. We don't have the budget for it. And since Taylor quit so suddenly, that strains everyone else. It's the way it works. You can thank Taylor for that."

Anne sighed, pulling her phone back and tossing it in her purse. "Taylor quit, that's the truth, but these issues have been going on for a while. Don't deny it."

"Not you, too." He tossed his pen down and finally looked up. "We are doing the best we can, spreading out our little staff. People quit, and that puts more work on the ones left behind."

"Have you thought maybe there's a reason people quit?" Anne asked in a huff.

He rolled his eyes. "I have meetings all day, and I can't discuss this with you, but I'll see what can be done." He stood up, and Anne stared at him. He was different than she once remembered. He ignored her concerns, and now she had to figure out the next steps.

CHAPTER THIRTY-ONE

NEAR HER BREAKING POINT

Anne

A*nne? What's the meaning of this? Lewis is allergic to Penicillin. You need to get your head in the game.*

Anne felt tears stinging the back of her eyes as she drove to Melanie's place. It'd been two weeks since Melanie's car wreck, and the girls and Melanie moved back to their house. Josh was moving in with the mistress, and Anne was relieved he'd be out of their lives once and for all. Josh signed both the divorce papers and his custodial rights.

Currently, exhaustion was Anne's biggest problem. She was making stupid mistakes, and Cecilia repeatedly called her out on them. How did she get to this point? Anne sniffled, a tear rolling down her cheek. She often thought about messaging or calling Taylor, but she would only look foolish. Taylor was right; the hospital didn't care enough to monitor their employees' stress levels and hours. She couldn't believe she had to face the same issues before realizing the truth.

Anne turned into Melanie's driveway and sat there momentarily, not even having the strength to get out of the car. She stared at the garage and waited until she saw Melanie open the front door and step out onto the porch.

Anne gave a smile and waved, then stepped out of the car. Melanie tilted her head as Anne approached her. "Everything okay? You've been sitting out here for, like, fifteen minutes."

Anne laughed. "It wasn't that long." Melanie arched her eyebrow. Anne looked away from her. Maybe it was that long, and she had dozed off or something. "I'm well. Where are my nieces?"

"They went to Josh's brother's house."

"Is that a good idea?" Anne asked. "Josh doesn't want custody, so I don't see why his family should be a part of their care. Any judge might question things if you shirk your responsibility onto them."

Melanie groaned. "His family isn't like him. The girls love their uncle and grandparents. I can't see leaving them out of their picture. Besides, his family has been great and supportive. His mom even said that I should have divorced him long ago." She laughed. "For his family to say that we're talking a major revelation. And I thought it'd be best. They don't need to be here asking questions." Anne wasn't convinced but was too tired to argue her point. Josh's family were good people. Melanie was right; the girls deserved to spend time with their uncle, even if she and Josh were no longer together. Melanie led the way into the house, where boxes lined the foyer and living room. "Josh said he would pick up his crap. He hasn't.

So, we'll load them up in the garage and wash our hands of them."

"Sounds good." Anne yawned and quickly covered her mouth.

Melanie sighed. "Are you sure you're okay? You look beat."

Anne smirked. "Well, you're not wrong. Work has been hectic. Ever since Taylor quit, things have been rough. But I'm hanging in there."

"Well, speaking of Taylor…have you spoken to her? You two could have something extraordinary, but it all disappeared."

"Yeah, well. We don't always get what we want. I'm not sure I'm ready to talk about her, but who knows what the future may bring." She moved to the first box. "But these boxes aren't going to move themselves. Let's go."

Melanie dropped it, and Anne was relieved. They started working on the boxes that Melanie had already packed. As they worked, they barely talked, which was alright with Anne as she focused on the task. Three hours in, Melanie crashed down to the couch. "Wanna stop for sandwiches? We're making good headway."

"Sounds good." Anne followed her to the kitchen, and Melanie pulled a pre-made tray from the refrigerator.

"What do you want to drink? Water? Milk? Juice box?" She laughed. "Or I've got something stronger." She wiggled her eyebrows.

Anne smiled. "I could go for some coffee." She turned her head and tried to mask a yawn.

"Coffee it is." Melanie grabbed a couple of pods to put in the Keurig and then turned to Anne. Anne saw that her eyebrows furrowed and her nose scrunched up in thought. She looked away, hopeful Melanie wouldn't bring up another heavy conversation. Being around her sister was good, but she wanted to keep the conversation light and fun. Getting rid of drama was always a plus. "I can see that you're more than just exhausted from extra hours, Anne." Anne lifted her gaze, concern etched on Melanie's face. "You look stressed, and being overworked is only a portion of that. Remember, I'm your sister. I know you well."

Anne rolled her eyes and dropped her gaze. Their relationship, especially the past six years, has been filled with her concern for her sister. Now that the tables were turned, she wasn't confident she liked that. She was the big sister and should be the one to have Melanie's back, not the other way around.

"I'm good. You shouldn't have to worry about me."

"Anne, I'm your sister. That's kind of my job. Besides, I owe you one for letting us stay with you when this all happened." Melanie winked, then turned around to grab Anne's cup of coffee. "Sugar?"

"Nah, I'm good." Anne took a sip, and then Melanie went back to her own. Anne nibbled on her sandwich and drank her coffee, taking in the extra energy boost she hoped the caffeine would provide. When Melanie sat down with her cup, Anne noticed that Melanie wouldn't give up on her quest to find more information. "It's just frustrating, you know? I put my heart on the line every day going into that hospital. I'm starting to feel like they don't care."

"Wow! That has to have taken a lot out of you to admit because I have seen the dedication you've given CAPMED."

Anne nodded. "That's why it's frustrating. The schedule is only half the battle. I've been working double shifts. It's exhausting, but I could handle it knowing that the hospital cared about its employees. All the nurses seem stressed and overworked. We're making mistakes." Anne sighed, sipping on her coffee. "I pride myself in not making mistakes, but they've almost become inevitable. You're bound to make mistakes when you live on caffeine and just a few hours of sleep. The management is mistreating its employees, and someone should take a stand."

"Oh, Hun," Melanie touched Anne's arm. "You deserve so much better than that."

Anne laughed, staring at her sister as Melanie flipped the script.

CHAPTER THIRTY-TWO

JOB INTERVIEW

Taylor

Maynard Pediatric's office was filled with seven kids aged two to ten. Unlike the dreary lobby of CAPMED, Maynard's lobby was decorated with bright green botanical wallpaper. Instead of fluorescent lights, large flower-shaped lamps lit the interior. The carpet felt soft under Taylor's feet. The mood of Maynard seemed significantly less frantic. The receptionist greeted her with a smile and told her to sit before taking a sip from a ceramic mug of tea. It was a far cry from the clipboards that constantly littered CAPMED's reception desk. Taylor watched as they played throughout the lobby, their parents watching them afar. A variety of toys covered the floor of the lobby. There was a train table in the corner and a pile of puzzles next to one of the chairs. They all seemed happy, albeit sick. Some were coughing to the point where they wore a mask. Others were most likely there just for their annual physicals.

"Taylor?"

Taylor jerked when she heard her name called. She'd been on four interviews thus far. But from the looks of the waiting room, Maynard Pediatrics could be a place Taylor could call home. Yet, she despised interviews, and as a resident nurse, she found that most offices were looking for someone more seasoned than she was. It was disheartening, but she could only hope she had finally found her home away from home.

"Hello, Taylor. My name is Jessie." Jessie held out her hand, and Taylor shook it with confidence.

"It's a pleasure to meet you." Taylor's voice didn't shake with nerves.

"Likewise. Take a seat. This interview will be short and painless."

Taylor hoped that Jessie was right. Some interviews lasted two hours, and she had to take a test before speaking with anyone. Others lasted fifteen minutes, and Taylor left, immediately feeling she had zero chance of getting a callback. So far, how she anticipated the interviews going, she was proven correct. She had gotten a call back from only one of them, but it was a polite no thank you.

"First, I want to give you a brief rundown of our office. We want to ensure that you'll not only be a fit for us, but we'll be a fit for you." So far, so good. Taylor liked the sound of that because every other place seemed all about what they had to offer and why she would want to be a part of their organization. She was left feeling like it was a big corporation, and she wanted a more cozy feel.

Jessie proceeded to go over the basics, from the number of providers to the specialties they serviced. She dove into the statistics and financial summaries, not holding back on anything.

"We have ten nurses currently and are looking to hire two more from our pool of applicants. The practice is growing, and the staff needs to grow with it." Taylor beamed. That was another great thing to hear. "Do you have any questions, currently?" Taylor quickly shook her head, feeling at ease at the start of the interview. "Why don't you start by telling me why you chose us."

"Well, I love kids. When I graduated college, I knew I wanted to work in Pediatrics. The resilience of children is amazing. They hold nothing back; they're relentlessly optimistic. They tell it like it is." Jessie continued to smile. "When I saw this job opening, I immediately applied, and when I got the call for an interview, I was overjoyed. I want to feel like I'm helping those who need it the most."

"That's great to hear." Jessie looked down at Taylor's resume. "I see that you worked in Pediatrics at CAPMED. If I'm being honest, many people tend to leave these doctor's offices to go to a big hospital. I find it peculiar that you're choosing to do the opposite. May I ask why, and can we call your previous employer for a reference?"

Taylor felt like she had been kicked in the gut. It was the one thing she was sure had lost her job from the other perspective employers. She still honored herself by being honest, no matter the cost; this would be no different.

"Jessie, the truth is, CAPMED was a good place to work. However, I quickly found that I was overscheduled with hours, working eight, sometimes ten, days in a row. I voiced my concern. Then, suddenly, he was looked down upon as a troublemaker and even weak. I pride myself on being strong, but the stress and hours just got too much. I know what my body could handle, and it wasn't that. I don't like making problems, but I speak my mind. If that's a downfall of mine, then maybe one day I'll work on it, but I thought CAPMED took advantage of their employees, and I had to speak my truth."

Jessie listened quietly and nodded. When she spoke, she smiled slightly. "I started as an intern at CAPMED twenty years ago." Taylor's face fell, and she looked down. Another interview went down the drain, and it was a job she honestly thought she'd fit well in. "Back then, I thought I wanted to continue my career there. However, the daughter of the CEO came in and swooped in, taking the job out from under me. Even back then, I would say that they had some less-than-ethical business practices. I appreciate your honesty, Taylor. And I'm sorry that you were treated that way."

Taylor heaved a sigh, not able to hide the smile on her face. "Thank you!"

"I think I've gathered the information I need here. I'll confess we still have a couple of candidates left to interview." Taylor's face fell. "But don't let that discourage you. You'll be hearing either way by the end of the week." Jessie stood up. "Thank you for coming in!"

"Thank you for having me." Taylor shook her hand, but it wasn't as strong as when she first met her. It felt like the odds were stacked against her, but she had to have faith that she would be a good contender.

She left the doctor's office, wishing she had a clearer idea of whether they would hire her, but plenty of other jobs were out there. She would have to strike out and continue the search, even if it were a bitter pill to swallow.

Taylor pulled into the driveway. Exiting the car, she saw their neighbor, Mrs. Milligan, standing at her flowers, watering the rose bushes. "Hello, Mrs. Milligan," she called. The older woman scowled and kept on watering. No matter how often Taylor attempted to get friendly with the neighbors, they always gave her a cold shoulder. She checked the mailbox and found no one had picked up the mail, then hurried to the porch to the front door. When she got inside, she heard Aunt Kristi and Joe talking in the living room. In the past couple of weeks, they hadn't spent a lot of time away from one another. Taylor found it sweet, even though her aunt hated it when Taylor pointed it out. Joe was much sweeter than Taylor thought he would be and wasn't bad-looking either. He was 5'9, with some silver around the temples and a Mediterranean complexion. He was muscular from his years as a mechanic, with beefy shoulders and defined biceps that Taylor could see beneath his denim work shirts. He was also a bit romantic; he'd been leaving flowers on their porch daily for the past week.

"Hey, you two!" Taylor looked in the living room.

"Hey, Hun. How'd the interview go?" Aunt Kristi asked. She crossed her fingers. "It went well. But several other applicants are interviewing, and I don't want to get my hopes up." She looked down at the mail and skimmed through them. Her hand stopped on an envelope; Willow's name was scrawled in a seven-year-old's handwriting. She had thought about the letter she left behind at the hospital and considered writing to Willow again, but she was too depressed even to pick up a pen. "Here's the mail." She tossed the other envelopes onto the coffee table. "You kids have fun." She winked and hurried to her bedroom.

She ripped into the envelope and sat down on her bed.

> Taylor -
>
> Thank you so much for writing to me. It meant a lot. I'm doing great. My doctor said that I could be getting out of here soon. The medicine I'm on is improving my numbers, whatever that means. Mommy said it meant that I might no longer have cancer. I hope so. I miss you so much. You and Anne are my favorites in the whole wide world. The Jell-O here isn't nearly as good as I got with you. Oh, and you're right, Taylor. I'm going to get all better. I know that I am. I can't wait to see you. I have to do tests, but Mommy will mail this to me.
>
> Love,
> Willow

Tears stung Taylor's eyes as she read the letter over again. She didn't understand. She hadn't mailed the letter, so how did Willow get it? There was a knock on her door, and she wiped her tears away.

"Come in!"

Gavin opened the door with a big grin. "Well, sis. How'd it go?" He plopped down onto her chair and wheeled himself over.

"Are you crying? Why are you crying? Was it that bad? There will be more interviews; I know it."

Taylor shook her head. "I'm not crying because of that." She looked up, brushing a tear from her cheek. She held up the letter. "I got a letter from an old patient, and I guess it just brought back a lot of memories ."

He snatched the letter from her and read it. "Awwww, that's nice."

She nodded, then grabbed the letter and reread it. "The interview went well. Unfortunately, there are a million applicants, so the chances of getting it are slim, but I can't have everything."

He reached out and touched her arm. "I'm sorry, Sis. But you never know, right?"

Taylor shrugged. Her phone rang, and she grabbed it and stared at the number. "H…hello?"

"Hello, Taylor? It's Jessie from Maynard Pediatrics. I know I said you would hear from me by the end of the week, but I don't need to wait that long." Taylor's face fell. She could sense the rejection from a mile away.

"Well, I appreciate you calling me so soon." Taylor sighed, tossing a look at Gavin. He frowned, and Taylor turned back to the conversation. "If you know, you just know, and there are other jobs out there, so now I can focus my attention on those."

"Taylor, I don't think you understand. I'm calling you to offer you the job. If you accept it, you can come in tomorrow and fill out the paperwork with HR, and they'll go over benefits and pay."

"What?" She squealed.

Jessie laughed. "You stood out, Taylor. I think you want to be a part of the team almost as much as we want you to be a part of the team. If you come in tomorrow, you can have a tour and meet the staff. I know everyone would love to meet you."

"Yes, I'll absolutely be there. Thank you so much, Jessie, for giving me this opportunity."

"It's my pleasure. See you tomorrow."

"See you." Taylor disconnected the call, tears back in her eyes as she turned to Gavin. "I got the job. I got the job." She jumped up, the letter falling to the floor, and embraced her brother. Everything was going to be alright. She could feel it in her bones.

CHAPTER THIRTY-THREE

FINDING HER VOICE

Anne

Anne paced back and forth in the hallway. She had been off work for an hour and was still working up the courage to talk to Henry again after giving it much thought, talking with her sister at the beginning of the week. Anne gave the schedules a chance to change, and when they didn't, Anne knew she had to talk to Henry. Unfortunately, she hadn't worked up the courage to schedule a meeting. So, that left her outside, pacing. His current meeting would be done any minute.

Fifteen minutes later, the door opened, and she stopped walking to turn to see Henry and a young woman exiting his office. He shot Anne a look, and his eyes darkened before turning to the woman.

"It was a pleasure meeting you, Carrie. I'll be in touch." He shook her hand, and the woman left. He then turned and stared at Anne. "To what do I owe this honor?"

"We need to chat." She didn't give him a chance to turn away. Anne stormed into his office and waited for him to shut the door. She had taken her concerns to two other members of HR and was all told the same. Money is tight, but we're working to hire more. She called BS. At what costs would they finally hire some nurses? She was about to crumble and liked to believe she was one of the strong ones. When he closed the door, she looked up at him. "Please tell me that is one of the many nurses you're interviewing to work with us."

He snickered, slumping down into the seat across from her. "Carrie is nineteen. She doesn't have any nursing experience. She'll be doing her externship next year for medical records."

"At this rate, we could train nurses, which would be better than what we're experiencing now. Please give us an extern that you don't have to pay. I don't care, but I'm on the edge, Henry. You promised that you would look at doing some hiring, and I'm getting more hours now than I was when I first complained."

Henry sighed. "I am hearing your concern. We all are. Don't you think we talk? I know you have pleaded your case to everyone else, and frankly, you're wasting your breath, so why even try?" Anne opened her mouth, then shut it and took a deep breath. "Anne, you are a good nurse. I saw that from the very first time you entered this hospital. We would be lost without you. But, if you can't take the stress, your duties may be placed elsewhere. Other hospitals are hiring that might be more up your alley. Any one of us would be happy to give you a reference."

Anne huffed and stood up. She started pacing again as those

words echoed in her mind. She hesitated and turned to him. "Henry, what happened to you?"

"Pardon me?"

Anne moved in closer to his desk. "You used to care. I don't know why I'm so surprised. You sat in the boardroom and allowed me to be humiliated that day and never once jumped to my defense. Yet, at the first mention that you threatened someone, I jumped to yours. Am I really that foolish?"

"Anne," he began.

"No, I'm seeing things clearer here. You have changed. Perhaps the power has gone to your head. It's sad. You were someone who could be the voice of those who needed you. I'm sorry you let some power go to your head. I don't want to give up on these children who still need a voice. I work my ass off, and now I'm just questioning if maybe that's another thing I'm being foolish about."

Anne turned and reached for his doorknob. "I haven't changed, Anne. I've always been this way. To get to the top, you have to be. You don't understand what it takes to run a hospital."

Anne looked over her shoulder. "With any luck, I never will because I couldn't do this. I couldn't watch the staff suffer for monetary gain. But you do you." She spun on her heel and left the office. She felt good about talking to him, even if it didn't get her anywhere.

Anne went home, the funk remaining with her, the conversation with Henry playing through her mind. She was hungry, but her stomach clenched whenever she tried to eat. Maybe the hospital had always been this way, and Anne refused to see it. She always thought CAPMED treated her well. She never wanted to abandon it. That was the point of going to school, right? Go to school, find a job that's not soul-sucking, and live your life. She covered her face, tears streaming down her cheeks as the realization hit her. Had her past screwed her up this badly?

Anne had put her loyalty in the wrong place. She should have trusted Taylor enough to know that she wouldn't make up false accusations. She had something wonderful going on with the younger woman, and she blew it to protect a place that didn't even care about her. Yet, the hospital management wouldn't protect them. That hurt more than anything. Taylor deserved Anne's support. Anne got up, dumped the soup down the sink, and shook her head. She wouldn't allow the management to have one more ounce of control over her. If they wanted to run the hospital on an overworked skeleton crew, they would have to do it without her because this was the last straw.

CHAPTER THIRTY-FOUR

DECISION MADE

Anne

Anne aimlessly walked down her stairs. She hadn't slept a wink the entire night, tossing, turning, praying, and looking for a sign. What should she do? She had always strived to be a supportive employee. She hated making waves and when she was getting into trouble. She was the first person to cower away from confrontation. Yet, in her heart, she felt the need to do something. She needed to take a stand and support her fellow nurses. Anne opened the refrigerator and stared at a fully stocked fridge. Yet, her stomach churned at just the thought of taking one bite. If only something could point her in the right direction, showing her the path. If only her mother were there. She felt a tear trickle down her cheek. She couldn't recall the last time she thought of how much she missed her mom. It never seemed to hit her. Sure, all women wanted the comfort of their mother's arms, but it'd been years since Anne felt she needed her mother's advice. She flicked the tear away and fell back against the counter. Decisions were tough, though, and how could she possibly know how to handle this based on intuition alone? A knock sounded on her back door, and Anne looked down at her messy robe. She groaned and headed to the door, peering through the curtains. "Tyler? What are you doing here?" She pulled her robe tighter around her.

"I'm sorry to bother you. You're always up so early and headed off to work, I just figured…" His words fell over her as he arched an eyebrow.

"I don't work until later. It's no bother. Wanna come in, have some coffee?" She stepped back to allow him to enter, but he stood there.

"Thanks for the invitation, Anne, but I can't stay. I got this in my mailbox a few days ago. Sorry I'm just now bringing it to you, but it's been a busy few days. Hopefully, it's nothing too important."

Anne grabbed the envelope and stared at it. Willow's name was neatly written in the corner. Her eyes widened. She had wondered if she had gotten the letters from her. Here was that answer. "Not a problem. I'm sure it's fine. Are you sure you can't stay for a coffee?"

He shook his head. "Thanks anyway. Take care." He waved and then hurried away. Anne sighed as she shut the door and stared at the envelope again. She ripped into it, anxious to read what Willow had to say.

Anne -

Thank you for the letter you wrote me. It made me smile. I'm not as sick anymore. The medicine has been working. I feel a lot better. Mommy and Daddy don't seem so sad now. Daddy visits when he can. I haven't seen my brothers and sisters at all since the move. Mommy will let me talk to them on the phone, and we'll FaceTime. I'm really good at it. Maybe they'll buy me a phone when I'm out of here.

Anne stopped reading the letter and sank into the chair, smiling as Willow's words seemed exuberant and hopeful. She talked about getting out of there, which was a great sign.

You always made me feel special. I don't have nurses here like that. They're nice but not as nice as you and Taylor. I miss you both so much. But the good news is that the doctors say I can leave here soon. And I would like to visit you when I do. Is that okay? I have to go. Mommy wants me to eat. The food isn't very good, but she says it will continue to make me stronger. I will talk to you later, Anne.

Love,
Willow

Tears stung the back of Anne's eyes as she tossed down the

letter and stared ahead. Willow was on the path to getting better. She could jump for joy over that. She got up from the table and went to the refrigerator. The girl was also smart enough to heed her mother's advice. Food was fuel. She pulled out milk, a bowl, and cereal and poured herself a bowl.

Anne sat back down at the table and ate as she spotted Whiskers. She jumped onto the windowsill and peered outside, staring at the birds. She was observant, tilting her head to the side like a person. It cracked her up as Whiskers chittered at the birds, banging her paw against the glass. She grabbed the letter and reread it, her tears replaced by smiles.

ANNE:
I know what I have to do.

MELANIE:
I look forward to hearing all about it, and I support you in every way. Love you, Anne.

ANNE:
Love you!

She closed her eyes as she laid down the phone and took another bite of her cereal. Sometimes, she saw the decisions of her life branching out in front of her like tree limbs. From owning her home to having a loving family with her sister and nieces. Has her life been perfect? Not by any means, but what life was? But she was still growing. She wasn't stuck. She always had choices.

Her life was hectic right now, but she would be okay. She had the strength to weather the storms, just like Willow did as a seven-year-old.

AT WHAT COST?

Taylor came floating into her life when she least expected, and while their first days were bumpy, she quickly became someone that Anne could see weathering the storms with. Whether they could continue to grow together was yet to be seen. She needed to experience that to understand what she wanted in life fully. Anne knew now that she wanted a woman by her side. She blinked back tears and tried to shake those images away. To think that things would be over between them was heart-breaking, but just another hurdle.

Anne stood up and walked to the sink, dropping the dish down. Even if Taylor was gone forever, she had to take a stand. All nurses deserved that.

With a new bounce in her step, Anne hurried to the office and didn't stop until she was seated in front of her computer. She quickly typed out an email and read it three times before deciding that she spoke from the heart and only spoke the truth. She then went to the website for the timekeeper and pulled up her schedule, saving a copy and attaching it to the email. Anne stared at the email address to verify inaccuracies. The Board of Ethics needed the truth, and she'd be damned if she didn't provide them just that. She sent the email and ensured the copy was saved on her drive.

There wasn't any turning back now, and Anne was alright with that because if she had a second to change her mind, she would have chickened out.

Anne quickly got dressed and was anxious to get to the hospital. She had to take only one more stand, and this was by far the easiest of her decisions. When she reached Henry's office, his door was ajar. She heard talking as she crept forward, but nothing could stop her.

Henry looked up and met her gaze. She didn't blink or waver; she just stared at him. "I'll call you back." He laid down the phone and leaned back in his chair. "This is a nice surprise."

"Is it?" Anne crossed her arms.

He snickered. "If I'm being honest, I'm a bit surprised after our last encounter."

"Yep, and that's why I'm here." Anne laid down her resignation letter and pushed it towards him. "It should all be in order."

He grabbed the letter and looked it over, then shook his head. "You're making a mistake, Anne. Sure, things get tough, but they always improve. Give it a few more days or weeks. Ultimately, you'll see."

"You're not getting it. I quit. I have made up my mind. This morning, I emailed the Board of Ethics explaining what shoddy management CAPMED has and how they should thoroughly review it. I imagine by next week, you'll all receive that call."

"You did what?" He slammed his fists down on the desk and stood up. "Anne, do you know the ramifications an email like that could have? You need to withdraw your complaint; say you were moody!"

"Or what, Henry? Are you threatening me as you did, Taylor?"

"Not this again," he groaned and sat in his seat.

"What? I shouldn't speak the truth?" Her voice got louder.

He looked up and met her gaze, his eyes darkening. "If you don't withdraw your complaint, I will ensure you're blacklisted in the city. No one would dare hire you." Anne stared back. "You think I'm kidding? Try me."

Anne shook her head. "You aren't the man I thought you were, Henry. But it doesn't matter. It's over and done, and I have made peace with it. Do what you think is best. It doesn't make me much difference because I'm quitting." She spun on her heel and stormed through his door, slamming the door behind him. Anne felt him staring at her but didn't make eye contact. She felt liberated as the tears started to fall once she got outside. Her past was behind her, and it was time to look toward the future.

CHAPTER THIRTY-FIVE

HEART'S CRY

Anne

Anne stared at the computer the same she had been doing the past week since leaving her job. "You did the right thing, Anne. You have to trust in that." There was little doubt that Anne could have continued the way she had, but it was still a scary place.

She scrolled the listings of another day until the list had reached its bottom. With all the places to work, she couldn't believe how difficult it had been to find a job she was interested in, or at least a bit intrigued. She turned from her computer and groaned. Another day, another dollar lost.

The fact that her house was paid off was the only reason she wasn't actively panicking. She had enough money saved up for her bills, such as her credit card and utilities, but eventually, that money would all run out, and that's when the panic started.

A text sounded on her phone, and she looked down to find a picture of Hailey holding her baby. Anne stared at it until tears sprung to her eyes. She was on the small side, as she was still born prematurely, but from the smile on Hailey's face, she was doing well—both of them.

> ANNE:
>
> OMG. Congrats to the parents. I want all the details.

She waited, staring at her phone for the text to pop through, when instead, her phone started ringing, and Hailey's name popped onto the screen. Hailey and Anne hadn't talked much since she was put on bed rest. A few times, she got the news of her health from Cecilia, but that was the extent.

"Hello?"

"Hey, Anne. Is this a bad time?" Hailey spoke so quietly, most likely not to interrupt a sleeping baby.

"No, it's a good time. How are you all doing? What's the baby's name? I'm sure you're both over the moon."

Hailey laughed on the other side of the line. "His name is Owen Michael. He was born yesterday. He's strong. Really strong. Just like his Daddy. He's definitely over the moon. We both are." She seemed happy, and that was important to Anne. "But I didn't call really to chat about Owen's birth. The truth is, I was calling to talk to you. I've been in contact with Cecilia. She's given me the details of the hospital. The good, bad, and ugly."

"Yeah, I'm sure she has," Anne mumbled. Anne had steered clear of two calls from Cecilia. She could imagine the disappointment from her mentor. But she wasn't the one who let anyone down. It was the hospital, which Anne had to tell herself. "Things haven't been great, Hailey. You've missed a ton."

"Yeah, it sounds like it." Then Hailey's voice turned small. "With everything that's going down, I don't think I will come back. I've done a lot of soul-searching and realized I want to be a stay-at-home mom. I didn't plan on saying that." She laughed. "Owen is the light of my life; if I can watch him grow up, I will do that."

"That's great, Hailey. You deserve it."

The phone went quiet, and Anne checked to see that she hadn't accidentally hung up on her. She opened her mouth when Hailey sighed. "So, how's Taylor? I know I didn't get to know her all that well, but I know that she didn't last long with scheduling. But she seemed like she could be the next Anne regarding nursing aspirations." Anne chuckled but didn't proceed in conversation. "I know the few times I did get a chance to talk to her, she seemed to have a draw towards you."

"What?"

"Yeah. I could tell that Taylor was quite intrigued by you. She would stare all awestruck. It reminded me of Mike when we first started dating. I guess there was a thought that maybe you two would develop into more than just a co-worker status."

Anne's brow furrowed. She leaned back in the chair, and her mind went to Taylor. "It's complicated. We had a falling out, so I haven't spoken with her."

"Well, that's too bad. You should act on it when someone looks at you as Taylor does. Trust me." Hailey giggled. Hailey was younger and didn't quite understand the reality of dating. She married her high school sweetheart. She didn't know what finding a spark with a near stranger was like. "If it was only that simple."

"Sometimes it can be. You should strive to be happy, Anne. How's the job search going?"

"It's not." Anne tossed a look to her computer and scowled at it. "But I imagine it will eventually work all out. You shouldn't worry about that. You have a baby to care for."

"You were a great mentor, Anne." The sincerity in her voice brought a tear to Anne's eyes. She quickly flicked it away. "You are going to do great things. That's inevitable."

"Thank you, Hailey." Anne sniffled.

"Well, I should let you go. Just know I'm here for you if you need to talk to anyone. Take care, Anne."

"You, too. Text me cute pictures of your baby, and I would love to see him soon."

"I will. Talk to you soon." Hailey disconnected the call first, and Anne slowly put her phone down. She glanced back at her computer, and Hailey's words came rushing back. She faced a huge regret, but Anne wasn't even sure where to find Taylor.

You have her number. You could give her a call.

She could, but it seemed way too impersonal if Taylor would even take her call. If she were going to get Taylor to forgive her, it would take a grand gesture, and that was not only for Taylor's sake but for hers.

CHAPTER THIRTY-SIX

HEART'S LONGING

Taylor

Another scream echoed through the living room as Aunt Kristi threw up her hands. "And I just bought your Boardwalk with a hotel. Hand it over." She wiggled her hand out over the table.

Marge groaned. "Has your aunt always been competitive? How did I never see this side of her?"

Taylor laughed, nodding. "I believe Aunt Kristi is changing." When Aunt Kristi met her gaze, Taylor gave her a wink.

"Not changing," Aunt Kristi argued. "Just going after what I want."

"Speaking of…" Violet asked. "How are things going with you and Joe?"

Taylor covered her mouth as Aunt Kristi's cheeks went red. Kristi and Taylor knew that would be the subject of conversation when they settled on game night. Typically, they got together monthly, playing games, eating snacks, and chatting about the opposite sex. But this had been the first girl's night since Joe and Aunt Kristi started dating. A loud noise sounded from Gavin's room, and Kristi jumped up. "I should go check on the boys."

"Sit down!" Marge argued. "It's just Gavin and the boys having fun on their video games." She laughed. "You are changing the subject, though. So do share all the juicy details." Four women sat around the table while Taylor hung back. She loved games, but for tonight, she was way too distracted to focus. "Earth to Taylor?" Taylor jerked from her thoughts, saw Missy had moved from the table, and joined her on the couch. "What's going on in that mind of yours?"

Taylor shrugged. "Not much," she lied. She tossed a look over to the table. "Don't you want to hear the juicy deets about Joe?"

Missy laughed. "I talk to your aunt at least twice a day. There's nothing she could say now that would be news to me. I thought I'd come over here instead. How's the new job going? Your aunt is so proud of you."

Taylor's cheeks were on fire, and she dropped her gaze. "The job is good." She shrugged. "You go in, work, get paid, then start over again." She had been actively working for two weeks now. And she couldn't lie that she couldn't recall ever being happier in the work aspect. She loved the patients, the co-workers, and, most importantly, the management. The pay was great, and she could see a lasting career working there.

Missy arched an eyebrow, to which Taylor gave a weak smile. "Are you coming back to the game?" Violet called out.

"Are you doing well?" Missy asked, ignoring Violet's call."

"Yeah, I'm doing okay." Taylor attempted to smile again. She looked away from the group. "I'm dying of thirst. Anyone else?" They each raised their glasses in response, and Taylor nodded. "Excuse me," she mumbled. Taylor hurried from the living room to the kitchen. She wanted to be okay or grateful for her job going well. But Taylor wasn't okay, not in any sense. Ever since Anne and her parted ways, she had this hole in her stomach, or maybe it was a little higher, such as her heart. It was hard to see if she'd ever have it filled again.

She reached into the refrigerator and poured herself another glass of lemonade. She was halfway through the glass when she spotted Aunt Kristi. She smiled.

"Did you change your mind?" She reached for a glass, but Aunt Kristi held up her hand.

"I didn't come for a drink." She walked over and wrapped her arm around Taylor's shoulders. "Are you doing alright?"

Taylor sighed. "Did Missy say something? I'm doing okay. Why can't that be good enough?" Aunt Kristi sighed, and Taylor dropped her gaze. "I'm sorry. I'm trying to feel satisfied with my job. I'm glad someone gave me the chance. I love my life and am happy to be living it. But…" Her words trailed off, and she looked away from Aunt Kristi's wandering eyes. She could feel tears stinging the backs of her eyes, and at any moment, she could have a downpour.

"It's rough losing the people you care so much about. When I lost my sister, I was heartbroken. She was on a downward spiral; no one knows that better than you and Gavin, but it didn't hurt any less."

Taylor frowned. She sometimes forgot that Aunt Kristi had lost her mom while everyone tried to get her better. "I'm sorry."

She smiled and shook her head. "You don't have anything to apologize for. Such is life, but I understand pain, and you were falling for Anne. I don't know Anne, but I certainly saw that in how you acted about her."

Taylor blushed and looked away. "She was the first person I could truly see a relationship with. I was getting to know her better, and so I guess that's why it's hard."

"You don't have to shut off your feelings." Aunt Kristi tilted her head. "And you don't have to lie about how you're doing. Not to Missy, not to me, not to anyone. We've all been there." She motioned with her head towards the living room. "Come in and play a game with us."

Taylor opened her mouth just as a text sounded on her phone. She looked down, staring at Anne's name.

> ANNE:
>
> Can we talk?

"Everything okay?" Aunt Kristi asked. "Your face just turned a sheet of white."

"Um, yeah." She held up the phone and showed her the message.

"Then, I'd say, you better get to talking." Aunt Kristi winked and leaned over, kissing Taylor's head. She left the kitchen, and Taylor returned to the text.

> TAYLOR:
>
> I'd like that. Do you wanna call me?

ANNE:
> Actually, come outside. I think we should do it in person.

Taylor frowned and left the kitchen, and went to the foyer. She opened the door, and Anne stood in front of the house. Taylor closed the door behind her just as thunder sounded. She looked up into the dark sky but then back to Anne.

"I don't understand. How'd you find out where I lived?"

"I have my ways," Anne smirked and moved closer to Taylor. Taylor didn't step in to close the gap. Anne snickered. "Joe. It took some begging, but I got him to give me the address."

"But why?" Taylor breathlessly asked.

Anne groaned and tossed back her head. "I'm not used to being vulnerable, especially around women I find intimidating, but I needed to see you. I needed to tell you how sorry I am for being a complete ass. I should have trusted in you. I should have been there to support you, but I was scared. I was scared to make a move. When I lost you, the world came out from underneath my feet. That's when I opened my eyes and saw what was happening."

"Anne," Taylor started.

Anne looked down at her phone and pulled something up before thrusting it in front of Taylor. Taylor grabbed it and read her message. It was powerful. It laid out everything Taylor had been feeling before leaving CAPMED. She looked up, and Anne had specks of tears in her eyes.

"I sent that to the Board of Ethics. Two days later, word spread and all the nurses at CAPMED revolted and went on strike. The Board came in and terminated the managers.

They're starting from scratch. But it should have been started earlier. I should have listened to you." Anne took a breath. "Will you ever forgive me?"

"I already have," Taylor said, tears stinging her eyes and finally releasing. She stepped forward and reached for Anne's hand. "I already have." She whispered the words before she moved in and kissed Anne. The hunger had never died. The hole in Taylor's heart closed. Her tongue dipped into Anne's mouth as the thunder sounded again. The skies opened and engulfed them in rain. Neither one parted, letting the kiss overpower their emotions, and Taylor's love started growing.

CHAPTER THIRTY-SEVEN

WHAT FOREVER FEELS LIKE

Anne

"Your aunt is delightful," Anne said as Taylor and Anne walked hand-in-hand up to Anne's front door.

"She loved you," Taylor replied, laughing as Anne stopped to unlock the door. Anne looked over her shoulder and grinned. "What?"

"I'm just wondering if Aunt Kristi is the only one that loves me." She winked, and Taylor's cheeks turned red. Taylor reached up and brushed Anne's wet hair from her eyes. They had stepped into the house and got dried, mostly, as they played games with the four other women. It wasn't exactly a night that Anne expected to play out, but she found herself letting it feel like home.

"Let's just say that I could be getting there."

Anne smirked. "Let's just say you wouldn't be the only one."

She opened the door and pulled Taylor in after her. She brushed her lips against Taylor's, and they kissed while standing in the middle of the foyer. "I've missed you," Anne whispered.

"I've missed you," Taylor whispered, followed by a moan as Anne cupped her hand around Taylor's ass. They parted from the embrace, and in the silence, Anne grabbed Taylor's hand and escorted her up the stairs. She had plenty to talk to Taylor about, but she wanted Taylor back in her bed for the moment.

In the solitude of Anne's bedroom, they faced each other. They slowly began to undress, watching one another, surveying each other's bodies as each piece of clothing fell to the floor. Anne just wanted to enjoy the moment and not rush things. She wanted to savor every second. When they were both naked, Anne looked Taylor over, her eyes latching onto Taylor's breasts. She was always beautiful, but in this moment, they were astounding. Taylor's beauty had grown during their absence.

Anne moved in, brushing her hand against Taylor's cheek. Taylor closed her eyes in response, but only for a split second. She opened her eyes, and this sensual glimmer danced in her eyes. Anne moved in, kissing Taylor and letting the kiss linger with their bare chests pressed to one another's. Her tongue slid across Taylor's, and Taylor moaned before Taylor slipped her arm around Anne, drawing her in even closer.

Anne's heart raced in perpetual heat. She pressed Taylor down to the bed until Taylor was seated. Anne straddled Taylor's body with her legs wrapped around her waist. Taylor held her in those solid and unwavering arms. Taylor leaned back, pulling Anne after her, and then pushed her way up Anne's bed, with Anne following like a blanket. The kiss never broke until they reached the pillow. Anne broke from the kiss and sensually massaged her hands down Taylor's chest and to her stomach. She pressed firmly before moving her hands back to massage Taylor's breasts.

Taylor watched, a heat coming from those two sexy eyes, growling as Anne groped her breasts, acting like she needed to learn them all over again. Taylor's jaw dropped, and she shifted her body underneath Anne. Anne could feel her wetness already seeping, and Anne knew it wasn't just because of the ten minutes they were stuck out in the rain. With one hand still massaging Taylor's breast, she took her right hand and lowered it to Taylor's opening, slipping three fingers inside her.

"God, yes," Taylor moaned. Anne pumped her fingers, bringing a moan echoing into her room. She thought it was only Taylor's sighing until she recognized her cries. She had been anxiously picturing this moment for over two weeks, and it was finally there. Anne pressed in her fingers and held them, applying force and waiting for Taylor's cries to crash through her body. Taylor lifted herself up and then crashed down repeatedly until she seized on the bed. Her juices flowed from her, and Anne was ready to appreciate them. Anne shifted herself lower and went back to tasting Taylor. She lapped up every trace of what Taylor had to offer, then pressed her hands against the bed and hovered over Taylor's lips. "Damn," Taylor groaned, then laughed.

Anne slid her hand behind Taylor's head and pulled her closer until they kissed. How long had it been since she wanted to feel this very emotion? Way too long. She slipped her tongue in, grasping onto another groan. Their bodies intertwined as they held each other. It felt right.

AT WHAT COST?

TAYLOR TWEAKED ANNE'S NIPPLES, AND ANNE STRETCHED OUT her legs and just watched Taylor ravish her body. They had an equal share of exploring one another, getting reacquainted, and indulging in their tastes. This time was no exception. Taylor replaced her fingers with her mouth and sucked each nipple as Anne closed her eyes and grinned. Sleep was overrated, and if Taylor continued to get down and dirty with Anne, Anne would never leave her bed. Like she'd ever want to.

Taylor wandered up her body and kissed Anne, with Anne stretching her arms around Taylor, holding her down to her body. Taylor broke from the kiss and fell beside Anne, her body limp, her exhaustion evident.

"Never in a million years," Taylor whispered.

Anne snaked her arm around Taylor and pulled her closer. Taylor's head rested against Anne's shoulder. "I'm sure you're exhausted," Anne whispered. Anne, however, was on her third or fourth orgasm. She didn't want to go to sleep. She just wanted to spend the whole night talking and enjoying each other's curves.

"Exhausted, possibly." Taylor laughed. "Yet, I don't know if I could fall asleep. I'm exhilarated. I want more."

Anne smirked. They had the same beliefs. So, that was a great start to healing their relationship. "Let's talk and see what the next few hours can hold." She looked at her clock. It was only two. They still had plenty of romance and sexual tension between them. "So, tell me about your job."

Taylor giggled next to her. "It's honestly great, Anne. It's one of those things that I didn't want to get my hopes up and have everything let me down. I wanted to believe I would get the job offer, but so much was stacked against me. When I got the call the same day, I could hardly believe it. But it's where I want to be." From the corner of her eye, Anne saw Taylor shrug. "Well, besides here."

Anne laughed and turned her head, brushing a kiss against Taylor's nose.

"Where'd you learn about the job? It's been two weeks, and I don't feel I'm any closer to landing a job with which I can see a future."

"Well, it happened kind of unexpectedly. Did you know that Reddit has a slew of ex-nurses discussing their unfair working conditions at CAPMED? I met one ex-nurse online. She still works at CAPMED but found a position that worked best for her. She's working in Health Informatics. She said it's a world of difference. Then, another had just moved out of the area and told me how she left this position and knew they were hiring. It sounded perfect, so I applied, and the rest is history. Since you've quit, being a part of the group might be beneficial, too."

"I don't know, Taylor. I think I'm ready to wash my hands of anything CAPMED. Getting pulled back in by ex-employees might be my demise."

Taylor snickered. "Don't tell anyone, but I'm an ex-employee."

Anne rolled her eyes. "Present company excluded, of course." She reached out and pulled Taylor closer, her breath up against Taylor's lips. "You're the only one from CAPMED I still need to associate myself with." She kissed her.

"Great answer," Taylor grinned.

"Anything new and exciting, besides the new job, that I've missed from your life?" Anne asked.

Taylor scrunched up her nose. "Joe and my aunt are getting pretty close. I guess bringing them together wasn't such a bad idea. I could see them getting married someday."

"When I spoke with him this week, he seemed nice. I'm glad it seems to be working out between them." Anne caressed her hand against Taylor's arm, thinking of Taylor's last words. "What about you?"

Taylor's brows furrowed. "What about me?"

"Can you see yourself getting married someday?"

Taylor tilted her head; a thoughtful look appeared across her face. She then shrugged. "For the right woman, of course. You?"

Anne nodded. She had her house paid off and only a few bills trickling in. It wasn't wild to consider it. She felt she already found the right woman, though. It was only a matter of time. She cupped Taylor's chin and drew her to her for another kiss. Why delay the inevitable when it was obvious what her heart had already craved?

CHAPTER THIRTY-EIGHT

DREAMS FOR A FUTURE

Taylor

Anne stared at Taylor, and Taylor blushed. "You're staring again, Anne." She looked down at her eggs and dug in for another bite.

"I can't help it." Anne laughed. "I'm just so happy."

Taylor beamed. Hearing Anne express the same things Taylor felt made Taylor feel like she was on top of the world. She had never been happier and appreciated Anne making the grand gesture and finding her address to apologize. They both had a lot to apologize for, mainly being stubborn for allowing so much time to go by.

"I'm happy, too, Anne." Taylor cringed. She was so happy that she didn't want the morning to end it all, but she had to get to work as there was a busy day ahead of her. "I don't want to leave."

"Then don't." Anne shrugged. "It's as simple as that."

Taylor laughed. "Nothing is that simple. I've already called off for the morning. It's a busy afternoon and duty calls. Besides, I didn't exactly come prepared to stay all day. I have to get home and get a shower and dressed." Anne made a face. "Maybe tonight we can get together. We could go dancing or maybe hit up Karaoke."

Anne smiled. "I wouldn't object to Karaoke. After all, you were a little drunk the last time."

Taylor rolled her eyes. "A little? I was smashed." That got laughter from both of them. "Well, I know tonight there will be some Karaoke. So, meet me there at 6, and we can have dinner and sing to our heart's content."

"It's a date," Anne stood up. "I almost forgot." She hurried from the kitchen, leaving Taylor confused. Taylor waited and then saw Anne round the corner. She had something in her hand. "For you." She handed it over, and Taylor clutched her heart. "Do you like it?"

"I love it." It was one of the knitted replicas of Whiskers. She leaned in and kissed Anne. "Thank you! Just for this, I spring for dessert tonight."

Anne snickered. "I'd rather we made you dessert tonight." She winked.

Taylor couldn't have beamed any brighter. "I think that can be arranged."

Anne kissed Taylor, then pulled back. "I do like the sound of that." Her heart was already pounding. They got up from the table. Anne grabbed her hand and walked her out of the house to Taylor's car. They stopped short of the car, and Taylor turned to see Anne staring at the car. Taylor waved her hand in front of her.

"Where'd you go?" Taylor asked as Anne focused her eyes back on Taylor.

Anne gave a weak smile. "I was just thinking back to our first encounter, you know, on the highway."

Taylor covered her face in shame. She shook her head. "Not my finest hour."

Anne smiled. "But look, we came out stronger in the end. I feel bad that you paid for it, though."

Taylor's jaw dropped. "Why? I caused the accident and should have paid for it. I never should have run. My biggest mistake in all of this."

"Looking back, I can understand why you did." Anne stepped in closer, and they kissed. As rough as that day was, things were getting better. That was what mattered the most. "I'm just glad we found our way to each other."

"And we have CAPMED to thank for that." Taylor laughed.

Anne groaned. "At least one good thing came from it." The best thing came from it. That was the truth. Taylor reached for her door and opened it, then turned back to look at Anne. "Goodbye, Taylor." Even though they would still be seeing each other by the end of the day, Anne looked distressed when she said farewell. Taylor closed the door and turned back to her. "What are you doing?"

"I can't leave without saying something. Anne, you are the woman that makes me want to be a better person. Spending time away from you kills me. Spending time with you, I never feel more alive. I love you."

Anne grinned. "I'm glad to hear that because I love you, too."

Saying the words healed Taylor's hole in her heart, and they passionately kissed one another.

"Now, I really have to go." She stole one more peck, then turned and didn't look back. If she had, she would never be able to pull herself away, and there was still so much to do before she went to work.

When she got home, she was alone. Gavin had started back to school the previous week, and her aunt was still working. However, her evening job was having a lull, so her schedule wasn't nearly as hectic.

She took a shower and thought of Anne throughout it, imagining Anne was there pleasuring her while she got soaped up. It was disappointing that she was alone. But it also was a good thing since Taylor would most likely be late to work if she was there.

Taylor got dressed and was out the door with plenty of time to spare. She got to work and saw the parking lot was full, waiting for the providers and nursing staff to get off lunch. Taylor went through the back door and made her way to the nurse's station. She clocked in and started looking over the schedule for the day. She was only a few minutes in when she heard the commotion and saw the others returning from their lunch.

"Hey, Taylor." Susie plopped down on the stool next to her. "Have a nice morning off?"

"Yep, it was nice." She didn't elaborate. She didn't know any of her co-workers that way. "I hope I didn't leave you guys too empty-handed."

"Nah, it was easy this morning. This afternoon will be a bit of a challenge. But I trust we'll make it. You'll be with Dr. Radcliffe."

Taylor shifted the schedule to Dr. Radcliffe's name and stared at the first patient. She closed her eyes and reopened them, sure she was seeing things. She clicked on the name and read through the notes. *The mother called to establish a new patient. Remission from leukemia.* She covered her mouth.

"Taylor? Are you alright? Are you crying?" She reached for Taylor's shoulder.

"Happy tears," Taylor replied. "I know this patient." The light flashed that she was checked in. Taylor jumped up and grabbed her stethoscope. She hurried to the waiting room and scoured her eyes around the room where children were playing and enjoying themselves, and then she saw her. She was in the corner, playing with another girl. Taylor cleared her throat. "Willow?"

Willow turned and looked in her direction. She jumped up, glanced over to where her mother sat, and then ran towards Taylor. "Taylor!" She ran into Taylor's waiting arms, and Taylor just hugged her; it was full circle.

Taylor rushed into Bar None. She glanced around until she spotted Anne sitting at a table on the other side. Ever since she saw Willow, there were so many times she thought about texting or calling Anne, telling her the great news. But then Taylor realized that she wanted Anne to experience the same shock she had felt. It made her heart sing when she recognized the name, and Willow ran into her arms. If Anne could experience that, too, she knew her lover would be equally happy. Anne got up from the table and greeted Taylor with a kiss. "I feel like it's busier tonight than it was even back then," Taylor started.

Anne laughed. "Probably just your nerves talking since you know you're about to upstage everyone with your singing talents."

Taylor groaned. "Don't remind me. I can't even get drunk because I work in the morning."

Anne smirked. "That's good because I don't think we need a repeat of last time." She winked. "But I figured you could use a beer after a long day."

"You were correct." Taylor took a sip of her beer. She fought the urge to tell Anne about Willow.

Taylor had everything planned and needed to trust herself not to blow the cover. She had a whole week to keep it under wraps, though. How would she ever be able to handle it?

"How was work?" Anne asked, sipping on her water.

"Great! How was your day? Or your afternoon since I know how your morning was."

Anne reached out with her leg and touched it with her foot. Taylor arched an eyebrow, and Anne laughed. "Just letting you know that I'm looking forward to dessert later."

"I'm sure you are." Taylor grinned, and Anne cleared her throat and dropped her foot.

"My afternoon was lonely. But, I took your advice and went on Reddit." Taylor looked up from her drink.

"Are you both ready to order?" Taylor and Anne turned to

the waitress and took a moment to get their orders in. When the waitress had disappeared, Taylor turned back to her.

"Oh, yeah? And?"

"I was amazed, honestly. I recognized some of the names, but I had no idea everything they were experiencing at CAPMED. I spoke with a couple of women, and it seems they are great advocates for finding new jobs. One woman even said she could get me a job with her office. It'd be as a lead nurse, though."

"You would excel at that, Anne. Specialty? Or Family Medicine?"

"Family medicine, and I think maybe that's my next calling. I mean, Pediatrics was great and all, but I feel like seeing the kids suffer all day was grueling. You know what I mean?"

Taylor nodded. She understood, but with her job, she didn't fear facing death like she would at the hospital. "You have to go where you feel the calling."

"It'd be a big change," Anne admitted. "I guess that's a bit scary, but I owe it to myself to go in for an interview. Nothing bad would come out of it."

"I agree. You definitely should."

"Oh, and you know what else I was thinking about today that we haven't discussed since we got back together? Willow."

Taylor looked at her from across her water glass. She placed it down and swallowed the lump. Did Anne already suspect something? One mention of Willow's name and Taylor was already mush.

"I think of Willow often. A couple of weeks ago she sent me a letter. It was in response to the letter I had written to her. Confusingly, though, I had quit before I got the letter. I had left it at the nurse's station. So, I don't know how she got it." Anne looked down, and her face was red. "You?"

Anne shrugged. "I couldn't imagine not sending it. But what's confusing is I didn't know your address then, so I'm unsure how you got it. I had written a letter to her, too. I sent it out the same day. I also got a response. Maybe she sent it to the hospital, and someone was nice enough to mail it out."

Taylor nodded. That was a likely possibility. But she was focused on the fact that Anne had been thoughtful enough to send out her letter. She appreciated that beyond words.

Their food came, and they ate, mostly staying in an easy conversation, with only a few stale moments where they had silence, but even in those moments, staring across the table, it felt right. As they ended the meal, there was a lull onstage. Taylor looked up there, then back to Anne.

"Are you ready?" Taylor asked.

Anne crossed her arms. "I'm ready if you are."

Taylor got up and reached for her hand. "As long as we're up there together." They walked up to the stage, and Anne broke from the grasp. She went to the DJ and requested the song, with Taylor watching. Soon, "Unchained Melody" started playing, and Anne reached for her hand again. With the bar watching them, they began to sing together, and their eyes were focused on each other, not paying attention to the crowd. It was a semblance of their romance and everything they meant to each other.

After "Unchained Melody," they sang "I Got You Babe," followed by "Don't Go Breaking My Heart." Three songs in, and it seemed like the audience wanted more, but Taylor was exhausted and wanted to get home to be with Anne, alone.

"Are you ready to go home?" Taylor asked.

Anne smirked. "Home?"

"Well, your home. You know what I meant." Anne looped her arm in Taylor's, and they got off the stage, despite some boos trying to keep them up there a little longer. They reached Anne's car, and Taylor stopped.

"Are you ready for some dessert?" Taylor asked.

"If that's you, then absolutely." Anne pulled Taylor to her, and she fell into her. Anne pressed against her car. A strong pull told Taylor to go home; she had to get up early for work. But on the other side, Taylor didn't want another night to go by where they didn't make love.

CHAPTER THIRTY-NINE

THROUGH A CHILD'S EYES

Anne

Taylor pulled into the park, and Anne turned to her. "So, is that the big surprise? A picnic in the park?"

Taylor looked around and then met Anne's gaze. "Did you bring a picnic because I did not?"

Anne tilted her head and then laughed and stared out the window. It'd been years since she had even considered hanging at the park, but from Taylor's wide grin, it was all Taylor wanted to do. She would have done anything to give Taylor everything she wanted.

"I'm excited."

"Are you?" Taylor reached out and touched Anne's hand. Anne looked down and stared at their hands clasped together. She looked up and moved in to kiss Taylor. "I love you so much, so if you want to spend the Saturday in the park, there's no other place I'd want to be."

"I love you, Anne." Taylor kissed her softly.

Yes, things had been going perfectly for them for the past week. They got out of the car, immediately joined hands, and started walking. The weather was gorgeous, the sun beating down on Anne's face. She took in a breath of fresh air.

"It's beautiful today," she replied with a gasp.

"Couldn't have planned for a better day. Then again, I had a stern talk with God." Anne laughed, and Taylor squeezed her hand. "Why do I think you're being serious?"

"Because I am. I didn't want anything to mess up this day." Anne nestled her head against Taylor's shoulder, and they continued to walk. Who knew how many days they would have with weather like this? There was no one she'd rather spend it with than Taylor. "Do you want to get some ice cream?" Taylor asked.

"I just want to wait here for another few hours, and then maybe." Anne laughed, kissing Taylor's cheek. However, Taylor didn't seem pleased by that answer.

"Are you sure? Because I want some ice cream."

Anne stopped walking and panned her eyes around the park, spotting the ice cream cart up ahead. She groaned. They had a late breakfast, and she wasn't all that hungry, but if Taylor wanted it, she would at least check it out. "Let's go."

They approached the cart, and Taylor looked around, hesitating. "Just a minute." She scanned the park and grimaced when she met Anne's stare; she shrugged. "I'm not really in the mood after all."

Anne frowned. "What's wrong?"

Taylor shook her head. "It's nothing."

"Aunt Anne." Taylor turned around, and Anne's two nieces, Melanie in tow, ran toward them. The nieces rushed into Anne's arms.

"What are you guys doing here?" Anne turned to Taylor. "Did you do this?"

Taylor shrugged. "I was afraid they weren't coming."

"We had a shoe crisis," Melanie said before she hugged Taylor. "Thank you for inviting us. Good to see you again." Melanie turned and hugged Anne. "Got the text and couldn't think of doing anything else this Saturday. The weather turned out perfect."

Anne laughed through tears. "Taylor's got an excellent track record with the man upstairs." She wiped her tears away. "But how? I didn't even know you had Mel's number."

Taylor shrugged. "I got it at the party. I guess I never deleted it."

Anne walked over and hugged Taylor. "This was the sweetest thing ever. I can never spend enough time with my sister and nieces. Thank you!"

Taylor nodded, but her gaze dropped. She eventually sighed. "There was more to the surprise, but I guess they couldn't make it."

"They?" Anne asked just as she heard her name.

Anne turned, her eyes narrowing on Willow as she ran toward them, arms open. Anne glanced at Taylor, who already had tears in her eyes. "Surprise."

Anne turned back to Willow, along with her brothers and

sister. Willow led the pack, her parents and siblings not far behind. Willow threw herself in Anne's arms, and they embraced.

"I've missed you, Anne," Willow replied.

Anne started to cry, the tears landing on Willow's hair. "I've missed you, sweetheart." She pulled back and stared at her. "How are you doing? Are you healthy?"

She nodded. "In re…re…" she looked up to her parents. "What's that word again?"

"Remission?" Anne asked. Her parents nodded, and Anne pulled her back into her arms. It was the news she had been longing to hear. Holding the little girl in her arms, she couldn't control her emotions. And knowing that Taylor had done this for her made the moment all that more special.

ANNE WATCHED THE KIDS AS THEY RAN THROUGH THE PARK. SHE never thought she'd see Willow outside of a hospital bed. But watching her laugh and enjoying time with kids her age brought her back to the zoo Anne would incorporate into the Pediatrics Department. Just hearing the kids laughing and having a good time was a sign that showed her what she wanted. Anne wanted to experience all that. And she needed to work in a place that would allow her to enrich kids' lives.

"She looks so happy," Anne replied.

Taylor reached out and took her hand. Willow's parents entrusted her with Willow's care for the day.

"I can't believe you did this. How?"

"I'd say it was a miracle," Taylor started. "Monday, I went to work. I was already in a great mood; my first patient was Willow. I nearly fainted. I was giddy seeing her. She was so happy, in remission, and you couldn't tell anything was wrong. We talked after the appointment, and I wanted to surprise you. So, I decided that I would plan this out. I texted Melanie."

"I was immediately on board." Anne turned to Melanie, and she was grinning like a schoolgirl with a secret. "You guys are perfect together."

Anne rolled her eyes. "You're going to scare Taylor away."

Taylor laughed. "Never!" She leaned in, and they kissed. Anne's heart had started palpitating once more. "I'm in for the long haul. When I got there, I couldn't see Melanie and the girls, and Willow and her family weren't there; I got scared. I thought it all was going to backfire."

"A shoe was missing." Melanie laughed. "That's the only reason we were late.

"And gathering so many kids is hard, so that's why Willow's family was late," Taylor added. "So, all my insecurities about it were instantly vanished. Now look at that…" She motioned toward the laughing kids. "They're having a great time."

Anne turned back to watch them running after a football. It was true that they were enjoying themselves as only kids could do. Taylor reached out and grabbed Anne's hand, squeezing it slightly.

"It makes you think we could have that someday, right?"

Anne turned to Taylor, and Taylor was grinning from ear to ear. "And on that note…" Melanie got up and walked away, leaving Anne and Taylor alone on the bench.

"You haven't thought of it?" Anne asked. "Having a family someday?"

"I have," Anne began. "I just thought that maybe it wouldn't be something you'd want."

Taylor shook her head, then peered out at the six kids running around not more than twenty feet away from them. Melanie stood on the sidelines watching them while Taylor and Anne turned serious.

"I've always dreamed that one day I would start a family. Find a loving woman with whom to spend the rest of my life, then add a child or two. But, as I got older, I feared that maybe my dream wouldn't come true. Sitting here, watching the kids, reminding myself of all the joy I tried to bring them at the hospital, I feel like maybe I gave up on things too quickly. I want that." Anne motioned to the children. "Not only in my personal life but in my career."

"So, you're saying family medicine isn't your calling?" Taylor's smile grew as she looked at Anne.

"I'm saying that everyone has a purpose in life, and that just happens to be my purpose. And once you find it, you shouldn't let it go."

"I couldn't agree more." Taylor leaned in and kissed Anne. The kiss deepened, with Taylor's tongue slipping into Anne's mouth.

"Excuse me!"

Anne smiled as they parted from the kiss and turned to see Willow. She was glancing between each of them, her eyes wide.

"Are you guys getting married?" she asked.

Anne laughed, pulling her onto her lap and playfully tickling her. She continued to laugh until she couldn't breathe and then held up her hands to surrender. Anne looked over to Taylor, who hadn't wiped that grin off her face, and Anne smiled in wonderment. She couldn't help but feel like the whole world was opening up for Anne and Taylor and their future family.

MT CASSEN BOOKS

Available In Paperback, Ebook, And Audio Formats. Click Here:
https://mybook.to/MELODYINHERHEART

Available In Paperback, Ebook, And Audio Formats. Click Here:
https://mybook.to/FIGHTINGHERTOUCH

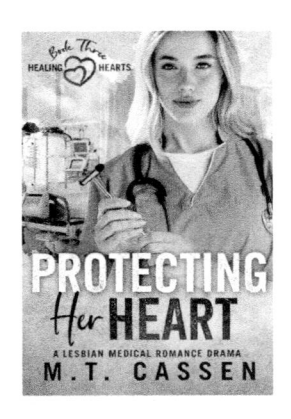

Available In Paperback, Ebook, And Audio Formats. Click Here:
https://mybook.to/PROTECTINGHERHEART

Available In Paperback, Ebook, And Audio Formats. Click Here:
https://mybook.to/TOOLITTLETOOLATE

YOUR OPINIONS MATTER

A big thank you for trusting my book with your time, attention, and support. Here are three points to remember about reader comments (aka book reviews):

1. I read all reader comments so I can fix any errors and make my next book even better. "**Get busy improving or get busy retiring**," is my motto as a writer.
2. Aren't reviews a boon for readers? I never buy books without checking out the reviews. What about You?
3. Now, you're all ready to drop a comment, but analysis paralysis gets the better of you. You might think: *What would I even write about? Who's going to read my review, anyway?*

Please snap out of your analysis paralysis. I have added here some questions on which other readers would want your opin-

YOUR OPINIONS MATTER

ions: a) What did you think of Taylor's temperament and personality? b) What kind of impression did Anne make on you? c) What did you think of the shady stuff in CAPMED and Anne's obliviousness to all that? and d) What would you like to communicate to other readers who may be interested in this book? Think of these questions as kick-starters for your review.

Please drop your honest opinions here:

https://www.amazon.com/review/create-review?ASIN=B0CHK41JPB
or click on the QR Code below:

That would make my day! Thank you!

YOUR OPINIONS MATTER

Please subscribe to my newsletter and grab a free full-length romance novel from:
https://BookHip.com/LJDAWWT
Or click or scan the QR code below:

Happy Reading,
Morgan

P.S: Thanks, www.kindlepreneur.com, for the QR code generator, and www.booklinker.com for the universal links.

ABOUT THE AUTHOR

Morgan Cassen
WITH ROXIE

Morgan Cassen writes Lesbian Romance. Her mission is to make the world safer for the telling of sapphic stories. Yes, she knows that there are millions of romance writers and billions of romance novels. Why would she even think of adding to the pile? Well, Morgan has seen enough to know that the truly interesting stories are not what happens between human beings. That gig can seem mechanical and unemotional — and better shelved in the action and thriller category, at least compared to its older, tempestuous sister. Let's bring out Ms. Inner Conflict, the queen of all drama in the human world -- the ruler of the emotional map. This is the conflict between everything you've worked for and everything your heart desires. You never imagined that all that hard work you put in over the years would put you increasingly far from everything your heart really wanted. Also, how about the conflict between the past and the future? Being true to the past would require you to push the future so far away from the present. But how long can you postpone the future? What if your whole framing of the past can't stand the scrutiny of thoughtful analysis today even as you resolutely keep the future out of your mental horizon? Huh, what do you do with that kind of conflict? The conflict between human beings can look so . . . what's the word? Tame? Yes, tame compared to the real thing: conflict between you and *you*. You are the hero and villain at the same time, but the nub of the problem is that the villain thinks she is the hero, while the hero is all caught up in doubt and indecision. Which you will you choose when nobody else will make that choice for you? You get to make that choice, and your comforting, trusty friend — procrastination — has indicated that help is running late. The time has finally come for you to choose. See, inner conflict is where it's at. Inner conflict in regular people living ordinary lives is what Morgan writes about in her books. Well, that's only half the story, so here's a more accurate sentence: Morgan writes about ordinary people living ordinary lives and finding life-changing love that will help them grow as humans. Fair warning: there are no perfect people in Morgan's books. These are lovable, kind, generous people with strong moral purpose. However, all these wonderful qualities sometimes (ok, often) come with quite a lot of maddening qualities as well, like being thick-headed and thin-skinned, clear in purpose but clueless in strategy, ready to fight the world for a cause, and unwilling to draw boundaries. Also, there are no billionaires here to rescue damsels from predicaments, nor are there any vampires to connect us to other words. Perhaps the only thing extraordinary is that ordinary people can relate to these characters. And that is all the motivation Morgan needs to keep on writing.

Please join her as she writes the stories of breakup and love that tug at heartstrings.

Stalk the author using the link below:

www.mtcassen.com

ABOUT PETER PALMIERI
(MEDICAL ADVISOR)

Peter Palmieri, M.D., M.B.A. is a licensed physician with over 20 years of practice experience in Chicago, Dallas, Houston, and the Rio Grande Valley in Texas. He received his B.A. from the University of California San Diego, with a double major in Animal Physiology and Psychology. He earned his medical degree from Loyola University Stritch School of Medicine and a Healthcare M.B.A. from The George Washington University. He is a regular contributor of original articles to a variety of health and wellness blogs.

ABOUT KAREN STOCKDALE
(MEDICAL ADVISOR)

Karen Stockdale, MBA, BSN, RN is an experienced nurse in the fields of cardiology and medical/surgical nursing. She has also worked as a nurse manager, hospital quality and safety administrator, and quality consultant. She obtained her ASN-RN in 2003 and her BSN in 2012 from Southwest Baptist University. Karen completed an MBA in Healthcare Management in 2017. She currently writes for several healthcare and tech blogs and whitepapers, as well as developing continuing education courses for nurses.

Karen's websites are:
https://www.linkedin.com/in/karen-stockdale-5aab2584/
and
http://writemedical.net/

ABOUT ROSIE ACCOLA
(COPYEDITOR)

Rosie Accola is a queer poet, editor, and zine-maker who lives in Michigan. Their writing explores how reality t.v. functions as autofiction and the intersection between pop culture and poetics. They graduated with their MFA in Creative Writing from Naropa University in 2022. In 2019, they published their first full-length poetry collection, "Referential Body," with Ghost City Press. You can find them on Substack, where they publish the RoZone, a monthly newsletter about the craft of writing and arts and crafts.

Printed in Great Britain
by Amazon